About the author

Evelyn Anthony started writing seriously in 1949 and before turning to spy thrillers she wrote a succession of ten highly successful historical novels, all of which were widely translated and two of which became Literary Guild Choices in America. More recently she has turned her hand – with even greater success – to writing novels of suspense, which include *The Tamarind Seed* (also available in Sphere Books) and *The Poellenberg Inheritance*.

Married to the director of a mining company, Evelyn Anthony has six children and runs two houses, one in Belgravia, the other a beautiful Elizabethan mansion in Essex.

*Also by Evelyn Anthony and available
in Sphere Books*

THE TAMARIND SEED
VICTORIA
ELIZABETH

The Assassin

EVELYN ANTHONY

SPHERE BOOKS LIMITED
30/32 Gray's Inn Road, London WC1X 8JL

First published in Great Britain
by Hutchinson & Co. Ltd 1970
Copyright © Padua Investments Limited 1970
First Sphere Books edition 1973

TRADE
MARK

Set in Linotype Times

Printed in Great Britain by
Hazell Watson & Viney Ltd
Aylesbury, Bucks

ISBN 0 7221 1179 7

CHAPTER ONE

'Could you give me the exact time, please? My watch has stopped.'

The desk clerk slid back his cuff, consulted his watch and said, 'I make it twelve-twenty-five, Signorina Cameron.'

He gave her a warm admiring smile with the information. The Excelsior was the finest hotel in Rome; all its staff were helpful and polite to their rich clients. Being an Italian, the clerk paid the blonde American girl this special compliment because she was beautiful as well. He remembered her last visit eighteen months earlier. Her mother had been with her; the two of them were obviously devoted; unlike many women of her wealth and connections Mrs Cameron was a gentle, courteous person. Everybody liked her at the Excelsior where she had been a regular client for years. They had all been sorry when they read the news of her death in the newspapers.

'Thank you,' Elizabeth Cameron said. She paused, adjusting her watch. There was an hour before she need start out for the airport. Outside the sun was shining, though the women huddled in fur coats. She had nothing to do but wait in the hotel lobby, and as always before a flight, she was nervous and unable to relax.

'I'll go for a walk, I think,' she said. 'It seems a lovely morning.'

The clerk watched her progress across the foyer. She was not very tall but she moved gracefully.

He enjoyed the way she walked, although it lacked the sexiness with which a Roman woman would have crossed the wide lobby to the doors. People were turning to look at her as she passed. They weren't just admiring a beautiful blonde girl in a fabulously expensive sable coat. They were staring after her because she was Huntley Cameron's niece.

Elizabeth stepped outside into the Roman street, and pulled her collar close against the sharpness of the air. It was a lovely morning, crisp and invigorating, the sunlight glittering on the shop windows of the Via Veneto, that most romantic of the city's avenues. She had always loved Rome.

It was one of the few capitals where she wasn't so acutely aware of being lonely. It was so beautiful, so much a mixture of the splendid past and the exciting future; it gave the feeling that anything could happen and when it did it would be pleasant. She turned right and began to walk up the incline. Rome was a place that had to be enjoyed on foot, or else in the piratically expensive little carriages, drawn by a single, slow-paced horse. She had been tempted to come back there after her parents died, but it held too many happy memories, memories of her first visit with her mother when she was still a schoolgirl, the discovery of architectural treasures concealed down every narrow street, the overwhelming experience of her first sight of the Vatican. She had even gone there to get over her first and only love affair. It had been her mother's wisdom and sound sense which helped Elizabeth to heal her savaged pride. One lover, one let-down. It was such an ordinary occurrence; perhaps if she hadn't expected so much she would have seen it in proportion. When it began she was old enough to have shed the kind of adolescent illusion which made her mistake an adventure for a love affair. But she had been a fool. A fool to let a man like Peter Mathews seduce her in the first place, and an even bigger fool to be surprised when he took off like a rocket at the mention of marriage. Thinking about it she quickened her walk, impatient with herself. It had been over for nearly four years, and she had not made the same kind of mistake again. It was colder than she realised, and she hurried towards Donis, where she could sit in the warm and play the national game of watching for celebrities to walk by outside. But the place was full; every table held a couple, and suddenly Elizabeth felt conspicuous and uncomfortable being alone. She didn't want to go in and sit by herself. She crossed the street and went on walking. She had been very much alone since she had lost her parents in a hideous plane crash over Mexico City. Her father she had scarcely known and never really loved. He was too much of a Cameron, obsessed by money and under his elder brother Huntley's influence. But her mother had been her refuge, her companion, and her ideal. Without her, Elizabeth had been lost. She had everything and nothing; nothing to fill her life or give it purpose. Was that why, in spite of her initial doubt, she was on her way to the Middle East with a man she didn't really know who wouldn't tell her why they had to go there—was it just boredom, or was it really family feeling for her uncle which was the reason for this journey she was making? Eddi King was a friend of her uncle Huntley; there was no complication in their travelling together. Perhaps that had helped her to decide.

She found a small restaurant, half-empty, and went in. She ordered coffee and lit a cigarette. King had asked her out to lunch. She had been a little wary of the invitation. He had never tried to see her on a personal basis before; he was amusing and an old family friend, but she couldn't think of him in any other way without a feeling of distaste. Over their lunch he had set out to make her laugh, gossiping about their friends, easing her into a pliant mood. And that was when he had suddenly told her Huntley Cameron needed her help. He, Eddi King, was going to the Lebanon, to Beirut. He had asked Elizabeth to come with him. She mustn't ask questions, she must go with him and take it all on trust. That was if she really cared about her uncle. King had leaned towards her, no longer playing the lightweight companion of a casual luncheon date. He had looked and sounded so serious that for a moment Elizabeth was frightened.

'But I can't just go off to the Lebanon without knowing anything about it!' She could remember herself saying that, and the look of surprise he gave her.

'Why not? If Huntley needs you, can't you just take it on trust? It isn't all that much to ask. To take a trip for a few days. It isn't dangerous or illegal, so you don't have to worry about that. But it will mean a great deal to Huntley. Incidentally, even if you don't come with me, he mustn't know I've asked you. It would ball everything up.'

'But there's nothing he can't fix,' Elizabeth had protested. 'He only has to raise a finger . . .'

'Not this time,' King answered. 'This time he has to depend upon his friends. And upon you, my dear. This time he isn't in a position to help himself. I'm leaving next Tuesday. Think it over and call me in the morning.'

Then he had changed the conversation, and nothing she said could make him reopen the subject. 'Think about it, let me know.' He wouldn't say anything more. After he had

7

dropped her at her apartment on East 53rd Street she had thought about it, as he said. She owed her uncle Huntley a good deal. After the accident he had taken her home to Freemont with him, shielded her from legal responsibilities for her father's huge estate, and offered the use of his complex resources if she felt a trip would help her get over the shock. He hadn't spent any time with her, or offered any personal comfort. But in his way he had been kind. And if she did go, Elizabeth thought suddenly, who was to miss her? What would an impulse journey mean beyond the cancellation of a dinner date with a man recently divorced who was conducting a bored investigation into his old girl friends, a couple of cocktail parties, and a tedious charity gala, of which she was a patron. She could pack now and go, without being missed. Even the terrier she had bought herself in a fit of grinding depression six months earlier had died of distemper in the Fall. She didn't wait till the morning to give King his answer. She called him the same evening and said she had decided to go with him.

Elizabeth looked at her watch and signalled for the bill. King hadn't stayed more than one night at the Excelsior with her. He explained that he had a meeting with a group of industrialists in Milan who might wish to part-finance an Italian edition of his political magazine. This would take him a day and another night. It was arranged that she would meet him at Rome Airport and they would catch the flight through to Beirut. While she had been sitting in the restaurant, Elizabeth had noticed a couple at a near table; he was middle-aged, the girl was young. They had been holding hands and whispering, intent and absorbed by each other. They looked fraught and unhappy. What was it? Elizabeth wondered. A love affair, a married man—whatever it was it must be different to her own experience. There had been no tenderness with Peter Mathews, no suggestion that what they did was connected with being in love. It was all sex for a laugh, and when it was over her self-contempt had helped to close the door on other men. The couple were going too; the girl clung to the man's hand, nuzzling it against her cheek. He put his arm round her. Elizabeth envied the Italians their emotional freedom, the naturalness with which they kissed their children, and showed their feelings for each other. She thought suddenly that all the Anglo-

8

Saxons could express coherently was lust. Sex on the stage was the ironic consequence of impotence in the bedroom. Those two leaving the restaurant, hugging each other, the girl wiping away tears—they wouldn't need to sit in a theatre to get the vicarious thrill. When their affair ended, as it must if he were married, at least it wouldn't be as arid and void of significance as the one she had experienced. When *they* parted it wouldn't be with a wisecrack and a wave. Elizabeth held nothing personal against Peter Mathews, her one lover. She just wished he hadn't taught her how degrading it was without love. She stopped a taxi as it cruised down the street, directing it back to the Excelsior to collect her luggage and then go on to the airport. She had sat on in the little restaurant, thinking backwards, which was an unprofitable thing to do. But at least it had stopped her thinking forwards, about going to Beirut with Eddi King. He had said nothing more during the trip out; nothing during the evening they spent together before he went to Milan. He would tell her what she had to do when they arrived. He had said that with a smile, and squeezed her hand. She hadn't liked the squeeze, it was too firm, and the one second while their hands touched became two, and suddenly she was alarmed, alerted by some instinct deeper than a dislike of being pawed. She hadn't liked the incident and she insisted that it was from that moment, not before, that she began to worry about going to Beirut. In New York it had seemed logical, even though mysterious, a means to do something for somebody and escape for a while from herself. Speeding down the broad Roman highway towards the airport and Huntley's old friend Eddi King, Elizabeth Cameron admitted to herself that the logic, the mystery and the chance to help her uncle seemed much less convincing arguments further away from home. If it was legal and without danger, why couldn't King have told her what she'd have to do—why hadn't she insisted upon knowing, instead of being outplayed and overborne, as if she had no right to ask ... but the cab had pulled into the airport entrance; her bags were being unloaded, and she was walking through to check her luggage. Eddi King was waiting for her. It was too late to turn back now.

Beirut was cold in February. The rich had gone in their

quest for sunshine and amusement as soon as the first cold winds came in from the Mediterranean and the famous blue seas reflected the changing grey of the skies. The sumptuous hotels, of which the St George was the most famous, more because of the spy Philby's patronage than for its established excellence, were empty, and in hibernation before the spring season. The beach umbrellas and bright canvas lounging chairs were under cover. At the St George the wicker pergola, under which it was so pleasant to drink gin or Turkish coffee in the boiling summer heat, was stripped of its creeper and shivered in the cold like a naked old man.

The man walking down the steep road towards the hotel entrance looked at the deserted terrace, and the wicker skeleton and turned up his coat collar. The wind blew in from the sea and it was very cold. His clothes were light-weight; he began to walk more quickly, and while he walked he paused in front of the hotel entrance and lit a cigarette.

Those were his instructions. They seemed meaningless, but he carried them out exactly. He didn't even look up to see if anyone was behind the glass doors in the hotel lobby, watching him, because he was sure that they were. He threw the match away and went on walking, sheltered from the cold by the hotel building, and then by the shops selling jewellery and Roman antiquities to the rich tourists. There was a bus shelter two hundred yards down and by the time he reached it he was shivering.

There was a woman waiting; she wore the jellaba, like all the poor-class Muslim women, but she had let it fall back from her face as he approached. Her cheeks were bright red, her eyelids and brows blackened like a clown's; she showed a pathetic prostitute's smile of invitation and revealed a tattered European mini dress. Her bare legs were blotched with cold. He didn't bother to look up when she spoke to him.

'I've no money. Go away,' he said in Arabic. He didn't curse her or spit on her, as her own people did when they refused her. He was a European, heavily built with blue eyes and a face that was common to many races and particular to none. He could have been Polish or German or French from Alsace. His name was Keller, because that was the name his mother gave him when she left him at the

10

orphanage. The nuns believed his father was a German but they didn't know, and he had never tried to find out. He didn't care. He came from nowhere and belonged to no one. His only background was a place for the rejects of society, dependent for survival on the Christian charity of the nuns. When he went out into the world he did so alone, and found no difference from the loneliness of bastardy and institutional life. The only change was for the worse. He had no rights, there was no one to shelter a waif in his teens from the brutal realities of a country ravaged by the German Army and occupied by Allied troops, where the only way to survive was by living outside the law. And that was where Keller had found himself from the start. Outside the law and outside the society the law represented. At twenty-five he joined the Foreign Legion; the war had been over for some years and he was only just ahead of the police. The Legion was not a romantic place of refuge or a leap into adventure. It was the last resort of the desperate.

The wretched little whore had moved away, and he was glad. She came from the filthy, overcrowded refugee camps on the outskirts of the city. She would be half-starved and venereally infected. She might be fourteen or even less. There weren't many of them because the Lebanese police discouraged amateur prostitution; it was bad for the flourishing tourist trade, for the elegant hotels and the opulent beauty of the Lebanon's great capital.

If Keller had money, he would have settled there. It was full of wealth; they were a trading people, and some of the richest men in the Middle East, excepting the oil-bloated sheiks, lived in the stucco palaces above Beirut. His journey took ten minutes. At the end of it he walked to a car parked on the opposite side of the road and got into the back seat.

There was a man sitting there, a thin, sharp-faced Lebanese in a warm overcoat with a velvet collar, bright black eyes and a smile that glittered with gold teeth.

'Very good,' he said to Keller. 'Right on time. Did you do it?'

'Yes,' Keller said. 'I hope whoever it was liked the look of me.'

'Why should you say that? What makes you say such a thing?' Fuad Hamedin was an arranger by profession. He

11

could and did arrange anything for anyone who paid enough, and for this the money was very big. It wouldn't do for this piece of rubbish to get clever.

'I say it because I'm not a fool,' Keller answered him. 'They want to look at me, all right. They've looked. When do I know about the job?'

'Tomorrow.'

'Tomorrow. Always tomorrow! I can't go on waiting.'

'You need money,' Fuad said. He spoke with tact when dealing with Keller. He knew the type; they were like dangerous animals, always ready to do with their fists what they couldn't achieve with their brains. He thought of Keller as rubbish because he was broke and obviously on the run. He had come through from Damascus, half-starved and ready to do anything, when Fuad heard about him. So Fuad had staked him to enough money to eat and sleep, and got him a job in the summer season as a bouncer in a sleazy night-club which robbed its customers. The club had closed in December. In the meantime he had taken a girl in to live with him, and offered to beat Fuad's face in when he suggested that she might be put out to a house to work.

Fuad feared Keller and therefore thought of him with contempt; it made him feel easier when Keller wasn't there.

'You need money,' he repeated. 'For both of you. And this is big money.'

'All I've heard is big talk.' The other man turned away from him. He felt in his pocket for a cigarette. The packet was flat.

'Give me a cigarette. You talk about a job and big money. But you can't say what kind of a job or how much money. You tell whoever it is, I want to know, or I'll find something else. I can still get to Israel.'

That was what had kept Fuad interested. Keller's original plan was to get some money together and make his way to Israel to fight for the Israelis. He had tried in Syria but the Syrians didn't want mercenaries. Fuad prompted him again, just to reassure himself.

'You're very sure the Jews would take you on,' he said. 'Myself, I don't see why. They've plenty of soldiers.'

'Maybe. But I've got something special to offer.' Keller took out a cigarette from Fuad's case and lit it. 'In their kind of war they need snipers. I can shoot a man's eye out at three hundred yards.'

'I hope you can prove that,' Fuad said, 'because that's what you've got to do. Tomorrow you must show just how well you can shoot. Walk past the St George at the same time tomorrow morning. And here's something to buy your girl a present.'

He put the money into Keller's pocket. 'Now you can take a taxi,' he said. The gold-capped teeth glittered in the cavern of his mouth. 'Enjoy yourself!'

Keller got out and slammed the door. He watched the car move off and called Fuad a short filthy name in Legionese, where the obscenities of half a dozen languages were blended. Then he began to walk back the way he had come.

'Did you get a good look at him?' Eddi King asked the question quietly, leaning towards Elizabeth. The manager of the hotel had recognised her face; the name of Cameron sent him rushing to check up. They hadn't been in the hotel for an hour before people knew she was Huntley Cameron's niece. The other patrons in the foyer were watching them with interest.

'Yes, I'd certainly know him again. I wish those two over there would stop staring at me. It's just because of that damned article.' Elizabeth turned in her chair, irritated by the unblinking scrutiny of an elderly foreign couple who were watching her and referring to the new issue of *Look* magazine. There was a picture of her uncle on the cover. Many articles were written about Huntley Cameron by people who got no closer to him than the gates outside his home, Freemont. He was a gift to the specialist in acid portraits. His marriages, his money, his personal tyranny as an employer, most of all his vicious right-wing politics, had made him a popular hate figure to millions all over the world. But what made him hated most was his arrogant avowal that his enemies weren't worth what the cat could lick off its ass. Some years back he had marshalled his newspaper, radio and television empire in a frontal assault on the Democratic Party under its then President Hughsden. All his life Huntley Cameron had been a right-wing reactionary, prepared to use his power and money to advance his views.

13

In the coming Presidential election he could have been counted with certainty among the supporters of the ex-Klansman John Jackson, with his bully-boy screaming about communists and niggers taking over the States. All Cameron's friends, and indeed many of his enemies, were behind Jackson, the ugly political phenomenon which had come up in the field of American public life like a poisonous fungus. He had spread like a fungus until the impossible had happened. The Ku Klux Klan was in the running for the White House. And that was where Huntley Cameron had shown himself of different stature to the rest. He had seen what a President like John Jackson could do for the United States. He saw beyond the present bitter Far East issues and social unrest to a future so bloodied by disruption and internal strife that it could cripple America for a generation. He had astonished everyone by swinging round completely and announcing that he was backing the Democrat Patrick Casey for the White House. He intended putting all his immense resources at the disposal of the most ardent liberal in American political life. Cameron had not begun poor; he was the son of a rich industrialist, but he turned his million-dollar inheritance away from chemical production and bought a steady circulation newspaper in up-state New York. By the time he was sixty he had a fortune which couldn't be counted with exactitude, and enough power to make or break anyone he chose.

By comparison Eddi King was a nonentity. He owned a small but select publishing house and an intellectual magazine which was widely circulated among conservatives in the States, and with some influence in similar circles in Europe. He was fifty-two years old, but he looked younger. His hair was slightly grey, but his skin was tanned and healthy, his figure kept in shape by rigorous exercising. Although he dressed immaculately, dapper was not the right word for him because he was too tall and thickset. The broad face, with its after-shave smell and even, American teeth, was still European, with a prominent frontal bone over pale green eyes. He said he had Latvian blood and women thought it was a rather smart thing to claim. He was a clever raconteur, a stimulating companion and an intellectual of consequence in a country where a sophisticated man of letters was more prized than a multi-millionaire. He was not

14

Huntley Cameron's friend; he was an intimate, but friendship was too close to describe Huntley's relationship to anyone. It presupposed equality in some degree, and no one was equal with Huntley but Huntley.

King sat back, crossing one leg over the other, and smiled at Elizabeth. Cultivating her had been a pleasure; he liked pretty girls and Elizabeth Cameron was exceptionally attractive, without the strident selfishness which desexed so many rich American women in his circle.

'You really got a good look at him?' he asked again.

'Good enough,' she answered. 'I certainly wouldn't pick up a Lebanese by mistake!'

'And it wasn't so terrible after all, was it?' He lit a cigarette for her and laughed in his easy way. 'I told you when we had lunch it wouldn't be illegal, or even dangerous. And you're quite happy about it now?'

'I'm sorry I made a fuss,' Elizabeth said. 'I suppose I'm not good at using my imagination; I'd begun to think all sorts of crazy things.' She had not made a fuss, or even a mild scene. She was too controlled, too self-disciplined, to do what she felt like doing, which was to walk right out and take the next plane home. Elizabeth kept restrained and cool, preserving her dignity. She hadn't demanded to know, she had merely asked, but in a way that showed Eddi King the time had come for him to give an answer. And he had ordered champagne for them both, made her sit down, and told her that all she had to do was travel back to the States with a man her uncle wanted to keep under cover.

It was perfectly simple; she had nothing to do but pick the man up, go to the airport with him and board the plane, see him through Customs and hand him over to somebody else at Kennedy.

'But why,' Elizabeth had asked him, 'why all the secrecy? Why couldn't you have told me before?'

'Because you just might have let it slip,' King's reply came back. 'Without meaning to; you're in the news, Elizabeth, people listen to what you say at parties. A columnist might have got hold of it, printed something and the whole plan would have fallen flat. Wham, like that!'

He had a way of making the flimsiest thing seem a substantial fact; a hint at a party, an eavesdropping columnist —it hadn't sounded ridiculous when he explained it. But

15

now, with time to think about it, and having just watched the man lighting his cigarette beyond the plate glass door, Elizabeth protested again.

'I still think you could have trusted me,' she said. 'If you'd said it was secret I wouldn't have told anyone.'

'Of course you wouldn't,' he agreed, 'but for Huntley's sake I wanted to be sure.'

'And I suppose that's why you won't tell me why he can't go to the States alone,' she said. On this question he was adamant. Again he demanded her trust, appealed to her family loyalty and made her feel in the wrong for trying to probe any further.

'He has an American passport,' King said. 'But he's not an American; that much I can tell you. Nobody must know he's making a special visit. Complete secrecy is the key. And because of Huntley being who he is, nobody else could be trusted not to talk, or be bribed, or try to make use of it in some way. Only you, my dear. And you're sure you're not worried about it? You've no reason to be, but even so ...' He shrugged prepared to understand and forgive if at the last moment she proved herself unworthy.

'Of course I'm not worried,' Elizabeth said. 'I can't see anything happening to me on a plane, can you? I must say, I wouldn't like to go walking down a dark alley with him.' She glanced back at the hotel door; the man had waited for a moment, lighting a cigarette, the match flame protected by his cupped hands, his face clearly turned towards them. King said nothing; her instincts were right. The man they had watched through the glass door was not a reassuring type. He moved like an animal; the simple act of throwing the match into the gutter was tight with violence. He tossed it away like a grenade. If Elizabeth was worried by what she had seen, King was very satisfied. The type was right. All that remained to establish was the degree of his skill.

'He won't give you any trouble,' King said. 'Don't bother about anything like that. You know I wouldn't involve you in anything I felt you couldn't handle easily. After all, my dear, I asked you to do this and I'm responsible for you.'

He had sometimes wondered what it would be like to take this particular product of the American social system

16

into a quiet room and stretch her out across a bed. He had been forced to put up with the spoilt and frigid foibles of the women he slept with, but he had never accepted them. He wondered whether this girl—in her beautiful clothes, her hair so sleek that no man would dare to ruffle it—he wondered whether she would be any different. She was certainly different from most American women. She had never been married and, as far as he knew, she didn't go in for casual affairs. She was aware of her own attractions without falling visibly in love with herself; she was intelligent and spirited without being masculine. He felt sure that sex with her would be an experience. Even an achievement. But thinking about it was one thing; he had never taken any action and he never would. She was Cameron's niece, and the only use she could be put to had nothing to do with his private imaginings. He took out a Tiffany cigarette case and lit her cigarette with a lighter that matched. He knew his role and he had been playing it so long that now it was natural. He bought the best because after fifteen years it was a habit.

'For the last time, I suppose you won't tell me what this is all about?'

'No,' he shook his head. 'I promised your uncle. Absolute secrecy. This is very important to him, Elizabeth. When you do know the story behind all this you'll understand why I can't say anything just yet. It's the biggest thing Huntley's ever attempted. And for him it could be dangerous if it blew up too soon. But if you're worried, like I said, you don't have to go through with it. I'll do it myself.'

'Of course I wouldn't do that,' Elizabeth said. 'You asked me to come to help out and I said I would. I owe my uncle a lot; he was good to me after the accident.' For a moment she looked away from him and her expression changed. When she was sad she was equally pretty to look at.

He leaned close to her again, restraining an impulse to touch her arm. He knew she disliked his occasional lapses, the signals he couldn't help giving that he might be tied up with Huntley Cameron, but he was nobody's uncle substitute where she was concerned. He knew she was afraid of him, and this excited his imagination. Other women accepted

17

him, pursued him. She must have a keener perception than most.

'Huntley's the only relative I've got,' Elizabeth said. 'I won't let him down, or you, Eddi. I'm sorry I've been so difficult about it all. I won't ask any more questions. You're a very good friend to him, you know that? I hope he realises it. He hasn't got that many friends.'

She had large brown eyes; they were an unusual combination with her yellow hair and fair skin. They were very expressive, very open. The eyes of a woman who had no real secrets from the world. And not all that much knowledge of it either. He could see himself reflected in them, a tiny miniscule in the bright pupils. Eddi King, the good friend, helping the man who had so few friends. Pity the poor rich; nobody loved them for themselves. It was just possible, he thought, looking into the girl's face, that it might be because they weren't exactly lovable ... 'Now,' he said, 'how about a drink before lunch?'

'I'd love one.'

As they walked through to the bar King noticed the men's heads turning, the way their eyes went from her legs up to her face. They were thinking what he was thinking. What would it be like ... It was a pity, a real pity, he would never be able to find out.

Keller lived in one room outside the Zone Franche, the Free Port where everything from carpets to coconuts was unloaded into the Lebanon. It was up three flights of stairs; a dank, urinous smell seeped up from the well of the house, mingled with fish. He had bought food, a bottle of wine, and some sweetmeats from the souk with Fuad's money.

The sweets were pink and of such high sugar content that Keller couldn't have eaten one of them. But the girl loved them; she had the Arab passion for sweet things, and he lay back on the bed and enjoyed watching her eat them. He had picked her out of the street one night, where she had fallen in a coma of hunger, and on an impulse, which he had never bothered to analyse afterwards, brought her in and fed her. It was like finding one of the stray cats that haunted Beirut, only they hung round the hotels and cafés and grew fat.

The girl was so thin and gaunt it was difficult to tell

18

her age, or even imagine what she would look like with a little care. Keller gave her food and a few shillings to buy more and told her to go away. The next morning she was sitting on the landing outside his door. Her name was Souha, and in the way of strays, she had adopted him and refused to go away. Keller tried. He raised his fist and pretended to be angry, but she only cowered and stayed where she was. She spoke French as well as Arabic and a little Hebrew. She had come with the refugees from Palestine, belonging to no one, her father dead, her mother, who had been a Frenchwoman, long buried in Jerusalem.

All she wanted, she insisted, was to work for him. To be his woman, his servant, anything, if he would only let her stay.

If he wanted to get rid of her, then Keller knew he would have to throw her bodily into the street outside. He had looked into the huge brown eyes, brimming with tears, so big in the taut face that they looked grotesque, and knew he couldn't do it. He knew what hunger meant, and what it was like to sleep in the open. He knew what happened to strays in this world because it had already happened to him. He swore at her and himself and let her in. That was the beginning of the association, which was not uncommon except that he neither beat her when he felt bad tempered nor put her out to whore for him when he was short of money.

And in return she loved him with the devotion of which only dogs and women are capable. She kept the dingy room clean; she washed his clothes and mended them and cooked his food; at first she refused to eat with him, serving him first in the Muslim custom, and then taking what was left on his plate for herself. She had offered him her body with downcast eyes and the doubtful information that he would get no sickness from her because he was the first man she had known. She was too young and vulnerable for Keller's liking. He had lived with one of the girls in the night-club for a few weeks; she came from England, and she was undomesticated and unreliable. She practised sex in a way that satisfied him without giving him any comfort, and one day she left him for a Lebanese she had met in the club. He had always picked up women when he needed them, from the unspeakably vicious Arab girls in the stews of Algeria when he was in the Legion, to the blank-faced Indonesians before the siege of Dien Bien Phu. He knew everything about what to do with a woman's body and his own and nothing at all about loving another human being. He had told the girl Souha to go away and sleep in her corner and not bother him. And then one night he had come home and needed someone. She was there, watching him with her beautiful eyes, and suddenly he realised that she was pretty. She had long dark hair, which proved to be brown instead of black, when it was washed, and her skin was as pale as any European from the Latin countries.

He had held out his hand and she had come to him trembling. And that was the first time in his life that Keller had been gentle because she had told him the truth. He was the first. When it was over and he wanted to sleep, she took his hand and kissed it.

'I love you,' she said. 'Now I belong to you always.'

In the morning when he woke, her face, watching him with adoration, was the first thing he saw.

Now he moved his arm, closing it round her, and kissed the side of her neck.

'If you eat any more of that filth you'll be sick.'

'They're not filth,' she protested. 'They're lovely. I wish you'd try one.'

'Not for me. For you, Souha, little greedy Souha. No wonder you're getting fat.'

She put the last sweet back and looked at him. 'You think I'm too fat? I don't please you any more?'

'You please me very much,' Keller said. It amused him to tease her but he dared not keep it up. She believed everything he said and it made her cry. 'Go on, finish that and then lie close to me. I want to talk to you. How would you like to go away from here? No, no, not without me! We would go together somewhere. We would have money.' He turned his head and looked at her. 'You've never had anything, have you? You don't know what money means.'

'We could have more food,' she said. 'I could go to the souk and buy some fine cloth and have them make an overcoat for you. I know what money can do. It can get all sorts of things we haven't got.'

'And there would be a new dress for you—perhaps two new dresses.' He watched the expressions flying across her face. Surprise, delight, disbelief. Nobody had two new dresses. Only he had ever given her one, and that she cherished so much he had to order her to wear it. It was the only way he could explain to her that things might undergo a change. She could understand it in the simple terms of more to eat and things to wear. But if Fuad was right, this could be a new life, like being reborn with a bank balance instead of a birth certificate. Only with real money you could get the certificate too, with any name on it you liked. Big money. That was what Fuad kept saying. And today the whole shadowy proposal had started taking shape. He had to pass some kind of test for marksmanship. Kneller took a cigarette from a new packet, and let Souha light it for him. If they wanted a marksman that meant they wanted a killer —whoever they were. They wanted someone who could shoot accurately from a distance. Who would it be? He drew on the cigarette, stroking the girl's thick plait of hair, winding it round his fingers.

One of the sheiks. Hussein of Jordan. He hoped it wasn't the King; getting away after shooting Hussein wouldn't be easy. Getting near enough to do it would be less so. A lot of professionals had tried for that target and failed. He would up the price on the bastards, if that was who they wanted to get. And get some in advance. At least Souha could be provided for in case he didn't come back. He tugged on the plait, turning her face towards him. 'Hello,' he said. 'What are you thinking about? New dresses?'

'No,' she said. 'I was thinking about money. Who would give us money, Bruno?' He had even told her his Christian name. No one had called him by it since he left the orphanage.

'Someone who thinks I'm worth it. Don't you think I'm worth money to someone?'

'I think you are worth more than all the gold in the Banque du Liban,' she said passionately. 'Don't play with me. Tell me, what would you have to do to get money? Is it Fuad Hamedin? I don't trust him ...'

'I don't either. No, it's not for him. Maybe for a friend of his. I don't know yet. I'll know tomorrow.'

After a moment, she said, 'Would it be a lot of money? Is that why you brought back all that food and wine—and the goujis for me—is it really big, this money?'

'It could be very big,' Keller said slowly. 'The more I think of it, little one, the bigger I believe it could be. The kind of money one dreams about. Enough to take us out of the Lebanon, enough so we could live anywhere we liked and never worry again.'

'Then I don't want you to do it.' She pulled away from him and sat up; he looked into the big eyes, fierce with emotion.

'That sort of money means danger. You would be in danger. I know it. Tell them we don't want anything. I can get money if you want. But don't do anything for Fuad. Don't get into danger, Bruno. I can earn money for us.'

He pinched out the red end of the cigarette, his skin was so tough he didn't feel the burn. 'I've never hit you,' Keller said, 'but if you ever speak like that again I will.'

'I won't say it again.' She put her hands to her face and began to cry. 'It's only that I love you.'

She was the first woman he had ever known who hadn't been sliding about on her back for years. He remembered the bedaubed child prostitute at the bus shelter that morning, and the sly, oiled smile of Fuad when he talked about the girl. His own mother had been some kind of whore. 'I know why you said it; I know you mean well, but you don't understand. You're my woman. No other man will ever touch you. And if we get some money our lives will change. You'll be a respectable girl with a house of your own.' He looked at her and wiped away the tears with the side of his hand. He might even marry her. But this he didn't say.

'Be a good girl now, and don't cry. Come and I will show you that I'm not angry any more.'

He was picked up in a taxi outside the St George Hotel. Fuad was in it. He made a gesture to Keller not to speak. They drove for an hour, and then the taxi stopped outside a restaurant. Fuad paid and got out. He went to another car, got into the driver's seat, and with Keller in the back, drove out on to the coast road. Keller noticed that after a few minutes another car was following them.

'Where are we going?'

'Out to Jebartaa,' Fuad answered. He kept glancing in the driving mirror. The car Keller had noticed was a black Mer-

22

cedes 2000 and it was still following. Jebartaa was two hours' drive from Beirut. Keller looked at his watch. They had been going for about that time.

They went through Jebartaa and turned off about a mile outside; the road became a track, the car jolted and lurched over ruts and chasmic pot-holes. There were no houses in sight. Nothing, so far as Keller could see out of the windows, but bleak fields.

'There's a case on the floor, by the other seat.' Fuad had stopped the car; he was half-turned round to look at Keller. He reminded him of a sallow rat in human clothes; his bright black eyes flickered back to the rear window. Keller followed the glance. The Mercedes was right behind them. The driver was Lebanese—he could tell that immediately. Not a regular taxi driver, more like somebody's chauffeur without his uniform cap. There was somebody sitting in the rear, but there was a partition between them and the front seats. It was made of smoked glass. Whoever was inside could see but couldn't be seen.

Keller found the case.

'Get out,' Fuad said.

Keller stayed where he was. 'I get out when you do.' All his back hairs were up; it was all very organised, very untypical of the Middle East. He didn't like the car parked behind them and that shadow behind the smoked glass.

'You must get out,' Fuad protested. 'Bring the case with you.' He was so nervous that he sounded shrill. 'You don't have to impress me, Keller. If you want this job you've got to satisfy someone else! !' He jerked his head back at the Mercedes, and slid out of the car. Keller got out after him. He didn't hurry; he turned his back on the invisible watcher, brought out the small case, and then lit a cigarette. All his life he had been pushed and only survived by pushing back.

'What are you doing?' Fuad was almost dancing round him; he was whispering and the whisper was pitched high with fear. Keller smiled; he took a last long draw on the cigarette before he dropped it and ground it out. He opened the case without answering and took out a small, slim-barrelled Lüger pistol. It was a superb weapon; he tested the weight and took a quick practice aim at a branch ten yards away. The Legion had taught him many arts. He could kill a man with his hands; he could walk for miles with almost no water and completely without food; he could adjust to scorching heat and bitter cold. He was an expert with automatic weapons, and even his French non-com, who hated Keller because of his German name, had to admit that with a rifle he was like the vengeance of God. He was a natural marksman. His eye and his trigger finger were in perfect co-ordination; he had an instinct for when his target was right, when it would cease to move for just that second which meant life or death. His regiment had notched up thirty Viet Minh in one day's sniper shooting in Indo-China, and twenty-five of them were shot by Keller. His skill with a rifle was no greater than his accuracy with a pistol. He was the regimental champion pistol shot.

'Ready,' Keller said.

'That's the target, up there, in that tree. Third from the left in that clump.' Fuad pointed at the mass of branches. Keller could see something tied among them.

'There's no ammunition,' he said. 'I can't shoot air.'

'I have these,' Fuad held out his hand. There were two cartridges in the palm. 'Two shots only, that's all you have.' He bit his lower lip; he had worried it till it showed raw. 'I hope you haven't lied,' he whispered again. 'I hope you're as good as you say you are . . .'

Keller looked at him. When he was angry his lead lowered on his powerful neck. 'Get out of the way!'

He loaded the two bullets into the magazine clip and replaced it, then he slipped the safety catch and cocked the gun. For a moment he forgot about Fuad the Lebanese and the Mercedes with its watcher or watchers behind the glass screen.

He raised the pistol to shoulder level; the target was a round rubber ball attached to a middle branch and as the wind blew, it moved.

He calculated that at that distance it was the same size as a man's head. He aimed and within a second he had fired. The little black dot in the tree disappeared.

'Is that the only target?'

Fuad had a pair of glasses to his eyes. He lowered them and suddenly his gold teeth glittered. He smiled delightedly at Keller. 'Yes! Yes!' he said. 'Nobody could have done better. First shot! Boom—first shot!' He wasn't whispering

24

now, he was shouting, gesticulating towards the Mercedes. His part had come out right. He would get his money and nobody could say he hadn't found exactly what he had been told to find.

'So,' Keller said. He raised the pistol in the air and fired the last bullet. It was the marksman's gesture after hitting the bull the first time. He laid the gun back in its case, dropped it contemptuously at Fuad's feet and climbed back into the car. To hell with them. To hell with the spectators in the Mercedes. He was the best of his kind and he had let them see it. At that moment he had self-respect; he really didn't care whether he got the job or not.

Suddenly the horn on the Mercedes sounded twice. They were long blasts, and Fuad sprang into the driver's seat.

'They want you,' he said. 'That was the signal. Once for no, twice for yes. You're a lucky man, Keller. I always told you Fuad Hamedin would bring you luck!'

'I'm not kissing your ass,' Keller said. 'You're getting paid. And it takes two to say yes to any deal. You tell me what the money is and what the real target will be. Go and tell whoever is in that car behind that I want to know now, and I'll give my answer the way he gave his. Once for no, and twice for yes.'

The Lebanese got out; the Mercedes engine had started up. Keller watched through the driving mirror. He saw Fuad go to the driver, who talked through the glass. When Fuad came back, his eyes were rolling in genuine excitement.

'Fifty thousand dollars.' He could hardly get the words out. 'American dollars. And a passport in any name you like. But you can't know any more for the moment. Take it or leave it, they say. Fifty thousand American dollars—*Allah ya ish Allah!*' He wiped his face with a bright silk handkerchief. It was oily with sweat.

'Make it two passports,' Keller said. He lit another cigarette. He too was beginning to sweat but he wouldn't let the Lebanese see any sign of excitement. Fifty thousand dollars. His throat was dry and now his hands were shaking too. Fifty thousand. 'Two passports,' he repeated. 'One for me and one for Souha. And ten thousand on account. For her. Go and tell them. Go on, you greasy son of a bitch! Do you want me to go round there and ask myself?'

Fuad was gone, and suddenly Keller pulled the collar

away from his neck where the sweat was trickling down. It was a fortune. He had killed so many men he had lost count for only a few sous a day. Fifty thousand dollars for one man. One king, one prince, one politician, one rival gangster in a billion-dollar empire like opium or cocaine. He had always thought of human life as cheap. He sat back in the car and laughed out loud at his own bitter joke. He had no idea it was so expensive.

'All right.' Fuad got in and closed the driver's door. 'A passport for you with the rest of the money when the job is done. Ten thousand now and a passport for the girl.'

'All right,' Keller said. 'All right then. Give two blasts. The deal is on.'

CHAPTER TWO

'I wish you would tell me what it is.' Keller had bought her a hundred dollars' worth of dresses and shoes. He had shown her the passport; it had come by messenger, and it gave her Lebanese citizenship.

'Now,' Keller explained, 'now you can go anywhere in the world. You have a nationality—look! You're a Lebanese, you're not a refugee any more.'

'I don't want to go anywhere,' she said. 'I'm happy here. I don't want to be a Lebanese; I'm a Palestinian. I don't want any of these things. What have you promised these people that they give you all this?'

Keller came to her and, putting both hands on her shoulders, he shook her. Just a little, as if she were an obstinate child.

'That's none of your business. I know what I'm doing and you should trust me. I've told you, we're going to have a new life. Instead of living like dogs, sniffing round the garbage for enough to eat, we'll be rich. Very rich, you little idiot. Now will you be quiet, and go and put my clothes into that suitcase?' The dark head was bent, hiding her face; he knew that she was crying.

'I am afraid,' she said. 'I don't know why, but my heart is full of fear for you.' She looked up at him then. 'I am afraid for both of us. But I will do what you say. I will wait here till you come back. Now let me go, Bruno, and I will get everything ready for you.'

He had lodged the ten thousand in the Banque du Liban, and arranged with them to pay her a weekly allowance. He hadn't told her how much money she owned, because it was safer for her not to know. If he didn't come back, the bank would go on paying her and she would be secure for the rest of her life. Even if he had told her, Keller felt sure she wouldn't have cared. She was the least mercenary human being he had ever met. She only cared for him. It made him feel uncomfortable to be loved like that. She had never asked if he loved her; with her sharp female instincts she probably knew that he didn't. It eased his conscience to think that no matter what happened to him, he had provided for her. She would never have to worry about money; she even had the displaced person's Holy Grail, a valid passport. If he had never been able to love her at least he had done something for her.

'I want you to be happy while I'm gone,' Keller said. 'I shan't be away for long. The time will pass very quickly.'

'It will be as long for me as my whole life,' she said. She was shutting his case. It was new, and so were the clothes inside it. He looked different in his dark suit, with a plain white shirt and a tie which she considered very dull. Different and somehow lost to her. She had wished and wished suddenly that he was in his shabby old suit. That was the image of him that she carried in her heart.

'I will write to you,' Keller said. It was a lie, but her thin body drooped with unhappiness and he would have said anything to comfort her.

'I cannot read,' Souha said. 'You know that.'

'Come here,' Keller said. 'Come here and listen to me.' She came and he put his arm around her. 'I will get word to you, somehow. And I will come back soon, I promise you that. And then we will be together and I won't go away again. Now will you be a good girl and smile for me?'

The tears were flowing down her face; she cried copiously, without the restraint of Western women, worrying about their make-up. She hid her face against him for a moment, and then raised her head and smiled. It was a very uncertain smile, quivering on the edge of more tears, and Keller didn't test it for too long. He kissed her, gently, on

27

the mouth, in the way that he had taught her, and then picked up his case and went to the door.

'Wait for me,' he said.

'I will wait,' the girl said. 'For all my life, I will wait for you.'

Then he closed the door and ran down the stairs to the street. He didn't look back at the window. He had said goodbye. Turning back was bad luck.

King had made the arrangements very quickly after the trip to Jebartaa. He had the contacts and the money. The passport was easy; his man had a stock of them. The money was transferred through from Syria, and the passport under which Keller would travel was waiting for him in an envelope at the airport. So was his ticket. He would know nothing until he was ready to board the plane.

'Miss Cameron here. Will you send up for my bags, please?' She put the receiver back and went to the dressing table to take a last look at herself. Everything was arranged. Eddi King had gone the previous night; he was travelling to Frankfurt to see his European office and discuss a sales promotion in Western Germany for his magazine *Future*. Elizabeth didn't like the magazine or its policies. They were too close to the savage reactionary views that Huntley's propaganda machine disseminated. Two dozen white roses were in a vase on the bureau opposite her bed. The card was in the wastebasket, torn in half. It said: 'You're a wonderful girl. Eddi.' She didn't know why the card made her uncomfortable, or why she had immediately torn it up. She didn't even like the flowers. White was such an odd colour to choose. But then King was an odd man. He had a lot of charm; he was a good talker, an amusing companion, men liked him and women were intrigued by him. Elizabeth liked him too, but not when he sent her flowers. Then she felt something quite different to the friendship for an old friend of her uncle; she felt repelled. It was silly, and unnecessary. King didn't mean anything; the white roses had no significance. She was just nervous about taking the man she had seen outside the hotel all the way back to the States. King wouldn't tell her what was behind the secrecy; why, if the man had a valid passport, couldn't he travel through

28

alone? It seemed ridiculous, until she took into account some of the stunts her uncle's papers pulled in order to expose them afterwards and throw a punch at the Administration. This could easily be yet another gimmick, probably planned with the slackness of the immigration system in mind. When the man was through and in the States he would be brought forward as one example of how many holes there were in the security net guarding America. It was the kind of thing Huntley enjoyed doing. Scandals were necessary; he kept repeating this. They kept the politicians jumping. They had to know the American people couldn't be fooled with all the time. Not so long as Huntley Cameron was keeping watch on their behalf. King had told her what to do. Pay the bill. Check out, and take the taxi which would be waiting for her at eleven o'clock. The man would be inside it. The flight was booked straight through, with only three stops. Rome, Geneva, and then New York. The bedroom door opened, and two porters came to take her bags. She followed them a few minutes later. As she left the room, she noticed the overpowering scent of King's white flowers.

Keller saw her come down the hotel steps. He noticed her because she was beautiful, even by the exacting standards of a resort like Beirut. She stood at the top of the steps waiting, her yellow hair shining in the winter sunlight, one hand holding the collar of a beige mink coat close under her chin. When one of the porters opened the door for her, Keller sat back quickly. He had brought the taxi as instructed. He hadn't known who was going to meet him. The last person in the world he had expected was a woman. She tried not to look at him as she got in. The door banged shut, and the driver turned to them over his shoulder. 'To the airport now?'

Keller answered. He had his instructions from Fuad. Pick up the contact, go on to the airport, ask for a package at the American Express counter addressed to Nahum. It would contain his passport and more money.

'Yes. And hurry.'

He took a packet of cigarettes out of his pocket and turned to the girl. 'Do you smoke?'

'Yes, thank you.' She bent down to the match he lit for

her, and he saw that she was as pretty in profile as she was full face.

What the hell, Keller said to himself, blowing the match out, what the hell was a woman like that doing in this kind of business? What sort of a cover was this supposed to be? He frowned, and broke the match in two. He didn't like it; he didn't like the way things kept turning out differently to the way they should have done. It was as sinister in its way as the Mercedes, with its smoked windows and unknown watcher, giving two blasts on the horn. They had no right to send a woman with him.

'If the traffic builds up,' he said suddenly, 'we'll miss the plane.'

He felt her looking at him and he turned to face her. He felt she was going to ask him something and he nodded towards the driver. The taxis were all automobiles; there was no partition between the man in front and his passengers. And all Lebanese listened; they couldn't help it.

She understood him, and she settled back in the corner of the cab. They made the twenty-five-minute journey in silence. He spent most of the time looking through the side window, and smoking. Elizabeth watched him when she was sure he wouldn't notice. He was very still; he never made an unnecessary movement. His age was difficult to judge. Somewhere between thirty and forty, his nationality was as indeterminate as his accent. If she could guess from the few words that had passed between them he was probably French.

He felt her eyes on him and turned round. His own were blue, set deep in a face tanned and hardened by extremes of climate. He didn't look as if he knew how to smile. 'We're almost there,' he said. He wished she wouldn't stare at him and then glance down, as if he were some kind of animal. It made him feel like an animal; hostile and on guard.

Until he opened the package in the airport he didn't even know where he was going. And a lifetime of living by his wits had honed his intelligence into a weapon of glittering sensibility. He didn't know what was ahead of him and he swore the bewildered girl who was escorting him didn't know either. It made the situation bizarre as well as dangerous. He decided to try her out a little when they were embarked for wherever they were going. He tried to judge by her

30

clothes, but failed. The mink coat was no indication. Most of the Middle East was cold at this time of year, excepting only the baking desert sheikdoms. The more he thought about it, the less likely any of the early possibilities became. Jordan was still probable, but his instinct was rejecting that too. He got out and paid the cab. A porter unloaded their luggage and wheeled it into the airport building. For a moment they stood side by side, and then Elizabeth said, 'I guess you have your ticket?'

'It's waiting inside for me,' Keller said. 'You have yours?'

'Oh yes. It's right here in my purse.'

'Then you go through. I will meet you in the departure lounge.' The man behind the American Express counter gave him an envelope, and he signed D. Nahum on the receipt form. Nahum was a Lebanese name; it had the same significance as Smith in Beirut. He slit the envelope open and there was the flat green passport with the American eagle stamped on the cover of it. He opened it and looked at the name inside. Teller. Andrew James Teller. Age thirty-eight, height five eleven, hair colour fair, eyes blue. No distinguishing marks. They were wrong there, he thought. There were some ugly scars on his upper body, relics of two Viet Minh bullets and a couple of drunken fights in Algiers. Teller. Very clever of them. It was near enough to his own name to make sure he'd answer to it automatically. Whoever had been in that Mercedes knew his business. There were a thousand dollars in a clip, and his ticket. It was booked through to New York. Keller put the money and the passport away in his hip pocket. New York. And he'd been thinking in terms of a little local assignment. What a fool he was; the amount of money, the currency involved, should have told him that whatever it was, this was right out of his class. He was just a stateless drifter, a man with no talent except one. He could kill accurately from a distance. He presented his ticket at the Pan Am office and went through to the departure lounge. The American girl was sitting reading a newspaper; he went past her to the bar and bought himself a double Scotch. He knew she was beside him by the way the two barmen looked up.

'I'd like one too,' she said. 'I hate flying. Can I have a whisky-and-soda?'

Keller put the money on the bar. 'You'll have to hurry.

We'll be called soon.' He wasn't used to flying; his experience was limited to French army transports.

'It's all right,' the girl smiled at him for the first time. 'It's not like a big international airport here. They're much more casual. We can finish our drinks and then go on board.'

'You know the Lebanon well,' Keller said.

'No, but I've travelled a bit in these sort of places. They're pretty much alike. I think Beirut is nicer than most. The people are nicer, anyway.'

'Yes,' he said. He finished his drink. 'So long as you have money. It buys most people.'

'Including you?' She hadn't meant to say it, but his contemptuous attitude seemed directed at her personally. He pushed his glass forward and snapped his fingers for a refill.

'Of course. You ought to know that.'

'I don't know anything about you,' Elizabeth said. 'I only know we're travelling together to New York.'

'And you're not getting anything out of it?' He turned towards her. The first whisky was making a little fire in his stomach. He sent the second down to join in. There was a slight, angry colour in her face. It amused him. She wasn't used to being spoken to as he had done; men like him hadn't come into her experience before.

'Only the pleasure of your company,' she said coldly.

'I shouldn't rely on that. As it happens, I am being paid. Another whisky!'

'We have a long flight ahead of us,' Elizabeth said quietly. 'I'd rather you didn't get drunk.'

She had guts; Keller gave her that. He kept seeing Souha's face, with the big brown eyes full of misery. He could have taken the American woman by her yellow hair and slapped her, just to see her cry instead.

'I never get drunk, mademoiselle. I'm not an American. That's the first call for our flight. Finish your drink and come on.' He took her by the arm; he had a grip like a vice.

They took their seats in the first class; for a moment Elizabeth was tempted to try and separate from him and take a single seat, but he was close behind her and she found herself being edged into the row where there were two seats vacant. He let her struggle out of her coat without helping her; he stood waiting, letting he hostess take the coat to hang it up, and when Elizabeth sat down he did the

32

same. He buckled his safety belt, took out the packet of cigarettes and after a moment offered her one.

'It's no smoking,' she said. 'The lights are on.'

'I'm not an experienced traveller like you,' Keller said. 'I don't usually travel first class. It's very comfortable.' She didn't answer. She wished he hadn't sat beside her. His physical presence was too positive to ignore. His body filled the seat; he smelt of the strong cigarettes he smoked. His hand on the chair arm was veined and powerful; she had to sit carefully so as not to touch him. She remembered her remark to King: 'I wouldn't want to go down a dark alley with him.' She didn't want to go anywhere at all with him beside her, but it was too late now. The Boeing began to nose forward, turning towards the main runway. The roar of its four turbo-jet engines reached a splitting crescendo as it began to taxi at increasing speed. Elizabeth closed her eyes, and clenched both her hands in her lap.

'You really are frightened.'

She opened her eyes and found him looking at her. He had a face which could be as cold as a mask. There was no smile, no alteration in the pale blue eyes.

'I'm all right now. It's just the take-off.'

The plane was airborne, climbing without effort into the azure sky. Already the winter clouds above Beirut were below them.

She took a copy of *Life* from the hostess and tried to read. The man had his head back and his eyes closed; he seemed to be asleep. Elizabth read the same two paragraphs of an article twice and then gave up. She couldn't concentrate on anything; there were too many questions she wanted to ask, and no one could answer them. It was all very well for Eddi King to say ignore her companion, but you couldn't sit with someone for twelve hours and just pretend they weren't there. Especially this man. Even when he slept she was aware of him.

Who was he—what was he—why did her uncle want him to come to the States? There were so many contradictions in the whole affair. He didn't fit in with her theory of a publicity stunt; he had a personality which wasn't exactly Joe Soaks. And the more she thought of him the more she believed he must have a purpose. He was coming for a specific reason; her trouble was that she couldn't think of

33

one which could account for him. He was not asleep. His eyes had opened and they were watching her. The look made her uncomfortable. Men didn't look at her like that, as if they were taking the wings off a butterfly to see how it flew.

'I don't know your name,' Elizabeth said. 'What do I call you?'

He wasn't expecting that question, and he had no answer ready.

'Some people call me Bruno. And what do I call you?'

'Elizabeth Cameron is my name,' she said. 'I suppose I shouldn't ask you questions but I would like to know one thing. Why are you coming to the States?'

For the first time she saw him smile.

'I was hoping you could tell me that.'

'You mean you don't know?'

'I'm not being paid to ask questions.' Keller said. 'Or to answer them. Don't you think it would be wiser if you took me on trust?'

'I haven't got much choice,' Elizabeth said. 'But I'm beginning to wish I'd asked a few more questions early on!' King had put it so simply to her; he had made it sound a trivial thing to do to please her uncle. Just come out to the Lebanon for a week and then come back, joining up with someone on the way. Just walk through Kennedy with them and then say goodbye at the terminal. It's all perfectly legal, he had promised her that. He too had asked her to take it on trust, like the man in the seat at her side. But without cynicism, without the subtle mockery which was in everything the stranger said or did. King had been charming and persuasive. She wished he were there now, he would have needed all his charm.

Keller saw the hostesses bringing the menus; the trolley with drinks was slowly approaching them. One way of stopping the girl asking him about himself was to cross-question her.

'Do you usually pick up strangers in a foreign country and take them home with you? Doesn't your husband object?'

'I haven't got a husband.'

'That's surprising. Most American ladies marry several times.'

'Not this American lady,' Elizabeth said. She took some

champagne and watched him swallow down a double Scotch.

'Don't worry,' Keller said. 'I have a good head. Tell me about yourself. You have no husband. You are American and you have money.'

'How do you know that?'

'I can smell it,' Keller said. 'Money has a certain smell which a poor man never forgets when it's been up his nostrils. I smelt it on you when you got into the taxi. Where do you live?'

'In New York. I have a small apartment in the city.'

'You have no parents?' He didn't really care. He went on talking without listening to her answers. He didn't want to know about her. He had his own woman in Beirut, who loved him. He was sorry he had taken the seat alongside her. Twelve hours and two stops was a long time.

'I haven't any parents,' Elizabeth answered him. 'They were killed two years ago in an air crash.'

'Is that why you don't like flying?'

'Maybe. Their plane just exploded, over Mexico. What about you—do you have a family?'

'Not that I know of,' Keller said. 'I never knew either of them.'

'I'm sorry,' she said. 'You're French, aren't you?'

'According to my passport,' he said, 'I'm an American. You mustn't forget that. Tell me something more about yourself.'

'There's nothing to tell,' she said. 'I visit quite a lot with my uncle, outside New York, and the rest of the time I live in my apartment.' She smiled a little, more at herself than at him. 'And I pick up the odd man here and there, as you said.'

'Just for the fun of it,' Keller remarked. 'Nobody pays you anything.'

'Nobody pays me. I'm just doing it for laughs. Actually as a favour to my uncle.'

Keller was listening to her now.

'Was he with you?' Whoever had been in the Mercedes while he used the gun, it certainly wasn't the girl. She must have a nice uncle to mix her up in this.

'No,' Elizabeth said. 'He never leaves the States. I came with a friend of his.'

'Why didn't he travel with us?' Maybe because he was shy, like the passenger behind the smoked glass. Maybe he used a pretty girl as a screen, so nobody would see his face.

'He had to go to Germany. He's a kind of publisher.'

Like hell he is; Keller lit another cigarette. Without thinking he took one out and handed it to Elizabeth. For a second their fingers touched. He refused to look up or take notice of her because of it. She was just a blind, a cover. When the journey was over he would never see her again. And he didn't want to see her. Suddenly he was tired of probing, or trying to find out who had employed him, and for what purpose. He knew the purpose. He knew it when he shot the target off the tree, and calculated it in terms of a man's head. He had been hired to kill, and the less he knew about the details, the safer it would be. All that mattered was the money. He rubbed out his cigarette in the ashtray and adjusted his seat back. He didn't look at the girl; he closed his eyes.

'Excuse me,' he said. 'I'm going to sleep.'

The room on the fourth floor back in the cheap hotel on 9th Avenue and West 39th St had been vacant for two months. When Pete Maggio booked it for two weeks, the superintendent took the rent and gave up the key without asking who or why or when. He knew Maggio by reputation; he had been born in the district and slipped down from petty hoodlum to running messages for the big boys. He had a collapsed lung after a three-year stretch in San Quentin, and he couldn't even beat up an old lady any more. He fixed things that needed fixing, and he made do with handouts here and there. He was a nothing, everybody knew that, but when he booked a place to sleep, or left something for collection, he was acting for the big boys. And always his money was good. The room was empty and it stayed empty until someone used the key Maggio had taken from the superintendent. Pete got his instructions by mail; he had syphoned off a few bucks from the rent money, and otherwise done as he was told. That morning in February he got up and dressed, put the hotel key in an envelope with the address inside, and took a crosstown bus to the eastern airlines terminal. It was a very cold morning; the stark New York buildings glittered like icicles in a frosty sky. The wind blew the Bejesus out

36

of him as he walked against it. He had to catch another bus to Kennedy Airport; Pete shivered and wondered whether he could run to a cab out there. All he had to do was go to the airport and meet the passengers off the Pan Am flight from Beirut, ask for Miss Cameron, give the package to the guy she was with and put him in a cab for West 39th Street. He had been told to do this on the telephone the day before. He had also been promised a hundred dollars when he had done it.

He thought about the hundred dollars and forgot the cold. He played the horses a little; it was his hobby, like women or booze or both were what kept other guys happy. There was a horse running down in Florida which Pete had been following carefully through last year's season. Monkey's Paw. On form it looked good, and he liked the name. He used to be called Monkey when he was a kid; he had a screwed-up face with deepset brown eyes, and a flattened nose. For a year or two it had been all right. Everyone knew Monkey. Monkey was good for making collections, and very good at hustling anyone who didn't want to pay. But he got caught and jailed and that was the end of it. He had a lousy lung and all he was good for was odd jobs when he came out. If he put the whole hundred on Monkey's Paw at eight to one that was eight hundred bucks. With eight hundred he could . . . He never saw the delivery truck. His mind was so full of what eight hundred dollars would do that he half-shut his eyes to concentrate and just stepped off into the street. He never saw the truck and he died without finishing the thought. It was a four-wheeler and it weighed two and a half tons. When they got Pete's body from under it all that that was left of his package for Keller was a blood-soaked pulp and a key.

When the plane landed Elizabeth was stiff with tiredness. Unlike the man beside her she hadn't been able to sleep properly; she had dozed uneasily for an hour or so, only to wake up with a sense of anxiety which she couldn't equate with the flight. And while Keller slept she studied him. He moved very little; she felt it must be her imagination but during the long hours she wondered whether he were really sleeping, or perhaps watching her under his eyelids, knowing that she was curious about him, uncomfortable in case he shifted his heavy body against hers. They disembarked in silence; again he made no effort to help her with her coat or even lift down her small hand-case. He ignored her; even as they walked towards passport control he said nothing. 'We're supposed to be travelling together,' she said. 'That's the whole point.'

'In that case I'd better take your bag,' Keller said. As they neared the immigration she felt his hand slide under her elbow with the same rough grip he had used to take her to the plane in Beirut Airport. She presented her passport first and waited, her pulse bounding, for the brief moment before Keller was through and beside her.

'Very good,' he said. 'Now where do we go?'

'Customs,' Elizabeth said, her voice sounded different. Her throat had constricted with the tension of those few minutes and she tried to clear it.

'Relax,' Keller said. 'It's over now. What happens after Customs?'

'Somebody meets us and you go with them,' she said. 'That's all I know.'

But nobody came forward when they were through into the main hall. There were crowds everywhere; hundreds of people in various stages of transit with the giant airlines whose tentacles reached out across the world. There were families with children, waiting for someone; business men and messengers and chauffeurs; airline officials; there was a constant stream of muffled announcements about arrivals and departures. At first they stood together in the eddying stream of people, waiting for someone to come forward. 'Maybe there's a message,' Elizabeth said. 'Wait here and I'll go and look on the board.' There was nothing for her; she didn't go back to Keller. She went to the Pam Am desk, refusing to be panicked, telling herself that King had arranged everything and she had no need to worry. But nobody at Pan Am knew anything. There was no message anywhere and nobody had come. She could see Keller standing alone at the edge of the crowds, his suitcase at his feet. She went back to him unwillingly.

'They must be delayed. The traffic in New York is terrible. We'll just have to wait.'

They waited for an hour. Elizabeth went down to the front entrance and back to the message board, but there was nothing. Keller grew more silent; she saw the expression on his face grow colder, more withdrawn, and had a panic impulse to just walk out of the airport and leave him there.

'I don't know what to do,' she said. 'I was told you'd be met as soon as we arrived. Something's gone wrong. Nobody could be this late.'

'I could have told you that half an hour ago,' Keller said. He picked up his case, and for the third time he held her by the arm.

'You're my only contact. We'll go to your place and I'll wait there.'

'No,' Elizabeth tried to pull back. 'No, you can't come home with me! I won't take you back to my apartment!'

'You haven't any choice,' he said. 'You brought me here; the contact hasn't come, but at least whoever it is knows I'm with you. That's how I'll be collected. If you pull away from me again I'll break your arm.'

They drove uptown the half-hour journey to East 53rd Street. She had a ridiculous impulse to burst into tears; it was like a nightmare. It couldn't be happening to her. This sort of thing was for the movies.

He paid the cab, but he kept her beside him; he moved through the hallway of the exclusive apartment block so close that they touched as they walked. He hadn't even looked out of the cab window while they drove from Kennedy; he hadn't shown the slightest interest in their surroundings or in the city which was one of the sights of the world. They went into the elevator and she pressed the button for the twelfth floor.

'I never asked you,' he said suddenly. 'You do live alone?'

'If I didn't,' she said, 'you wouldn't be able to force yourself on me like this.'

'Don't be too sure,' Keller said. 'American men don't frighten me. And stop looking at me as if you thought I was going to rape you. I don't want to stay any longer than you want to have me.'

The apartment was small, but elegantly furnished with a modern décor and some of the surrealist and abstract pictures her mother had collected. Keller dropped his case in the hall and stood for a moment, looking round him. He had never seen an apartment like this one. It was incredibly warm; the heat lapped over them like waves. He stared at the linen-covered walls, the Swedish furniture, the large and brilliant painting by the Belgian artist Magritte, which was the best in her collection.

'What an ugly place,' Keller said slowly. 'Why do you spend so much money to make such an ugly place to live? Jesus Christ . . .' he pointed to the Magritte—'how could you put that on a wall?'

She didn't answer him; he was just ignorant; a peasant. Her back conveyed exactly that as she walked past him into the living room.

'Where's the bedroom?' he asked her.

'Through there. And don't tell me you find that hideous too, because it's the only place you have to sleep.'

The guest room had its own bathroom, and one of her decorator friends had done it out in natural-coloured hide. The bathroom was fitted up like a ship's cabin. Keller turned to her; his eyes were like stones.

'This is a man's room. You told me you lived alone.'

'It *was* a man's room,' she said. 'But nobody uses it now.'

'So you're in between lovers at the moment?'

The slap she gave him was instinctive; there was no thought behind it or she would not have dared to hit him. But her hand came out and struck him hard across the face. 'Don't you dare talk to me like that!' And then because he moved towards her, 'Don't you dare touch me. Don't you dare come near me . . .'

He would never have done it if she had not said that. He would have let her slap his face because she wouldn't have been the kind of woman she was if she had let him get away with that last insult. But it was the cry of fear, physical fear and revulsion that tore through his jagged nerves and sent his temper to explosion point. He had come seven thousand miles to kill a man he had never seen for the kind of money he had never even dreamed about. He had his head stuck out so far on the end of his neck that he could feel the cold, and everything had gone wrong. The carefully laid plan, the meticulous organising, had broken down. Nobody had come to meet him at the airport and he was left with this girl, hostile and defiant, forbidding him to put his hands on her as if he were some kind of dirty animal. Not to touch her. Not to dare touch her. All the way from Beirut, with her

40

scent in his nostrils and her legs brushing against him, he had wanted to do just that.

He caught her arms and twisted them behind her back, pulling them upwards; he bent her against his braced body, and forced her head back. Her mouth was open with the pain of his hold; when he kissed her it closed against him, her head jerking in a hopeless effort to get free. He hurt her deliberately to begin with, to teach her that he was a man and she had better not struggle with him. She didn't surrender at once; she kicked and writhed and made little sounds under his mouth, but then she quietened, and he opened her lips. It was as if she were suspended, as if time had ceased to run. Nothing was real but the pressure of his body against hers; her arms were free and they hung down, numb and useless; his fingers were in her hair, holding her head in position for the assault on her unprotected mouth. The sensations of sight and sound deserted her; she hung in his arms, rising and sinking with the rhythm of his kisses, feeling her arms move upwards as if they were controlled by someone else, and slide round his neck. Lovers, she thought, wildly, in between lovers. She had been to bed with one man, and tried to delude herself that this was what being in love meant. Peter Mathews for whom that bedroom had been decorated. There had never been a moment, not even at the climax of his possession, when Elizabeth had lost herself as she was lost now.

It was Keller who stopped. He put her away from him and held her. Already, without conscious intent, they had both moved near the bed. Another moment and he would have pulled her down on it. Her face was deathly, tears had seeped under her lids and smudged down her cheeks.

'Now we know where we are,' Keller said slowly. 'I can take you any time I want. And I do want, so be careful. Be very careful.' He moved her to the bed and made her sit down. 'I didn't mean to hurt you,' he said slowly. 'You made me mad. I'll get you a drink. Where do you keep it?'

'Through there.' She didn't recognise her own shaking voice. 'In the living room.' She watched him go through, heard him move round, open the door of the single unit standing against the long wall, with a Klee drawing above it, listened to the noise of glasses and his heavy tread as he came back. I should move from here, she tried to say it to herself. I should get away from the bedroom, get off the bed. If he touches me again . . .

'Drink this,' Keller said. He put the glass of brandy into her hand, and finished a four fingers' drink in one swallow. 'You'd better go to your own room,' he said.

She looked up at him, the brandy dulling her exhaustion into a kind of calm. 'Why didn't you finish it? Why did you let me go?'

'Because I'm in enough trouble without getting mixed up with you,' he said. 'I wanted to show you what happens when anyone tries kicking me around. Now you know. You needn't be afraid. I won't touch you again.'

'You made me hit you,' Elizabeth said slowly. 'And I'm not in between lovers. There was only one. Years ago.' She got up and went out of the bedroom, Keller following. She saw her reflection in the mirror as she passed; she looked dishevelled, her hair hanging down over her shoulders. She tried to push it back, feeling for the combs that held it up on her head.

'Leave it alone,' she heard him say. 'It looks pretty like that.'

'What are you going to do?' She should have gone to her room as he said and locked the door. She should have pretended, lied, acted as if she were injured by what had happened between them. But Elizabeth couldn't. She was too honest with herself to try to fool him. She had ended up willing; if he had come back and taken her in his arms at that moment she would have welcomed it.

'I'm going to get something to eat,' Keller said. 'You don't have to bother about me.'

'I'll make us both something,' she said. 'If you're going to stay here, you might as well be comfortable. And I might as well make you welcome. Whatever this whole business is, we're mixed up in it whether we like it or not. I'll get some eggs and some coffee.'

He didn't answer her. He went into the room they had left and started taking his shaving kit and pyjamas out of the bag. With any luck he wouldn't need them. With any real luck somebody would call and he'd be out of that apartment and away from the girl that same day. He didn't like what he had done to her; it was a bad sign, a sign that he wasn't

42

in command of himself. He didn't like the look on her face, or his own irritation when she tried to put her yellow hair up. The whole thing was a crazy ball-up, and he threw his clothes out of the case and swore. He wouldn't go near her again. That was the first thing. He'd keep well away, away from the scent and the accidental contact in case it ignited that sexual spark again. And anyway he didn't want to mess around with her. He had a woman, a woman who loved him and was waiting in Beirut. To earn his fifty thousand dollars he needed to keep clear of all involvements.

In the kitchen Elizabeth closed the door and leaned against it. Her arms were throbbing; there were marks on the skin which would turn into bruises. He had a body like a tank; crushing, unassailable. She thought suddenly of Peter Mathews and the memory was blurred and sloppy, like the man himself, with his pettish ephemeral desire. He had lied her into bed, and lied himself out of it when he had got his own way. She had never understood why her friends wanted the casual affair, or plunged in and out of marriage like divers at a swimming gala. Once was enough for her. She had only to think of it to feel the disillusionment and the hurt all over again. Keller had promised not to touch her again and she believed that he would keep his promise.

She began to boil eggs and make coffee; her hands were steadier now. She brushed the hair back as it fell against her cheek. Later, after they had eaten, she would pin it up again.

King made his rendezvous in Paris. He felt he had earned a few days' rest before he went on to do his legitimate business in Germany. He booked in at the Ritz Hotel in Paris, and enjoyed an excellent dinner and early night. He believed in the refreshing powers of sleep; when he was tired or travelling he napped whenever an opportunity came along. Next day he amused himself going round the antique shops in the Quartier Lebrun, bought a handsome eighteenth-century *boulle bureau plat* and spent the morning arranging for its shipment to his Frankfurt office. It was a beautiful piece of furniture, a fine example of French craftsmanship which he had decided to possess on impulse. For this reason he was sending it to Germany instead of to his New York apartment. It would be easy to move it from Frankfurt.

In the evening he took a taxi to an address in the street one block down from the Rue St Honoré. He got out at a splendid nineteenth-century house with an imposing front door, and rang the night bell. He was shown into a large hall, decorated in Empire blue, with several pieces of fine Louis-Philippe furniture and a magnificent crystal chandelier. His hat and coat were taken from him by a maid. He presented his card, and agreed to wait for a moment. When the maid came back she was followed by a woman in her middle fifties, elegantly dressed in a black couture cocktail dress, surrounded by an aura of 'Joy'.

'Good evening, Monsieur King. I have a room ready for you. Would you like to come through and see some of the young ladies?'

There were a dozen girls in the green-painted salon, some were dark, others blonde, three were red-headed. All were fashionably dressed in costumes ranging from Pucci-type evening trouser suits to severe cocktail black. King made an inspection. They looked up at him and smiled. A girl with a pointed gamine little face and a curly black head, ruffled and trimmed into clever disarrangement, caught and held his look. He indicated her, and at a sign from the proprietress she stood up and came forward. She had a beautiful figure, with large breasts and a neat waist. King imagined her naked. It was as if his mind were read.

'Go through there, and Monsieur will follow.' She turned to King, her even teeth displayed in a professional smile. 'You wish to see her undressed,' she said. 'I can promise you, she won't disappoint you. Her name is Marcelle. She is a charming girl, very amusing, very cultivated. Please, Monsieur King.' She held out her hand, gesturing towards a side door like a duchess showing the way to royalty.

'No,' King said. 'I don't wish to embarrass the young lady. I think she will be a perfect companion. I will go up to the room first, and then if you will send her in about half an hour ...'

'As you wish,' she smiled again, inclining her head a little. 'Come with me. The other gentleman is waiting for you.'

The room was furnished with the same luxury as the rest of the house; the bed was a draped couch, and from the look of it, probably genuine First Emipre, with a comfort-

44

able mattress. A table with drinks, ice and three glasses was placed under a yellow lamp. A bottle of champagne was in a separate bucket at the side. The room was warm and scented; there were fresh flowers in the vases. A man was sitting waiting for King. He had already poured himself a large gin-and-Dubonnet, and he had been reading *Paris Match*. A faint blue haze of Gauloise cigarette smoke hung over him like a halo in the lamplight. He was older than King, fat and coarse, with a shadowed chin and deep-set black eyes, with heavy rings under them. He looked like a meat porter from Les Halles in his Sunday suit.

His name was Druet; it was not the name he had been born with, but that was long forgotten. He didn't stand up when King came in; he put down the magazine slowly, and looked up slowly. He was more important than King. There wasn't a man in Europe for whom Druet had to get out of his chair.

'Good evening,' he said. He spoke with a thick Marseilles accent. 'Get yourself something to drink and let's not waste time. You should have reported yesterday.'

'I was tired,' King explained. He wondered whether his expedition to the Quartier Lebrun was known. He had met Druet several times before, and he knew what to expect. He disliked Druet, because he was a vulgarian with the manners of a brute; but he was brilliant in his own line, and for that King respected him. He decided to begin as he intended to go on after the interview with Druet. He opened the champagne.

'Well,' Druet said, 'get on with it. From the time you left the Lebanon.'

'I chose the man. He'll do exactly what we want. I saw him shoot and he's first class. I arranged for Cameron's niece to take him through when I was well clear and I heard from my contact in Beirut that they had gone together. I got someone to check with the airline in New York and they were crossed off the passenger list as arrivals. So that part is going according to schedule.'

'Where is the man now?' Druet asked.

'In the room booked for him, waiting. I intend to make contact with him when I get back. By telephone.'

Druet lit a cigarette; he had a hoarse nicotine cough.

'Everything's going well from the other side. Casey has

45

accepted Cameron's official support for his candidature; it should fit in perfectly.' He used long words with the pedantry of the self-educated.

'There will be a big reaction to this killing,' King said. 'I predict the biggest public outcry since the assassination of Jack Kennedy. Bigger than Bobbie, bigger than Martin Luther King. This deal will tie up the racial and religious vote into one screaming knot. And this time the public won't be fobbed off with any Warren report; they'll want to know who and why, and why and why again.'

'A two-part question . . .' Druet coughed up smoke, 'to which you'll have supplied both sets of answers—if you've done your job properly.' He didn't like Eddi King; the type irritated him. He resented King's expensive clothes, his well-barbered face, his self-confidence. Druet knew that his only asset was his own brain; he was fat and ugly and he used fear on his subordinates the way a man like King used personal charm. He needled him deliberately.

'I always do my job,' King said. 'When have I ever failed?' He didn't show anger. He just asked the question, knowing how Druet would have to answer.

'Never so far,' the Frenchman said, 'but there's always the first time. Have you laid the trail properly? Left the clues where our friends can find them?'

'Huntley Cameron's niece brought our man in from Beirut. Sure, she'll implicate me, but I'll be gone by then. And Cameron himself is involved up to here.' He brought his hand up level with his eyebrows. 'He's financed the whole operation. I told you, it's all going to work out perfectly.'

'It better had,' Druet heaved himself up from the chair and poured gin into his glass; the Dubonnet was only a splash. 'A liberal of Casey's stature could put our progress back in the whole North American continent by a hundred years. One point. You will be implicated by the Cameron girl but you will be gone—one of the conspirators who got away ahead of the law and is probably hiding in South America, right?' King nodded. 'But what arrangements have you made for security in the Lebanon? Your killer comes from there. How can you be sure there's no lead left to connect him with us?'

'The man never saw me; it was all arranged through a

46

third person who doesn't know me either; everything was fixed by our people in Beirut. They won't leave any pointers.' He hesitated, remembering something. 'But there was a woman. The man asked for money to be paid to her and for a passport. The arranger spoke of her. Between them they might know something.'

'I'll send instructions to dispose of them,' Druet said. 'We don't want any loose ends. I'm going now. You want to stay on?'

'I've arranged to spend the evening,' King answered. 'I leave for Frankfurt at the end of the week.'

Druet finished his drink. He wiped his mouth with the back of his hand, which made King wince because it left a smear on his cuff, and opened the door.

'Good luck,' he said. 'Just be sure your man doesn't miss.'

'He won't,' King said. 'Not the way I have it planned. It'll be the TV feature of the year.'

Five minutes after Druet had gone out there was a knock on the door. The pretty girl from the salon downstairs came into the room and smiled at him. She wore a négligé trimmed with emu feathers, and as she crossed the floor towards him, King saw that she was naked underneath it.

'Good evening monsieur.'

'Good evening,' King said. 'Will you join me in a glass of champagne?'

That first night Elizabeth didn't sleep. Keller went to his room first, and as hers was adjoining she could hear him moving about, taking a bath, and then the creak of the mattress as he turned. They had eaten together, and because of what had happened between them there was a silence which became a strain. Even when he helped bring the plates through to the kitchen he moved very carefully so as not to touch her, even by accident. Elizabeth undressed slowly, and then began to unpack. The Lebanon seemed so unreal it might have been a place visited a year or more ago. There was a smell about the dresses she took out of the case, a mixture of her own scent and the smell of the wardrobes in the Beirut hotel. Twenty-four hours earlier she had been there, getting ready for the plane journey with the man she had glimpsed for a moment outside the hotel doors. Now he was next door in her apartment and the marks his hands had made were on her arms. She went into the kitchen and began to make coffee.

'Did you sleep well?'

Keller slid down on to the banquette opposite to her. 'Very well. The bed was very comfortable.'

'Would you like bacon and waffles for breakfast? I'm going to make some.'

'I've never tried them. What are waffles?' He found himself talking quite naturally. All the hostility which had quivered between them on the flight was gone. He could notice how pretty she was because it didn't give her any victory over him. The victory was his, won in the brief, explosive struggle. He also thought she looked as if, unlike himself, she hadn't slept.

'They're difficult to describe. Try some, see if you like them. They're very American.' She watched him eating; he didn't pretend with the waffles. He shook his head and pushed them to the side of his plate. 'Too American for me,' he said. He poured out more coffee for her and lit two cigarettes.

'What are you going to do?' Elizabeth said.

'Wait here,' he said. 'Read your books, eat your food, and wait for someone to phone or come for me.'

'Have you ever met my uncle?'

'No. I don't even know who he is. You keep on talking as if I should know, but I don't.'

'It's so odd,' she said, 'you not even knowing about him.'

'Is he so important?'

'Yes, very important. Even in the Lebanon you'd have heard of Huntley Cameron.'

'It means nothing to me. Tell me about him. Is he rich?'

'One of the richest men in the world,' Elizabeth said. She saw him put his coffee down without drinking it and she smiled. 'He's worth a hundred million dollars, maybe more. He owns newspapers and television networks, real estate, oil wells, an airline—I don't know what else. He's a big man politically, too. He has a lot of power.'

'With all that,' Keller said it slowly, 'he could be President.'

'No,' she shook her head. 'He's never wanted that. But he's suddenly taken it into his head to help someone else be President. I think he feels it's more fun to pull the strings.

He's decided to support Casey. You know who he is, surely?'

'No,' Keller said. His mind was working while the girl talked. He had forgotten her yellow hair, the pale skin showing at the collar of her housecoat where the top buttons were undone. He was thinking about the rich politically powerful uncle. If he was going to point the target he would never have used his niece . . . But if he were the target . . . It didn't make sense.

'Can I ask you something?' Elizabeth said. He drank his coffee and waited. 'What have you come for? You said you didn't know, but that can't be true. What have you really come for?'

She had a directness which surprised him. She asked a question and expected an answer, without guile. Perhaps American women were like this; perhaps they behaved with equality towards their men. 'I don't know,' he said. 'You shouldn't keep asking questions; I told you before. The less you are mixed up with me the better, just in case I find myself in trouble.'

'Oh, you won't,' Elizabeth said. She had a pretty laugh and it was the first time he had heard it. 'You don't know my uncle. If you're under his wing, nobody can lay a finger on you.'

'I'm glad to hear that,' Keller said. 'I feel much easier.'

'Forgetting about the passport—what are you really, then?' she said. 'French?'

He nodded. 'I'm French. Half-French anyway. I think my father was a German, but I don't know. I was brought up in an orphanage and they didn't have much information for me. I know I'm a bastard and that's about all.'

'That makes us both orphans,' Elizabeth said. 'My parents were killed two years ago. All I have is my uncle, and though I'm fond of him he isn't exactly a second father.'

'You loved your parents,' he said. 'You must have had a happy life as a child. That's what gives you that look.'

'What look?'

'The look that says, "The world belongs to me!" I thought it was money. I think it was your happy childhood. You're entitled to that look.'

'I'm not,' she said. 'Even if I had it. My childhood was extremely happy because of one person. My mother. She was what made my life from as far back as I can remember.

She was the most gentle, interesting, artistic person—how she ever married my father I can't think! He was such a Cameron, just like my uncle. Nothing existed except business and money; he adored my mother but he couldn't have been further from her than we are now to Beirut. They had nothing in common at all, except me.'

'Maybe your mother loved him,' Keller said. Suddenly he thought of Souha. 'Women can love without any reason in it. Which is nice, for some men. Like your father.'

'I don't think she loved him,' Elizabeth said. 'But she was too kind to let him know it. She was that sort of person. Camerons don't think about themselves like ordinary people; they don't think about whether they're loved or not. They take it for granted they are.'

'Are you like that too?'

'No,' she said. 'No, I've no illusions about myself. In spite of the "look", or whatever you call it. I thought I was in love once, a long time ago, and I thought he was in love with me. I found out very quickly that it wasn't so. He came. He saw. He conquered. And he went. I believe I mentioned marriage or some silly joke like that. He used to stay in your room,' she admitted. 'I had it done up for him. But it was a long time ago; four years. Nobody's been there since.'

'You don't have to explain to me,' Keller said. 'It's none of my business. By the way, you cook well. I didn't know rich women knew how to cook.'

'Maybe in Europe they don't. In America we're brought up to be useful, independent. There's none of this servant fetish I find abroad. I can cook, I can sew, I can drive any make of car on the market, and I'm pretty good with children. I don't do a job because—well, I don't need to—and after Mother died I didn't want to be tied down. What do you want for lunch? Or we could go out, if you liked. You've never seen New York! We could have a real tour—Central Park, the Frick, the Metropolitan Museum, the Statue of Liberty! Why don't we do that?'

'I can't go anywhere,' he said. 'Someone may telephone. But you don't have to stay here. You don't have to be shut in all day.'

'What a pity,' Elizabeth said. 'It would have been fun. I love the city; I would have enjoyed showing it to you.'

'I would have enjoyed seeing it,' Keller said. He hadn't wanted to go out anyway. Parks and museums were not his line. She looked flushed and young, very young, like a child deprived of a treat. Immature—that was the word for her. Rich and sophisticated, with a knowledge of the world which the women he knew could never claim, but compared with any of them this American girl was basically naïve, someone who had looked through the window of life but never opened it. He thought of Souha again, of her hungry face and cavernous eyes, already full of the knowledge which this girl lacked; the knowledge of pain and fear and deprivation. He had always thought of Souha as a child, even when they made love. He had treated Elizabeth Cameron like a woman the day before, and she had crumpled. She had nothing behind her but a lover who didn't want to get married. And not much of a lover either, to have left that innocence behind him.

'I'm always asking questions,' she said suddenly. 'I'd like to ask another one. Are you married? Do you have a girl?'

'I have a girl,' Keller said. 'In Beirut,' He stubbed out the cigarette and slid back a little from the table. He was not going to talk about Souha to anyone. He was not going to describe her or discuss her. He could imagine what Elizabeth Cameron would think of a refugee from the Arab camps. He stared deliberately at the open neck of her gown. It was made of some soft green stuff, with a long row of velvet buttons. He didn't want to talk about the Arab girl he lived with in Beirut to this girl, with her breasts showing their shape under the row of little buttons.

'Maybe you'd better get dressed,' he said.

'All right.' Elizabeth stood up; she saw his eyes on her, and one hand came up defensively. 'It's none of my business. I'll go out and get something for lunch. You make yourself at home.'

Martino Antonio Regazzi, Cardinal Archbishop of New York, was born in downtown Manhattan, where the Italian immigrants were living in such fecundity that the district was known as Little Italy. His parents were poor even by neighbourhood standards; his father worked in a shoe factory uptown, which closed in the Depression, and for the next three years he drew Assistance, and hung around the streets making a few dollars getting other people cabs, or sweeping, when the weather ran foul. Snow was a godsend because it meant money. There were ten children in the two rooms where the Regazzis lived. All his life until he went to the seminary, Martino spent his days and nights in a crowd of bigger and small children, relatives, his mother and father. When his father died it didn't make any more room. He was never alone, never quiet. Life was a noise that altered in volume but never became silence. Even at night it was noisy. Some snored, the baby cried, his mother woke up to feed and crooned while she suckled; the truckle beds with two and three bodies in them creaked. The tap in the kitchen living room had a maddening drip, and a knock that seemed to come only between four and six in the morning. There were big families up above and Sicilians on the floor below. They fought like jaguars, and the woman used to scream and pray when her husband hit her.

It was a nightmare in which to grow up; his family lacked everything material. They were often hungry, nobody ever had new clothes, and when his parents sought comfort behind the old curtain they hung across the corner to hide their bed, the children lay awake and listened. It was the happiest place Martino had ever been in, and in twenty-eight years since the war he had been in many places, from the foxholes in Iwo Jima, to the Archbishop's Palace in New York where he lived. His description of his home and his family was one of the best things he had ever done on TV. It brought a hundred thousand letters, jammed the studio switchboards all night, and won nation-wide coverage.

He had made them live for the watching people of America, his brothers, his sisters—the brother who went to reform school, the other two who went into the Army and got killed, his sisters who married and began their lives in the same environment as their parents. The statue of the Sacred Heart which stood in their kitchen in the place of honour; the lamp which was never without oil, no matter what they had to do without to buy it. The way Regazzi told that story made the professionals cry with envy. He spoke with clarity, with simple phrases describing simple people. He dignified their poverty and their squalid conditions, he spoke of his mother with gentle pride and his father with compassion. He was a poor man who had become a Prince of the Church. He hoped that this title wouldn't deceive anyone into thinking he wasn't still a poor man. As poor in possessions as the Carpenter who had only a seamless cloak when he died. And then the soft narrative became an impassioned attack upon poverty, drawing the distinction between the poor as people and the infamous conditions in which they had to live. Regazzi spoke and socialism thundered from the screen, from the mouth of a Catholic cardinal. It was for this he had exposed his family, describing their sorrows, their relationships. To rouse the conscience of the people. And not just his people; but the people of America.

What really made the cynics weep was that they knew he meant it. Those close to him, like his secretary Monsignor Jameson, knew that Regazzi spent an hour in prayer before he made his famous TV appearances. He knew that he prepared for every public appearance, perfected every sermon, presented himself with a film star's flair for the best profile and the winning smile, for just one object. To better humanity in the name of God. Regazzi had many critics; most of them were within the Church itself, where his publicity seeking and rhetoric from the pulpit were disliked and contrasted with the dignified neutrality of his predecessor. Regazzi was in his early fifties. He had a good war record as a young chaplain with the Marines, and a dazzling career as a theologian and sociologist. When he became Archbishop of New York it was part of the revolutionary process taking place within the Catholic Church. The fiery Italian was made Cardinal as a proof that in spite of the conservative element in the hierarchy, reform was blessed by the Vatican. Monsignor Jameson was ten years older than the Cardinal. He liked a quiet life and a comfortable routine. For the last three years he had been chased like a hare, travelling, investigating, following Regazzi into his furious leap into the public eye, and loathing every moment of it all. Privately he described the Archbishop's Palace as a three-ringed circus, with Regazzi in the centre. He would have liked to retire but the Cardinal wouldn't let him. Most of the former Cardinal's officials had been replaced; for some reason Jameson couldn't understand, he was kept on and there was no release in sight.

The Cardinal worked until one or two in the morning,

and was saying Mass by six. He expected his secretary to be available, and this meant that while Jameson might doze in a chair in the outer office, he dared not go to bed. It was past midnight, and the Cardinal's light was shining under the door. The Monsignor settled into the chair, trying to get comfortable, and drifted into a light sleep. He woke with a jerk that brought the spectacles balanced on his forehead down on to his nose as if it were a party trick. The Cardinal was beside him. He blinked into the handsome, sallow face, gaunt with secret fasting and regular lack of sleep, and was relieved to see no sign of anger. Regazzi never allowed himself to lag; he sometimes showed impatience with those who did.

'I have some letters for you, Monsignor,' he said. 'Will you come in please?'

'I'm so sorry, Eminence,' Jameson was stammering. 'I just closed my eyes for a moment to rest them and I must've dropped off . . .'

'You're tired,' the Cardinal said. He was behind his desk and in the harsh light of the anglepoise lamp he looked exhausted. Jameson hadn't noticed it before, and he was shocked. The man was driving himself beyond endurance. In the first month after his elevation to the See, someone on the administrative staff had said, 'The guy's a fanatic. The caretaker told me he spends half the night in the chapel. He thought someone had broken in! We're all going to have one hell of a time with him—you'll see.' And they had seen —those he hadn't replaced with younger men, men who shared his crusading ideals. Only me, Jameson thought wearily, I'm the only one he kept. It'll be another hour before I get to bed!

On a sudden impulse he said, 'You ought to get some rest, Eminence. You look buttoned up. Give me the letters and I'll have them ready by the morning. You go to bed.'

Regazzi smiled when he was being interviewed; he smiled when he spoke in public and when he was being photographed. Those who worked with him were not often favoured in the same way. He smiled at Jameson then, and patted the top of his desk very lightly. 'Sit down a moment. I'd like to talk to you.'

It's coming, the older man thought. He's going to tell me I'm being replaced. I'm too old, the job's too much. I gave him the opening by saying *he* was tired. And for some reason he felt disappointed, and not relieved at all.

'We've worked together since I came here,' the Cardinal said. 'I've often meant to tell you how I appreciate your help, but somehow I never seemed to have the time. I'd like to thank you now.'

Jameson only nodded. This was it. At twelve-forty-five in the morning of all times to get the push.

'I want to ask you something. What do you think will happen to the people of this country if Johnny Jackson gets to the White House?'

It was such a surprise that Jameson opened his mouth and couldn't bring out an answer. When he did open it again he said what he thought, without trying to be intelligent. The Cardinal had a way of challenging people to measure up to him. Jameson always felt this and struggled, but that night he was too tired even to try.

'I've never thought about it,' he said. 'Because it won't happen. We wouldn't elect a thug like that.'

'We're running him,' the Cardinal said. 'A couple of years ago it wouldn't have seemed possible. He was just a dirty word in a dirty state. Now he's right up there fighting.'

'He can't win,' Jameson said. 'He can only split the vote.'

'Exactly. He can do that. He can weaken both parties so that if he doesn't get in this time, the next election he just may. Provided the conditions are right for him. But you haven't answered me. What would happen if he did get elected?'

Jameson hesitated. 'The Negroes would revolt,' he said. 'I'd say that was sure. We'd have a civil war on our hands. I guess his labour policy would bring out the unions, there'd be strikes. Foreign policy I don't know; some kind of isolationism, I suppose. He'd have a lot of power behind him, though. I can see whole sections of this country going along with some of his ideas. And then again, like the coloured people, whole sections more who'd fight 'em.'

'Civil war and chaos,' the Cardinal said. 'A man like Jackson causes them, but what causes a man like Jackson? Isn't that equally important?'

'I guess so.' There was a pipe in Jameson's pocket but he didn't like to bring it out. Regazzi never smoked or drank.

'Ignorance and poverty and social injustice cause men

like Jackson to get into public life,' the Cardinal said. He was speaking quietly, keeping it intimate between them. 'Those sort of people breed anyway, but they never get further than the street corners or the local lynch mob, except that the rest of us create a suitable climate for them. Jackson is contesting for the Presidency simply because that climate exists. There is so much poverty and ignorance and inequality in our society that the people who are its victims have turned to violence in despair. And their violence brings more ignorance and fear from a whole lot of other people, who can't answer any problem except with fire hoses and riot police. A man like Jackson just naturally climbs on their shoulders and tells them what they want to hear. This is the danger.

It was, and put like that, there was no argument. Jameson nodded.

'That's what I'm fighting,' the Cardinal said. 'I'm fighting the climate. The misery, the ignorance, the arrogance that says that if people suffer from these things it's their own fault. And I'll use all the means at my disposal. I'll let them make up my face and go on TV. I'll act it out and pray it out loud, and beat it into people because God has given me these gifts and he wants me to use them. I know you don't approve of me, Patrick, I've always known it. But I hope that you can understand why it has to be done. I'd like you to support me from your heart.'

It was the first time the Cardinal had ever used his Christian name; Jameson felt his face and neck begin to redden. Shame and embarrassment fought for possession. He actually grabbed the pipe out of his pocket and began to stuff tobacco in it. 'If I've ever shown—if I ever conveyed anything to you—Eminence, I just don't know what to say!'

'Say that you understand,' the Cardinal said. 'You're a good man and a good priest. And you've borne with me like a real Christian. I believe we have something more to do than just our ministry within the Mass and the Sacraments. I believe we have to fight for good in every level of society. *In* the world, as well as in the Church in the world. I believe I must fight for my people, and I mean all my people, black and white, Catholic and Protestant. I must fight in politics, in social work, in industrial relations. I am going to fight Jackson. I've been drafting a sermon for St Patrick's Day. I'd like you to read it tomorrow.'

'I'd be honoured,' Jameson said. 'I surely would be honoured.'

'It's late now,' Regazzi said. 'And you are tired. We both are. I hope you'll go on working with me, in spite of the late nights.'

He got up and Jameson scrambled out of his chair. He put the unlit pipe back in his pocket, and in the light he saw Regazzi's hand held out to him to shake. He didn't shake it. He went down on one stiff knee and kissed the Episcopal ring. He remembered that the Cardinal had substituted paste for the twenty-five-carat amethyst, and sold the stone for a Vincentian charity.

'If you can stand the pace, Eminence,' he said, 'please God I can. Good night.'

When he had gone Regazzi put his papers in order and locked his desk drawers. He switched out the harsh little working light on its long flexible neck, and except for a single corner lamp the room was dark. He flicked that off at the door and went out. His room was on the same floor as his office; he had moved out of the comfortable suite occupied by former cardinals, and the bedroom was bleak, with nothing but necessities for sleeping and keeping his clothes. He spent little enough time in it. But that night he didn't go there; he walked on down the corridor and down the stairs. By his orders the chapel was never locked; he went into it, and paused. There was no austerity here, none of the ruthless pruning of luxuries which had made him so unpopular with his priests and staff. This was the Tabernacle of God, the golden shrine of that supreme mystery which had brought Martino Regazzi from the delinquent slum background of his youth in a crusader's quest for glory. But glory for God, not for himself. He genuflected and went to the altar rail to kneel. Perhaps it was this silence, so different from the chaos of his ordinary life, which had stirred the vocation in his heart. He didn't know; he had spent a lot of time thinking about it, examining his motives for pride or psychological slants. No doubt there were other explanations beside the call of God, but he was not aware of them. He loved the peace, the isolation of the empty chapel, empty of people but to him full of that other personality. And when he needed comfort or encouragement, this was where the Cardinal found it. He had made a decision that night; perhaps the biggest decision of his life since he became a priest. He was going to commit the unforgivable sin and enter into politics. It was not an easy choice; he was brave and there was more than a streak of braggadocio from his Sicilian grandmother, but what he was going to say from the pulpit of St Pat's Cathedral would open the skies on him. The Church was political; but when people said this they weren't paying any compliment. Even for Catholics it was a facet of their religion which they preferred to play down. The Vatican was far enough away to conduct itself like a national government in international affairs, but God help the priest who started weighing in for candidates at home. That was one reason why Regazzi had stayed neutral, refusing to ally with the obvious choice, an Irish Catholic democrat whose family counted the last Cardinal as their closest friend. Also he didn't like them. Millionaires were not his kind of people, however similar their background might have been. The Cardinal believed in that unpopular saying that no good man dies rich; he went further still and said he couldn't live rich either. He hadn't supported Casey, because he wanted to be independent, to be everyone's champion, rather than the Father Confessor to the White House. But not supporting was different from not condemning. The sins of omission were more heinous than the rest. That way was cowardice, indifference, sloth. John R. Jackson was the worst thing to happen in American politics in anybody's memory. A lot of people were fighting him, but it seemed to Regazzi that from the citadels of American Catholicism the voice had been tactful if not mute. The Church of God was the Church of the poor, the coloureds, the underprivileged, the dropouts, more, in his opinion, than of the respectable people whose security was threatened by these elements. Had society been less selfish, more Christian in its distribution of the great riches of America, there would have been no problem population and no threat. The rich had many champions. He, Martino Regazzi, was about to become the champion of the rest and throw his Christian challenge in Jackson's face; literally because he would be sitting there among the congregation on St Patrick's Day. He had worked on the first draft of that speech; there would be many more before the final text. And that was why he had woken poor old Patrick Jameson, whom he knew was asleep in the outer office. He had needed somebody to turn to, somebody to confide in, and the impulse overcame him. He had judged his private secretary long ago. He had told the truth when he said Jameson was a good priest and a good man. He was simple and kind, without pretensions except a natural yearning for a little ease in life. His loyalty was something the Cardinal wanted very badly. That night, with this burden of decision on him, he had been human enough to come right out and ask for it. He knelt for a long time, praying for courage and strength, and he thanked God for the generosity of Patrick Jameson, who had suffered him for three long years and not refused him in his need.

CHAPTER THREE

In the four years since he walked out on Elizabeth Cameron life had changed direction for Peter Mathews. He had done the usual things rich men's sons did—gone through Yale and into his family's broking business; slept with pretty girls and taken a few amusing trips; involved himself in a divorce case and come out without marrying the woman. He had been conventional in all the conventional ways of wealth and amorality and been bored to death in the process. His affair with Elizabeth had been one of many; it was no landmark in itself. He only remembered it in detail because right after he escaped, and he used the word in connection with the marriage he felt she expected him to offer, he decided to change his job as well as his bedmate. He took a plane down to Washington to lunch with an old class-mate who was with the State Department, and over the third J. & B. whisky he asked him outright if he could think of anything, he, Peter Mathews, could do before he went berserk and reinvested all his clients' money in a South American gold mine.

He came back to New York with his question unanswered; by the end of the week he had forgotten ever asking it. And then the class-mate called him up and this time there was another man at lunch. The same man, who was sitting behind his desk in the New York offices of the C.I.A. four years later, asking Mathews about that old affair with Elizabeth Cameron. He had taken the bored, spoiled loafer out of his broker's office and made him into one of the best local operators in the Agency. Peter Mathews looked the same, mixed in a wider circle than before, but kept them amused with the old blend of flippancy and good nature which had always opened doors. And sheets. Inside, the restless, unscrupulous instincts had been channelled away from the bed, the bottle and the jetting junket from one resort to the next; Mathews had all the interest and excitement he needed. In return he had willingly toughened and disciplined himself. Francis J. Leary wouldn't have covered one lapse that could be traced to sloth or carelessness. Mathews knew that. He liked his boss; he had liked him over that lunch four years ago, and he still did, in spite of his being an Irishman. Mathews found the Irish tricky people; so many of them had a chip on their shoulders. Leary had no irritability; he was affable, with a generous allotment of his people's charm, a quick sense of humour which enjoyed Mathews' slick wit, and he was also the most exacting and pitiless bastard in his profession that Mathews had ever met.

Now Leary wanted to know about Elizabeth. He knew of the association because Mathews' own background had been thoroughly checked. The idea didn't worry him. He found it rather amusing to have his girl friends catalogued and filed away.

'Have you seen Miss Cameron at all since you broke up?' Leary asked.

'A few times, but only at other people's parties.'

'Did you part on friendly terms?'

'Medium friendly. I said I didn't want to get married; she said okay. That kind of thing. No malice; no scenes. She's a very civilised girl.'

'She sounds it,' Leary said. He didn't make it a complimentary remark.

'Can I know what this is all about? It's a bit late for a paternity suit ...'

Leary laughed. 'You're a bastard, Pete,' he said. 'It's not about anything much—yet. I just want a character check on the girl, and I knew you'd been connected with her.'

'You could put it like that,' Mathews said innocently.

'Shut up. Did she ever discuss politics with you?'

'No sir. She had a good little brain, but I never encouraged it. I don't think she had any opinions.'

'When you were with her,' Leary went on, 'who were her friends? Were they in your set? Did she have any odd acquaintances, people from a different strata? Any intellectuals?'

'No. Her mother was arty; she had the house full of bloody painters and musicians, but Liz didn't pick up any herself. Her mother was a kind of patron. Liz was just like all the other girls; we all went around in the same crowd. She certainly wasn't Left, if that's what you mean. Not with her money!'

Leary took his glasses off and put them away in a cloth case. 'She's going around with someone we don't like the smell of,' he said. He always used the word smell to describe a suspect. 'You know anything about Eddi King, man who owns *Future*?'

'He's an egghead, right-wing Republican. The magazine is an influential monthly, mostly concerned with politics. Why? Does he smell?'

'Never mind why,' Leary said. 'He just does. That's what interests us in Miss Cameron. Would you say they were sleeping together?'

'Unlikely,' Mathews said. 'It took all my charm to make it; maybe he's got a lot of charm. But it doesn't sound like her. She never went for older men and this guy's well in his fifties, isn't he?—I don't know, of course, but I wouldn't think so.'

'Could you go and see her? Talk to her—would she talk to you?'

'I don't know,' Mathews hesitated. 'I could try, anyway, if that's what you want. Just brief me.'

'Okay. Sound her out about King. If she's involved, leave it alone. But strictly alone, understand. If she's not, get her to come round and see me. I have something to show her which might interest her. But keep that to the last. Just make contact and scout the land first.'

'All right, Mr Leary. I'll call her this morning. Ask her out to lunch.'

When Mathews had left his office, Leary got out a file from his top drawer. It was a new file, with a green sticker, marking it extremely confidential and most secret. The name of Eddi King was printed on a little card slotted in the cover. There was not much inside. Everything Leary had been able to gather about King was on the three sheets of paper. He had begun the investigation in a hurry, and these things needed lots of time and patience. He glanced through it again. King came from Minneapolis; his birth date was given as December 9th, 1918. Educated at Minneapolis High School and Wisconsin College. Parents died in late '28, King being the only child inherited the whole estate. Worked for ten years with a publishing firm in New York, now extinct, and then went to Europe; interned in France during the war. Returned to the U.S. in 1956. Not married, started magazine in '58. His address in New York, and a weekend house at Vermont. Close friend of Huntley Cameron and frequenter of right-wing circles. Ref. *Time* Magazine Nov. '67 issue. No scandals or deviations apparent from the first checking. Lately escorted Elizabeth Cameron, with whom he flew to Beirut for a week's holiday. And that was all his people had uncovered. And there wouldn't have been a file on King at all except for a report received from Leary's own agent in the Sûreté in Paris. The C.I.A. were often accused of penetrating and subverting the intelligence services of other countries and inducing agents to act for them. It was accused of many unorthodox and ungentlemanly acts, and it was Leary's private boast that much of what was said was true. He had men working within the French Intelligence who passed on anything they thought might interest the C.I.A. And it was one item in just such a report that was pinned to the bottom of the last page on Eddi King. The proprietress of a fashionable Paris brothel had mentioned in her report to the Sûreté that the leading French communist Marcel Druet had visited the establishment in order to meet an American called King. Leary's man had followed the lead right up to the cab which took King back to his hotel, the next morning, and identified him from the hotel register. That was the smell Leary had in his nostrils. Druet was one of their top men. He didn't go to brothels to meet anyone but another top man. Eddi King, the wealthy intellectual publisher. It didn't just smell; in Leary's view it stank. He just hoped that Miss Elizabeth Cameron didn't have the same kind of odour. It was possible that she might know a lot more about Mr King than his people had been able to uncover. And what she didn't know she might be able to find out, right from the inside. He hoped Peter Mathews didn't ball it up. He made a note on the file, and closed it. He had men working on it in Minneapolis, going through the school records, checking at the college. Somewhere, someone had got at King. Most probably during his internment in France. The French would follow that one up. In the meantime Leary had ordered a thorough check on everyone who worked for *Future*. His superior might think that this activity was going too fast and too far on a single lead, but Leary had one argument which silenced every protest. An election was coming up. Anything could happen.

Keller had been a week in America; he thought of it with amusement, but like all his jokes the humour was thin and inclined to bitterness. One week, spent cooped up in the luxury apartment with the Magritte painting staring at him from the wall, reading the books he found in the guest bedroom, one after another, watching television and waiting for a call that didn't come. Nobody had contacted him. Elizabeth Cameron came and went, pretending to act normally while the strain grew more apparent every day. She cooked for him; she went out for lunch and disappeared during the day to do whatever rich women did to waste their time, and then they spent the evenings together. At first he had gone to his room early, thrown himself on the bed and tried to sleep.

After the fourth day he gave in; he felt stifled, savage with tension and uncertainty. He was a man who couldn't bear confinement and inactivity. He let her take him out and show him New York, and in spite of himself he began to relax and enjoy what he saw. It was a fabulous city; it couldn't be compared to Paris, which was the only European capital he knew, and the cities of the Middle and Far East were so different that they might have existed on another planet. She was right when she described New York as an exciting place; it reminded Keller of an enormous glittering hive, peopled by a species of human he had never met before. Always hurrying, driven by time, by that curious American word hustle, which couldn't be translated and yet described so much, living at a pace that frayed the nerves and made the Martini into a national emblem. It had a beauty which was peculiar to itself; the glacial buildings, towering into the sky, the two great rivers, the Hudson and the East, running through the asphalt island like twin arteries, the oasis of Central Park—above all the unbelievable panorama of the city at night. She had taken him driving one evening, and as they crawled through the long traffic jams, Keller was reminded of a firework display, a city of Golden Rain, where the lights were squandered on the night, dispensed like a sackful of jewels over the heads of the moving crowds.

'It's beautiful isn't it?' Elizabeth said. 'Not like Europe, but it's not meant to be. It's so essentially American. I love it!'

'You have a lot of enthusiasms,' Keller said. 'It must be good to feel like that about a place.'

'You've never cared about your country?'

'I have no country,' he said. 'I was born in France, but that means nothing. I have grown up anywhere; one orphanage is the same as another.'

They had stopped at a traffic intersection. When the lights changed they moved on; he noticed that she drove very well. She had told the truth when she said she was efficient and resourceful, but what had surprised him was the erratic feminine streak, the sudden hesitancy that made him grab her arm to cross the street. He had never felt protective about a woman before; his attitude to Souha was almost paternal, as if he were dealing with a child whom the world had already knocked to the ground too often and he were angrily determined to prevent more bruising. But there was nothing of that in his feeling for Elizabeth Cameron. She was a mixture that confused him, constantly arousing new impulses which he had not experienced before. She didn't need protecting, not like the Arab girl who had been born on the defensive. She was rich and self-assured, she could do most things as well as most men, but whenever he was near her he wanted to take her arm, or carry her parcel, or just stop the car and turn her to him. He watched her as they drove. She was unselfconscious about her beauty, as if she didn't realise how he was affected by her. But when they came close or touched by accident, there was a pleading in her eyes that begged him to be gentle, not to take advantage

64

of her. He understood desire; he knew what it could do to a man's nerves and how it could distort his judgement, albeit temporarily. He knew because that was just what he felt for her; but resisting the temptation to just walk into her room at night and take her in his arms was only possible because of other, unfamiliar feelings which he refused to name, even to himself. Love was not a word he would admit. When she went out he prowled round the apartment, bored and irritable, waiting for the sound of the elevator and the click of her key in the lock.

When she was with him he forgot why he had come to New York, he forgot to listen for the telephone call which still hadn't come; he forgot about Souha and the Lebanon as if his past were a dream, and the days spent with Elizabeth were the only reality.

They were back at her apartment; they got out of the car and the doorman climbed in to drive away. Keller was accepted; he even rated the head doorman's salute. Elizabeth turned to him in the hallway and smiled.

'Would you like a drink?'

'No.' Keller took her coat as she slipped out of it and for a moment his hands closed over her shoulders. It was a mistake to touch her, a dangerous indulgence in something he had promised both of them would never recur. He felt her stiffen and immediately he stepped back.

'You don't have to be afraid of me,' he said. 'I told you that.'

'I'm not afraid of you,' Elizabeth said. 'Only myself.'

'I can't go on staying here,' Keller said suddenly. 'It won't work. It could be a long time before anyone contacts me. And I can't answer for myself much longer. I've got enough money, I can go to a hotel. You can take a message for me. It would be better that way. Better for you.'

'Please don't go.' She came close to him; he looked down at her and saw her eyes had filled with tears. 'Don't go away. I don't want you to leave. All right, I know what it'll mean if you stay, but I don't care. Do you understand that— I don't care what may happen. I'm in love with you.'

She put out her hand and he caught it. They moved towards each other and he closed both arms round her.

'You mustn't say that,' he said. 'You don't know anything about me. You don't know what you're talking about;

65

you should have a good man, someone to marry you.' With one hand he stroked the blonde hair back from her face. 'If I ever got my hands on the one who left you, I'd beat his head in.'

'You wouldn't need to,' Elizabeth said quietly. 'I thought I was in love. I thought that making love to him was real, but now I know it wasn't. I guess you're the only real man I've ever met in my life. When I think about him, all I wish is that it hadn't happened.'

'If you regret your nice clean-living American,' Keller said slowly, 'how much more are you going to regret me?'

She put both arms around his neck; immediately his hold tightened, gripping her body against his.

'I don't know,' Elizabeth whispered. 'If I lose you, probably for ever.'

'Where did you get those marks?' Elizabeth leaned over him, tracing the savage scars down one side of his chest. There was no shyness, no inhibition left in her now. Every day she learned more about love. It wasn't all passion; it was just as much the slow contentment of lying close and talking in the half-light. It was the way he kissed her now, after they had made love, and soothed her to sleep in his arms. Mathews had never been gentle afterwards. He had separated quickly and made jokes, as if he was afraid of being taken seriously. With this man it was all different. So many contrasts, from the fierce masculine possession to the silent tenderness that made her love him more each day. It didn't seem possible that they had become lovers only a week before. She repeated the question.

'How did you get those scars? Tell me.'

He put his finger on a jagged weal that ran down from his left shoulder. 'That was a fight in a brothel in Algiers.'

'I don't want to hear about the brothel,' Elizabeth said. 'Tell me about the fight.'

'There was this German Legionnaire—he called himself Beloff,' Keller said. 'But that wasn't his name. He was a bastard. A mean one. He hated my insides and I hated his. He was supposed to be an officer in one of the S.S. regiments. We had a fight over one of the whores in this place. He was no officer—he used his feet too well. Not as well as I used mine, so he found himself a bottle.'

'Don't,' she pleaded, closing her eyes against the picture of the jagged glass tearing into his skin. 'Please don't . . .'

Keller laughed. 'He was in the sick bay for a month,' he said. 'If he was a war criminal I did him a favour. His own mother wouldn't have recognised him. Most of us were Germans on the run anyway. The non-coms were French; they were bastards too.'

'You were in the Foreign Legion?' She sat up a little, staring at him. 'I can't believe it. I thought that was just something they made movies about with Gary Cooper.'

'Who do you think was doing the fighting at Dien Bien Phu?'

She shook her head at him and smiled. 'I never heard of it.'

'It's a place called Viet Nam,' Keller said. 'Now you must have heard of *that*! That's where I got these two holes.'

He put her fingers against his ribs. 'I was three months in hospital in Saigon. When we pulled out I'd had enough. I deserted. I'd spent my whole life looking at the world from the gutter. I wanted to get some money and see if it looked better from a different angle.'

'You know something,' Elizabeth said. 'I've told you everything about myself. I know practically nothing about you, Bruno. I want to know what happened before I met you. I want to hear about the orphanage and afterwards and the Legion. Will you tell me?'

It was true that she had told him everything about herself. She had lost all reticence; it seemed to have disappeared with her reserve and all the inhibitions which Peter Mathews had left intact; the first night spent in Keller's arms had blown them up as if they were dynamited. Elizabeth had told him about her childhood, her parents, intimate details of her life which she had never imagined sharing with anyone else, and he had listened to it all.

He had never talked about himself to anyone before; it was difficult to find the words. He had never told Souha anything, and she had never thought of asking. But Elizabeth had taught him that a woman could be a companion, an equal and ally. He pulled her down and kissed her. She had a soft mouth and he loved running his hand down her smooth hair. It was like fine silk; he could blow strands of it in the air. You're a fool. He said this to himself a dozen times. A fool living in a fantasy and what you're doing with this girl is insane for both of you. But he couldn't stop what was happening. It had gone too far and too fast. He couldn't stop making love to her and now he couldn't stop the deadly, insidious joy of loving her for every other reason too. Like the colour of her brown eyes, which had green lights in them, or the way she kissed him to wake him in the morning. He loved her because she was intelligent; she could talk and he forgot she wasn't a man. And he loved her even more because she was suddenly silly, and had never heard of Dien Bien Phu.

'What do you want to know about me?' he said.

'Everything. What was it like to be in an orphanage?'

'I don't know,' Keller hesitated, trying to remember. What could he say to describe the long years of an existence so uniform that time itself had no relevance? The routine, the smells, the discipline, the punishments, the crushing lack of privacy. He couldn't explain them except by one word, and this was a better summary than most.

'It was lonely,' he said. 'But it was better than being outside. I knew that much from some of the other children who came later. My mother didn't keep me for long; she gave me to the nuns when I was a few weeks old.'

'How could she?' Elizabeth said angrily. 'How could she have abandoned you?'

'I used to think that,' Keller said. 'I used to brood about it and call her names—whoever she was. But afterwards I understood a little. She must have been poor; she'd been seduced and left with a bastard. With my name, the man must have been a German, maybe a visitor—I saw women trying to keep a child. It isn't easy for them.'

'It wasn't exactly easy for you either,' she said. 'Were you well treated? Were they kind to you?'

'There were three hundred of us, and a war going on,' he said. 'They were as kind as they could manage to be. One nun was good to me; she used to pay me some attention, more than the others. She asked me to write to her when I left. I did, once, but I had no address so I never got an answer.'

'What did you do then, after the orphanage?' Elizabeth asked him. She was beginning to regret having asked. There was such a bleakness in his description.

'I tried working. I was fifteen. I worked for a grocer in Lyons. He paid me nothing and his daughter kept trying to get me to sleep with her. I remember her; she was a little older and she had a way of coming round me all the time and looking at me.' He laughed. 'I hadn't seen any women except the Sisters; I didn't like that one much, and so she got me thrown out. She told her father I was stealing.'

'And were you?' Elizabeth asked.

'Yes, of course. I didn't get enough to eat. So I stole and sold the stuff on the black market. There was a lot like that; a job here and there. Never enough money to live, so I started to live the other way. And I'm not going to tell you about that.'

'All right,' she said gently. 'You've told me enough anyway.'

He lit a cigarette and smoked it silently, remembering the things he wouldn't tell her. The beating-up he got from the couple who took him in to work in a café after he hitch-hiked from Lyons to Paris. He had misunderstood the job and let the American troops get out of the place without importuning on behalf of the brothel which was running at the back of the café. He had been kicked black and blue and left in the street outside, retching blood into the gutter. It was not his first beating, but he was sixteen and he had decided then, wiping the tears and spittle away from his damaged face, that it would be his last. He had never taken anything again without making sure he gave it back, and doubled it.

'I was a thief,' he said. 'I worked for the black market and I sold everything I could get money for. But I lived like a dog, sniffing round dustbins, hungry and hating the world which had so much and wouldn't give me any of it. So I took. It was the way I learnt to live. When it got too hot for me I joined the Legion. It seemed better than getting arrested.'

'It wasn't your fault,' she said. 'Whatever you did, you had no choice. You were only a child, and there wasn't anyone to give a damn what happened to you.' She put her arms round him and held him. 'You never had a chance. But do you know something? When I think of you as a little boy, growing up like that, being alone in the world—it makes me love you even more!'

He smiled and let her hold him. 'I thought you might be shocked,' he said. 'I left the Legion to make a new start.'

'And that's when you came to Beirut,' she said. 'Will you tell me about your girl there—how did you meet her?'

'I found her in the gutter as I was walking home one night. She had passed out with hunger. There are hundreds of refugees like her, selling themselves for a few pence. But she wasn't a whore. She was too thin and ugly, poor little devil. Nobody would have wanted her.'

'But you did,' Elizabeth said slowly.

'I didn't know what to do with her and she wouldn't go away,' Keller corrected. 'Have you ever had a human being lie outside your door and try to kiss your feet? I took her in. And she cared for me.'

'She must love you,' Elizabeth said. 'She must love you very much.'

'I think she does.' He reached out for the cigarettes; they both smoked for a while without speaking. 'Most Arabs would have robbed me naked the first night and then run off. But not Souha. The only thing she wants is me.' He turned and looked at Elizabeth. 'If we were in Beirut she'd poison you,' he said, 'and think she was right to do it.'

'How nice.'

'Don't judge,' Keller said quietly. 'It's a different world to yours. When you have nothing you fight very dirty to keep even that. In your world I'm nothing; to someone like her I'm a prize. A man who doesn't beat her or put her out to whore, someone to buy her sweets and make her laugh. I gave her some money before I left. Maybe it would buy that fur coat of yours. But she's rich for life now. Whatever happens she'll be all right.'

'What could happen?' Elizabeth drew back from him. In the dim light he could see the anxious eyes, the changing look of fear in her face. He was talking too much. And he had nearly made a dangerous admission. He took her in his arms and told a lie.

'I might decide not to go back,' he said.

Fuad Hamedin had bought himself a new car. He had a passion for sleek American models with chassis like space-ships; he loved the huge parking lights that opened a monster red eye in the dark, the heaters, the radio, the electrically

70

operated windows, the power-assisted steering. He bought a beautiful Ford convertible, two-tone blue and beige, with white-walled tyres, and he stroked it as if it were a woman. The money for fixing Keller had been very good. He had been paid through the post, and that was the end of it. He wondered what that bum was doing to earn his fortune, or if he'd ever earn it. Fuad thought not; those sort of jobs carried a double risk. Capture by the law and disposal by the employer. Keller would be very lucky if he saw a dollar of his money. That would leave his girl with a nice little cache he had provided for her. She might be worth visiting later on, when Fuad was sure it was safe. He drove his new car home and took his wife and their three children for a long drive. His wife was a pretty girl, his two sons and a daughter were plump and pampered; the youngest boy whined continually because both his parents spoiled him. They settled back in the new car, talking and laughing, shouting at the children and at each other, the radio turned on a frequency with high-pitched Arab music. It was a fine day and Fuad took his family up in the hills behind the city, where the view was magnificent, the sea spread out from the curving green land like a sheet of blue silk. The sun shone, and inside the car it was warm. Fuad had only taken delivery that morning. It drove like a bird; the narrow roads wouldn't allow him to accelerate and he changed direction, bringing the car down from the heights to the broader high-way leading into the city itself. To try it out properly he drove down to the coast road, and on towards the airport. It was two in the afternoon, and there was little traffic. He nudged his wife, and she laughed. The speedometer said sixty. Fuad began to press on the accelerator. They had reached eighty when the mechanism attached to the speedometer needle fired the explosive charge. Under that speed he could have driven the car with safety for a year.

Ten miles from the airport where he had first acted as a tout twenty years before, Fuad Hamedin and his family blew up in a tangle of steel and scything engine parts. The remains of the car and the bodies were scattered over fifty yards. Druet had kept the first part of his promise. Only Keller's girl was left to silence.

'It's nice to see you again, Liz. You're looking great.' Peter

Mathews smiled at her across the table. He had contacted her as Leary wanted; the phone call had been difficult; on the other end her voice was cold, disinterested. Mathews didn't feel snubbed; he had been told to see her and that's what he was going to do. No, she couldn't lunch. Or dine. Or let him come up for a drink. Mathews had a real instinct that she was not alone in the apartment while they talked. Another boy friend? It wasn't Eddi King; he was in Frankfurt. They had checked on that. In the end she agreed to have a drink with him and he chose the 21 because it was a place they used to go. She did look good; he meant the compliment sincerely. They faced each other over the little table, and he noticed that the position was her choice; she deliberately avoided the banquette. She hadn't always felt like that about him, he remembered. She used to be the one who wanted to hold hands all the time.

'You're looking well too,' she said. Keller had thought the call was for him. Only relief that it wasn't had trapped her into accepting Peter's invitation at all. That and the fear that he might just come on up to the apartment if she refused to meet him. He hadn't changed at all; in the few encounters since they split up she had never really looked at him. Now she could and did, because he meant so little to her that it might have been a stranger with the Martini in his hand and the same old grin on his mouth.

'Why the reunion?' she asked him.

'Why not? I thought it might be my last chance. I've wanted to call lots of times, Liz, but I felt maybe you wouldn't feel like Auld Lang Syne just yet. You were a bit sore at me, weren't you?'

'A bit,' she admitted. 'But not any more. Is that what you wanted to hear?'

'Partly. Partly that you're not sore and partly that you wouldn't say no if I called you up now and again. It was like getting a diamond out of a showgirl persuading you to come tonight.'

'You must have a lot of diamonds back, then,' she said. 'For here I am. Aren't any of your other girl friends free tonight?'

'I didn't try them,' Mathews said. 'It was just you, my darling, only you I wanted.' He put his hand on his heart; in spite of herself she laughed.

'You really haven't changed at all. Still the song-and-dance man, aren't you. And not married?'

'No. No, no, no. If I wouldn't marry you, Liz, who else would get me? Or want me. Okay I said it for you. But how about you—how about those rumours I hear that you're going to marry that publisher guy Eddi King?'

'What!' Putting on an act wasn't in her line; that one word and the expression on her face was all the denial Mathews needed. But she went on, angry and incredulous. 'Eddi King? He's a friend of my uncle's. I've never heard of anything so ridiculous!' She put down her drink and some of it spilled.

'You look great when you're angry too,' Mathews said. 'But what's so ridiculous about it? He's only middle-aged, and you're not seventeen; he's loaded, and he knows all the right people. After Onassis all the old guys are shaking out the moth balls. Besides, if you go off on holiday with a man, what do you expect people to think?'

'What do you mean, on holiday?' she said. How had he heard about Beirut?

'It was in the Suzy Knickerbocker column.' Mathews told the truth. ' "Seen strolling along the exotic back streets of Beirut"—you know the kind of crap.'

'You couldn't have chosen a better word,' Elizabeth said. 'He went on business for my uncle; I'd never been to the Lebanon, so he suggested I come along.'

'Well, if it isn't King, then stop getting mad and tell me who it is that's putting the stars in your eyes. You never looked like that when you were with me.'

'No,' Elizabeth said slowly. 'I imagine not.' She kept seeing Keller when she looked at Peter Mathews; the talk about herself and King had made her feel as if something were creeping over her skin. It was funny to think that it showed. Stars in her eyes, he called it, and she didn't bother to retort. She was happy, and fulfilled and in love. Sitting there in the warm atmosphere of the smart people's night haunt, the scene of so many dates in the past, she knew that this described what Mathews saw. She was in love. In love with a man who had as much in common with all the pleasant pre-packed types like Peter Mathews as an Apache Indian. Ugly. Keller was ugly, thick and broad without the flippant graces that were a part of looking down at life from

73

a mountain of dollar bills. Mathews was watching her; the expressions shifted quickly on her face, but there was a self-containment about her which didn't change. She had changed a lot; she had always been beautiful, smartly dressed with the *chic* of the best New York couturiers, but the gleaming hair hung loose over her shoulders, and the eyes were wide with a knowledge that they had never held before. Now, she was really something a man might want.

'There is a guy, isn't there? I don't want to come calling if it's serious and get a busted nose.' This wasn't part of his job, but he was curious. They moved in a small circle, exclusive because of its wealth and social activities. It couldn't be anyone he knew or someone would have mentioned it. Elizabeth didn't answer him.

'Tell me about yourself,' she said. 'How's Wall Street these days?'

'I don't know,' Mathews shrugged. 'I left Hannings; money bores me. Making money, anyway. I'm in government service now.'

'Don't tell me,' Elizabeth leaned back and smiled, mocking him. 'Don't please tell me it's the Peace Corps?'

'No, Internal Revenue Service. I hunt down tax evaders.'

'You're joking,' she said. '*Tax*—you? It's not possible.'

'Oh yes it is. I change the carbon in the typewriters and if I go on at this rate I'll get to change the ribbons next. As a matter of fact, Liz, that was another reason why I wanted to see you. My boss is dealing with some of the overseas aspects of your father's estate. Sorry to bring this up, but when you leave ten million bucks it can get complicated. Did you know he had property abroad?'

'No,' Elizabeth said. 'Why haven't you got on to my lawyers. They handled everything.'

'My boss thinks it would be quicker if he talked to you direct.'

'You're not suggesting there's been an evasion!'

'Of course not. There's just something we can't sort out. Look, Liz, I'll come right out. I said I knew you pretty well; my boss wanted to see you and I opened my big mouth and said I could fix it. It might just get me to change the ribbons if you'd call on him. Please?'

'All right,' she said, 'if you want to get inky fingers. Who is your boss, anyway?'

'His name's Leary,' Mathews said. 'You'll like him; he's quite a guy.'

'I can't imagine you and anything like income tax. It's so respectable!'

The old casual grin flashed back at her. 'Don't worry; I'm still a shit in private life. I suppose you won't change your mind and have dinner with me?'

'Sorry.' She held out her hand. 'I already have a date. I don't want to keep them waiting.'

'What the hell do you mean—there's no one there?'

King's voice began to rise. He had got in from Europe in the late evening; he had enjoyed the week spent in Frankfurt, although he didn't like the Germans. He had become quite attached to his little publishing empire over the last fifteen years. But he was tired; there had been a three-hour wait at London because of some engine fault and he hadn't been able to relax for the rest of the flight. First he had dropped into a hot bath and given himself a large Bourbon, then he called his middle contact just to check that the arrangements for Keller were satisfactory. There were still three weeks to go and he wanted to be sure he was kept happy and out of trouble. He made the call as a routine; when he asked the prearranged question about his friend from overseas, hoping he liked the accommodation, he was in no way prepared for that answer.

'He never showed up.' The man at the other end had been frantic for two weeks; he had a job to do, and that was to take over Keller when he got to the rooming house on 39th. But he never came, and because it was forbidden to contact King in Germany under any emergency the middleman could do nothing in his absence. He had found out that Maggio was run over by a truck and that told him where the link was broken. He tried to get this across to King.

'You remember my chauffeur?' Chauffeur was a pick-up's code name between them.

'Yes.' King stiffened. Christ, if he'd got arrested. He had never been happy about using the petty criminal element like Maggio, but this was not his responsibility. That section of his network was controlled and organised by someone else. He had the use of it but no say in how it operated. 'Yes, what about him?'

'He got run over. Killed outright.'

'Too bad.' So that was what had happened. Keller hadn't been met at Kennedy. His contact had been killed, and the whole elaborate set-up fell to pieces. Just wait till I put in a report about this. King's mind raced ahead in fury at the incompetence which hadn't prepared for any emergency including sudden death. Just wait, you stupid bastards.

'All right,' he snapped down the phone. 'I'll just have to phone round some of the hotels and see if I can trace my friend. But keep the room booked. I'll be in touch as soon as I've located him.' He crashed the receiver back on its cradle; the whole instrument jangled in protest. His hands were shaking; Keller had got lost. Just because he had gone to attend to other business and left the last hook-up to the New York people, it had got completely out of control. He remembered his confident remark to Druet in the Paris brothel. 'Everything's going according to plan.' He could imagine the report Druet would send him once this was known. Blaming his own reception network wouldn't help him. This was his operation; he had emphasised that too strongly to slide backwards now. If it misfired, if his killer was lost, picked up, traced back to Beirut. He wiped his face with a handkerchief; the sweat made a stain on the white silk. There was one chance; one hope. It was just possible that Elizabeth hadn't walked out on him at Kennedy without waiting to see he was met. Unlikely. She had said very clearly that she didn't like the look of the man, and he had been emphatic yet again, telling her to just walk him through and leave. He looked at his watch. It was eleven-thirty. He picked up the phone. It rang for so long that his hand was going down reaching for the cradle to hang up when through the distance he heard Elizabeth answer.

They had been watching television. Keller was fascinated by it; it was such a childish quirk that Elizabeth indulged him through every B movie, quiz game and series. He had never seen anything like it. And it was comforting to sit together, close in his arm, watching him discover this facet of America. They had been watching a news programme; he had turned to her at the beginning and suggested that they might be tired. And she had laughed, and taken his hand away from her breast and said that this time there was something *she* wanted to watch. 'That's a remarkable man,'

76

she said. The image of Cardinal Regazzi had come on the screen; he was giving a news interview on the problem of drug delinquency in the pre-teens.

Keller sat forward a little and listened. 'You mean your *children* take the stuff?' He sounded shocked; in the countries he knew where life was lived in such a sub level anything was possible, but here, in this rich indulgent city, bursting with opulence like an overfilled shopping bag, it seemed incredible.

'More and more. Listen to Regazzi. He really knows about poverty.'

'There isn't any poverty here,' Keller said. 'And I've never seen a poor cardinal. You're not a Catholic, are you?'

'No.' Elizabeth shook her head. 'But you must be, brought up by nuns.'

Keller didn't answer. He sat watching the small screen; the man could really project himself, even in a few minutes.

'What do you think is the cause of this?' The interviewer's voice came through, off camera.

'When a child wants to escape from his world so badly that he can't get enough fantasy from books and movies and television, all the escapist aids we have to offer, then that means he's getting starved of everything he has a right to—opportunity, security, love and hope. If some of the money spent on keeping these children in reform schools was spent on re-housing and better education they wouldn't need drugs.'

Keller said, 'He's not making sense. Everybody's rich here.'

'Oh no they're not,' Elizabeth said. 'All you've seen is this little golden acre. There's desperate poverty in this country. Regazzi knows what he's talking about, he came from that kind of background himself, and he's spent his life fighting for the poor. I think his religion's all wrong, but he's a great man.'

'All religion is a lie,' Keller said. He remembered the Sister of Charity who had given him a rosary when he left the orphanage, and stood by the gate wiping her eyes. 'Catholics are no more wrong than anyone else.'

And that was when the phone began to ring. 'Answer it,' Keller said. 'It may be for me.'

'That's what I'm afraid of.' Elizabeth stood up slowly.

'Nobody rings at this hour. Leave it, Bruno. Let them call tomorrow.'

'Answer it,' he said, 'or I will.' And that was when King heard her speak.

She turned her back to Keller, trying to keep her face hidden. 'Why, hello—how was your trip?'

'Fine,' King pitched his voice just right, sitting on his anxiety like a box lid. 'What about you—how was our friend?'

'Stranded,' Elizabeth said. There was no use pretending to Keller, she turned round and nodded to him. He got up and came beside her. 'Nobody picked him up. No, we hung around waiting and so I thought he'd better stay with me.' She made it sound casual. 'No, no trouble at all. I've hardly seen him. He spends his time sleeping mostly.' There was a sudden gleam in Keller's eyes; he put both hands round her waist and squeezed.

'With you,' he said under his breath. 'Give me the phone.'

'Do you want me to call him?' Elizabeth asked.

King sounded very gay on the other end of the line. He was so relieved he couldn't hide it. 'No thanks, my dear. I'm so upset you've had this trouble.' He injected some concern. 'You're sure he hasn't bothered you? You should have put him in a hotel—Elizabeth, I can't tell you how sorry I am— look, let me arrange for someone to pick him up first thing in the morning. Let me come round and take you out to lunch and make it up to you.'

'I can't lunch,' she said. 'I've got an appointment at the tax office; I don't know how long it'll take.'

'Just leave everything to me from now on,' King said. 'And of course you did the right thing keeping him with you. I'll explain when we meet. I'll get him out of there tomorrow.'

She put back the receiver. 'That was the man I was with in Beirut,' she said. 'Eddi King. He's fixing to move you out tomorrow. Bruno, I don't want you to go.'

'I've got to go. I'm being paid.'

'But paid for what? We're lovers, darling, why can't you trust me?'

'I'm being paid to do what I'm told,' Keller said. 'And I go tomorrow if that's what your friend said. What I do tonight is on my own time. Come here and let me teach

78

you something. Tomorrow is a question mark. Tonight we can be sure of, so don't waste it.'

Francis Leary's office was on the seventh floor of a big office block on Lower Broadway. Two complete floors were rented by Leary's people under the title of the Trans-Oceanic Shipping Company, which was registered and traded on the eastern seaboard. It provided a working cover for Leary's New York headquarters.

Leary had his desk facing the window, so that the panorama of the great city moved constantly before his eyes. He found the changing scene a powerful stimulant to thought; aesthetically he loved it for its typical admixture of beauty and ugliness. The sluggish stream of cars, the hurrying crowds in the street below, its perimeter cut by the jagged horizon of tall buildings, the glimpse of trees, festooned with flashing lights as the evening came—this was part of the city where Leary had been born, where his grandparents had landed from a starving, desolate Ireland, to found a family and a new life. Leary was part of America, but more especially he was part of the beautiful, violent city itself; it had spawned him from the squalid ghettos of the West Side where the immigrant Irish congregated. Leary had fought his way out into the affluence and taken a piece of it for himself. He had a successful business selling commercial-radio advertising space when the war broke out. He had been transferred to Intelligence from the infantry and that was where his life changed direction until he ended in the office on the seventh floor. He had spent an hour reading everything available on Miss Elizabeth Cameron. Like Eddi King there wasn't much material with which to make a file. She was twenty-seven years old, born of money married to more money, orphaned in a crash that killed eighty-four people. He had underlined this in thick pencil. He made marks on all his papers; the most confidential dossiers were scrawled and smudged by that pencil. Leary's files were famous for their untidiness. There was a Presidential memo to that effect. Leary had it framed and hung it in his study at home. She had been living with Peter Mathews but there was no evidence of any association with another man, and from Mathews' own report that morning, she was not involved personally with Eddi King. Mathews

79

had emphasised her devotion to her mother. Leary looked at his watch. It was eleven-forty-five; she should be there any moment. He picked up a wooden box about nine inches long, and moved it till it was in front of him. It looked as if it contained cigars. The buzzer on his desk announced both Mathews and Miss Cameron.

Leary buzzed back to send them in. When she came into his office he came round the desk, his hand held out to her, a neat almost dapper man, with a thin Irish face and bright blue eyes.

'Good morning, Pete. Miss Cameron? How nice of you to come along. Take a seat here, won't you.'

He hadn't expected her to be so pretty; photographs weren't that reliable because they missed the expression; in the clips on the file she looked like any other well-dressed socialite posing for the camera. The expression was the person; even without the advantage of her colouring and the honey haze mink coat, she hit right over the heart when she looked at him. What the hell, he thought immediately, had she seen in a bed-hopper like Mathews?—even allowing it was four years ago. 'Do you smoke?'

'Thank you.' Elizabeth took one and he lit it for her. He noticed that she held it steadily.

'Pete, I know you've got things to do. Miss Cameron and I can have our little talk and I'll send down for you when she's ready.'

'Okay, sir. 'Bye Liz.'

Elizabeth watched him go out. He had never called anyone sir, not even her uncle. He had changed a lot in the four years; the easy-going grin was like the laughing mask on the Roman god with two faces. Mathews at his work, calling Leary 'sir', was the Janus side she had never suspected.

'You must think this is an odd request, Miss Cameron.' Leary leaned forward and smiled at her. He wanted her to feel at ease, and like all his race he had abundant charm. He wanted her perfectly relaxed and off guard before he showed her what was in the wooden box.

'How much did Peter explain to you?'

'Not much,' she said. 'He mentioned something to do with my father's estate and some tax problem you wanted to discuss. I must warn you that I'm not very good at this sort of thing. My lawyers deal with everything for me.'

'I see.' Leary leaned backwards, tipping his chair. Income tax. Trust Mathews to think of something like that. Of course she was disarmed. 'Miss Cameron, I don't know how annoyed you're going to be, but I'm afraid I don't know anything about income tax either.'

'In that case,' Elizabeth stared at him, 'in that case, Mr. Leary, what am I doing here? I'm afraid I don't understand . . .'

'This office has nothing to do with anybody's tax,' Leary said. 'I told Mathews to bring you here, I didn't tell him what to say to you. This is the New York office of the Central Intelligence Agency. I'm one of its senior officials. If Peter Mathews told you he was with the Internal Revenue then he's a lying s.o.b. But I guess you know that already.' He looked across at her and smiled his engaging smile.

'Actually, he's one of my best men. Will you help us? He was sure you would.'

'He's a little too sure of himself, I think,' Elizabeth said. 'In what way can I possibly help you?'

'You can listen to me for a while and answer a few questions, if you wouldn't mind,' Leary said. 'I'd be very grateful to you. You know the publisher Eddi King, I believe?'

'Yes, I know him. He's a friend of my uncle, Huntley Cameron.'

'He's friends with a lot of influential people,' Leary said. 'Politicians, industrialists, well-known figures in the literary world. Pretty far over to the right, isn't he?'

'I don't know,' Elizabeth answered. 'I've never discussed politics with him. I don't think he approves of my uncle supporting the Democrats. But what is all this about, Mr. Leary? Why are you asking me about Eddi King?'

'Before I answer that question,' Leary said, 'I have something to tell you. You lost both your parents in a plane crash last year, didn't you? B.707 blew up coming into Mexico City. Everyone on board was killed.'

'Yes,' she said. She shrank back a little, away from him. She didn't want to talk about it, or let him. But he went on without mercy.

'I've heard about your mother from Peter,' he said. 'She was a wonderful woman. You were devoted to each other, weren't you?'

'Please.' Elizabeth made a movement as if she were going to leave. 'Please, I find this most upsetting . . .'

'I apologise,' Leary said. 'I know how you must feel. Believe me I hate to do this. Your mother didn't die in any accident. That plane was sabotaged. She and your father were murdered as surely as if they had been shot.'

There was the sound of Elizabeth's bag falling. She went so white that Leary got out of his chair; he thought for a moment that she might collapse. He bent down and gave her back her handbag, found the cigarette which had fallen to the floor and ground it out in an ashtray. He put one hand on her shoulder.

'I'm sorry,' he said. 'I know how you must feel.'

'It isn't true,' she said. 'It just isn't true. I don't believe it!'

'I've got the proof right here—in this box.' He opened it and held out the jagged piece of metal. It was about six inches long and four inches wide, with a seared and blackened mark right through it. He put it into her hands, making her take it. The steel was cold and the edges were so rough they could have cut her skin.

'That's part of the tailplane,' Leary said. 'We dredged up a few bits of the wreckage here and there; some of it was in shallow water. We had a reason for suspecting something, Miss Cameron, and the way that plane blew up was just too damned convenient to be accidental. That piece of fuselage is one of several pieces from the same part of the plane— the rear, where the baggage was stowed. That mark is the result of an explosion; there are definite traces of tetrachlorine; one of the most powerful explosives we know. There was a bomb in the baggage, Miss Cameron. It was put there to destroy a certain person who was travelling on that plane. The Vice-President of the Republic of Panama was their target, and they got him. There's been a communist revolution in Panama which has caused an awful lot of trouble for this country, and if Miguel Mantonarez had been alive it wouldn't have happened. So they murdered him, and your parents and all the other people on that plane.'

'They?' Elizabeth whispered. She turned the ugly lump of shattered steel over and over; her hands were trembling. 'Who is "they"?'

'The communists,' Leary said. He went back and sat down again. 'They don't mind killing people; to them that old calumny against the Jesuits is really true. The end does justify the means. They killed your mother and father; they killed all the other passengers and the crew. There were children on that plane. Would you like some coffee?'

'No,' she whispered. 'No, I wouldn't. You mean—they could have been alive now except for this bomb put there to murder someone else? My mother could be alive now?'

'Surely,' Leary said.

'Why have you told me this?' She moved forward and laid the evidence of death down on his desk. She couldn't stop staring at it, at the mark left by the explosion. They must have been sitting back, relaxed in their seats, preparing to land. Her mother loved Mexico. She had bought a house at Cuernevaca. Elizabeth had helped her mother furnish it. The room began to move, as if it were on castors, and she closed her eyes, shutting out the evil, blackened splinter. The plane must have been ripped like a paper bag. One moment they were alive, perhaps leaning sideways to catch the first sight of the city, the next they were destroyed, their bodies blown to fragments, their last thoughts, the instinctive cry before death, lost in eternity, in a single convulsive flash.

'Oh my God.' She sank forward, and the blinding tears came with a rush. Leary didn't move. He waited, letting her cry. If she hadn't she would have fainted. He buzzed and his secretary answered.

'Get me two cups of coffee and a brandy, Nancy. And no calls. I don't want to be disturbed.'

Elizabeth didn't hear anyone come into the room. She felt somebody touch her and it was a light hand, not the heavy hand of Leary which had rested on her shoulder after he had explained how her mother and father died. A girl was beside her, holding a glass in one hand. She had a pleasant face, with curly brown hair, and a calm voice.

'Drink this,' the voice suggested. 'You'll feel better.' She did what she was told, and they left her in peace for a while. Leary began to look through some papers, his secretary poured the coffee and then went out.

'I'd like to go home,' Elizabeth said.

'I understand how you feel,' Leary said. 'Could you hang

83

on for a while longer? I didn't just ask you here to break your heart. I need your help. What would you say if I told you Eddi King was working with the people who put that bomb in the plane?'

'I wouldn't believe you. I couldn't believe anyone—I couldn't . . .' She stopped, the words falling away. Eddi King. Eddi King working with political assassins, communist agents—it was like a nightmare from which she couldn't wake up. It was impossible, horrible; the man sitting there a couple of feet away from her, leaning his hands together like a schoolteacher addressing a class, he couldn't be real either.

'Eddi King is not what he seems,' Leary said. 'My department have reason to suspect that he's a communist, that he's working with an international communist organisation.'

'Why do you think this?' She sounded calmer now; the brandy was anaesthetising her shaken nerves. The man sounded so cool, so factual.

'I shouldn't tell you this, but I'm going to. I need your help that badly. King went to Paris a couple of weeks ago. He met a top communist while he was there, in very secret circumstances. The man responsible for half the industrial and political upheavals in Western Europe. He started off as a bully agent; beating up strike-breakers, intimidating opponents of the party. Then he graduated to big-scale operations. There's quite a few murders to his credit. Now he's one of their best men. Can you tell me what King was doing, meeting him in secret?'

'No,' Elizabeth said. She shivered, trying to pull her coat closer. She felt very cold, as if all the windows in the room were open.

'It looks bad,' Leary said. 'It looks so bad I can't afford to keep a watch on the guy from a distance. I need help from inside. I need you to help me, Miss Cameron. That's why I told you about your parents. So you know exactly what we're dealing with in men like Eddi King.'

He paused then, letting her take his words and examine them; he made no more attempt to press her or convince her. If she said no, that was it. She wouldn't be any use to them even if she did change her mind because they couldn't be sure why she'd changed it. From his assessment Leary felt there was a good chance.

When she answered him, she looked directly at him; her eyes were swollen, her make-up smudged. She looked white and ill.

'Just tell me what you want me to do.'

'I want you to tell me everything you know about him,' Leary said. 'Who his friends are—where he travels to—and everything you can remember about Beirut.'

She wouldn't let Peter Mathews drive her home. He put her in a cab and before closing the door he hesitated. 'You're sure you won't let me ride back with you? You're sure you're okay, Liz?'

She looked very pale, and her eyes were red. Mathews knew Leary; he could be kind and charming if he felt that was the way to get what he wanted. If that method didn't work he could be the biggest bastard unhung. Mathews felt uncomfortable; he would have liked to go back with her; he knew Leary was going to take the lid off that plane sabotage and use it as an argument. And by the look on her face it must have worked. She even tried to smile at him.

'No, thanks, Pete. I just want to be alone for a while. I promise you, I'm fine.'

He watched the cab move out of sight and then went back into the building. As soon as he reached his office there was a buzz from Leary.

The room was thick with cigarette smoke when he went in; Leary was behind his desk, making untidy notes and drinking coffee. He looked up and gave Mathews his brief, professional smile.

'Sit down, Pete. You did a good job getting her here. How did she seem when she left?'

'Shaken,' Mathews said. 'She looked as if she'd had a hard time.'

'I tried to go easy,' Leary said. 'She's an attractive girl. I kept wondering what the hell she ever saw in you.'

'I wonder that myself,' Mathews said. 'Will she work with us?'

'She said she would,' Leary answered. He pushed his papers into an untidy heap and began playing with his pen, turning it over and round between his fingers. 'She's clean, as far as Eddi King's concerned. You were right about that.'

'But what?' Mathews prompted. He knew his chief; he wasn't completely satisfied.

'I think she's holding out on something,' Leary said slowly. 'She told me a lot about King and everything about Beirut, except the real reason they went there together. She said it was a holiday; I don't believe her. There's something she's hiding.'

'What are you going to do?' Mathews said. He didn't argue with Leary, there wasn't any point. He had an instinct which never failed.

'Put a tail on her,' Leary said. 'The first thing is to keep a watch on her apartment. And you're going to pick up your romance right where you left off. I've cleared it with her, you're her contact from now on. Everything she finds out about Eddi King she passes on to you.'

'You mean she agreed to this?' Mathews couldn't believe it. 'She looks on me like a bad smell.'

'Sure she does; don't we all?' Leary grinned at him. 'But she saw the logic in it. You won't be suspected; you've called before, so to speak. Besides, she's got a score to pay off against the people who sabotaged that plane. Apart from keeping her little secret—whatever it is.'

'What could it be—the secret?'

'I don't know,' Leary admitted. 'My guess is there's a man mixed up in it, and sure as hell it isn't Eddi King. From now on she's your assignment, Pete. You get her apartment under twenty-four-hour watch, and start reintroducing yourself. I have another hunch. I believe we're on to something more than just a big-time fellow traveller. I think we're getting close to something really big.'

Keller had followed instructions exactly. He left Elizabeth's apartment within half an hour of the telephone call, took the subway to Times Square and began to walk to the address he had written down on the piece of paper in his pocket. It was the first time he had been out on the street alone; several times he stopped to check that he was going the right way. He had never imagined that New York could be a dirty city; driving within the perimeter of Elizabeth's golden circle had given him no indication of the littered streets and sleazy houses, peopled by sullen drifters in the

86

district he now entered. 9th Avenue was very wide; it reminded him in some way of the strong-smelling markets of the East, with its stalls packed with fruit and vegetables and the stench of the fish markets. Traffic roared and lumbered up the centre, shoppers hung around or jostled irritably, their arms full of packages. There were Negroes and hybrid Puerto Ricans accompanied by hordes of screaming children running races through the crowds, shouting cheerfully to each other in Spanish; down-at-heel women arguing over the food prices, a single drunk slumped against a shop front, his feet sticking out, his face turned upward to a sun that wasn't shining, his eyes tight shut in a blissful alcoholic dream. It was different in detail but essentially the same as most of Keller's other stopping places. Dirt and smells and mean humanity. This was where he belonged, with all the other members of that universal brotherhood of the poor. Who so far had shown no sign of inheriting the earth. He looked at the piece of paper again and tried to stop someone to ask, but no one waited; they just shouldered past him and one man turned and swore. Morries Hotel. He crossed, avoiding a large truck on its way to the Port Authority building. The ground floor of the hotel was a bookstore. As soon as Keller walked in he recognised it for what it was. Naked girls in coy erotic poses cavorted from racks of magazines; cheap paperbacks with pornographic titles were on display, and these were only the façade on what the store was really selling. The collections of perverted photographs and really filthy publications were kept out of sight. There was a narrow stair which smelt as stale as the inside of the store itself, as if the customers had impregnated the air with their furtive scent. On the second floor there was a desk or a table that did duty for it, with a man in his shirt-sleeves leaning over it, picking his teeth with a splintered match. He didn't even bother to look up at first. He was thin and round-shouldered, with greasy hair stuck down in streaks over his scalp, and glasses wedged on the knobbly bridge of his nose. When he did look up the lenses were so thick that the little eyes behind them almost disappeared.

'Yeah?'

'There is a room booked for me. Name of Maggio.'

The superintendent dropped his match. The eyes behind the glasses flickered. Even if he hadn't just learnt this was a Maggio set-up, with its criminal implications, he would have recognised the big, fair man, with the look like splintered glass, as a familiar type. He took a key down from a rack behind him. 'Four dollars sixty a night.' Keller counted out the money slowly and put it on the table. The super clawed it up and came out from behind. 'Upstairs,' he said. 'I'll show ya.' Two flights further up, he stopped and unlocked a door.

Keller held out his hand for a key. 'Where can I get something to eat?'

'Drugstore round the corner on 9th. If you want anythin' I could maybe get it.' He didn't exactly present his dirty palm, but Keller saw the gesture. He nodded towards the door and the super backed hastily out of it. He looked round at the room. It was small and furnished with a bed, a chair and a closet. He tried the bed; it was hard. He went to the window and tried to open it; it was stuck fast in its frame; even so, he could hear the rumble and roar of the traffic, the strident human noises. He put his few clothes away in the closet and slumped down, searching for a cigarette. And because he had nothing to do he had no defence against Elizabeth. If he closed his eyes she came into the dingy room, so real he could have reached out to touch her. The man who called him had ordered him to disappear while she was out, to leave no means whereby she could contact him again. Keller had done what he was told. But he had sent the flowers to say goodbye. The night before he had told her he loved her. He had taken some of his money and bought yellow roses for her, thinking at the same time he could have lived for a month on what they cost. He wanted her so badly that his body ached.

She hadn't been experienced in making love; she had been helpless and untutored, completely at the mercy of his skill, a skill picked up with whores who used the word love as they quoted a price. Elizabeth wasn't poor or in need like Souha. She would never follow him, unquestioning and childlike, ten paces behind. After she had got over him, when she accepted that he was never coming back, she would put up her blonde hair again, and go out with her smart American men who didn't know what to do to make her love them. The idea of it brought Keller up off the uncomfortable bed, sweating with jealousy. The thought of

88

another man touching her, kissing the mouth he had kissed, playing with the beautiful hair, falling asleep with her in his arms, contented and warm, made him feel like a madman. He paced up and down the room, trying to calm his imagination. What the hell had become of his coldness, his indifference?—pity for Souha was one thing, but this sick fever for a woman was taking possession of him. He sat down again; he had to stop thinking about her, because the reality was that they would never see each other again. He had to control himself and banish the desire for her and the sickness of spirit that missed her so violently he felt like an abandoned animal. He had to forget her eyes and her laugh and the smoothness of her body, almost virginal, it was so soft and unmarked. A woman like Elizabeth was not for him. He had never come nearer one of them before than watching them drive past in big cars, or walking on the same street. It had happened to him by chance; he had been allowed through the gates of the good life for a short interlude, but now they had closed on him and he was yet again on the outside. He was back where he belonged, in a sleazy bedroom among his own kind. Elizabeth was gone for ever. The man who had lived her life and learned that it was possible to love another human being had gone too. Also for ever. The man prepared to kill for money was the reality. If he thought about the money, perhaps it would help him keep her out of his mind, until he could believe that it had been a fantasy, that he would forget her as he already feared she would forget him. The money. He lay back on the bed, kicking off his shoes. He could think about the money. Fifty thousand dollars was a fortune. Maybe not here, not in America where they spent that on a picture and then hung it in the men's room. But in Beirut he could live like a merchant prince. He could dress his Arab girl in beautiful clothes; he could pay to have the sheen of elegance and taste applied to her, so that perhaps he could find in her love what he had discovered with Elizabeth. Perhaps he could buy the kind of happiness which had been shown him by chance. He went to the window again and looked out. The man on the telephone had said it would be soon. Elizabeth had called him King; Eddi King, but to Keller he hadn't given a name. He had just given his orders. Get out of there; cut all contact with Miss Cameron.

Your fee depends on it. Go to this address and wait. And keep indoors. You'll be contacted very soon. Then the line had gone dead. Keller let the window curtains fall. He went back to the bed and lay down on it again. Think about the money. Think what fifty thousand dollars can buy in the way of a new life.

Think about anything but Elizabeth. And if you can't stop yourself then use your old army training and fall asleep.

When Elizabeth opened the apartment door she knew he had gone. Her head had begun aching in the taxi; the driver was a talker, directing a constant stream at her over his shoulder. She had sat through the journey with her eyes closed, not even bothering to answer. The President, the Viet Nam war, the wave of hold-ups on cab drivers after dark. It washed over her, competing with the pounding ache behind her eyes. Her mother and father had been murdered. Their lives and the lives of all the other innocents on board that plane had been extinguished as deliberately as flicking a light switch to 'off'. That shock was bad enough; the discovery of King's connection with those responsible for their death had been a secondary shock; in her subconscious the last and greatest blow of all was building up. Keller was one of them too. She had told Leary everything she could remember about Beirut, everything she could think of about Eddi King from the first time she met him. But she hadn't mentioned Bruno Keller. She walked through the hall into the living room, and even before she called out she knew he wasn't there. That was the worst of all the things which had happened to her. She had left the apartment that morning, and now nothing would be the same again. If she had found him there Elizabeth didn't know what she would have done or said. The one fact cast everything in doubt. She had protected him, even when she knew what King was, and therefore what he must be. Even with the evidence of that dreadful act of sabotage lying on Leary's desk in front of her.

'You can't just walk out on me,' she had pleaded with him when they woke up that morning, and he had only said he couldn't promise. He might have to do just that. There was no letter in the living room; she walked through to her bedroom and the one he had slept in for the first few days. There was nothing. Why didn't I tell Leary? She asked the question aloud. I knew it was something vital, and I sat there lying and holding back. All I have to do is go over and pick up the phone and call Peter Mathews. They'll find him. Loving him is no excuse.

When the doorbell rang she started to run to it, and then the crazy hope died in her. He had never gone out alone. She wouldn't find him on the other side. It was the hall porter. 'Good afternoon, Miss Cameron. The gentleman asked me to bring these up when you came back.'

They were a sheaf of yellow roses, wrapped by the flower shop down the block. There was no card, no message. She held them in her arms and sobbed. That was the thing she had feared most, the callous vacuum left by a man to whom she had been nothing but a means of passing time. He had sent her flowers to say goodbye. And that morning, just before she left, he called her back and kissed her. She went back into the living room, holding the roses, crushing them without knowing. Thank God she hadn't told Leary anything. Thank God she would have time to find him first. He had talked all the time about being paid. If money was the only object then she could match whatever King was offering. She got up, meaning to put the roses into water, the paper had fallen to the floor, a pin gleamed on the telephone table. When she picked it up Elizabeth noticed that the top page of her telephone message pad had been torn off. She forgot about the flowers. No one had come to get him. He had been rung up and given an address to go to; he had written it down on the pad and taken the page with him. She held the pad up to the light; there were white marks on the paper, indentations made by the pressure of the pencil on the sheet which was gone. She couldn't make anything of them. She gathered the flowers and went to put them in water. Her hands were shaking very badly; she poured a neat Cognac into a glass and sipped it slowly. He drank a lot of whisky; never once had she seen it loosen his tongue or have any effect upon him. She had told him he had a hollow leg, and he had laughed. She sat down with the drink and the pad. It was meaningless, indecipherable. And then, calmed by the brandy, Elizabeth remembered something. White on white didn't show. But children knew that old trick about making secret writing and then running a pencil over the page to show the indentations up. She took the pencil and began, very slowly and carefully, covering the page from left to right with a dark background. The first two words showed up halfway down. Morries Hotel. And then a whole word written with the sloping capitals of a foreigner. West Thirty-ninth Street. He hadn't used the numerals; that would have been easier. He had written it all down as a stranger would. Morries Hotel West 39th. That was where Keller had been told to go. She tore the page off and put it in her handbag. Her first impulse was to go straight to him. It was wrong and she wouldn't give way to it. She wanted to find him. She wanted to tell him what had happened, weep and exhaust herself in his arms and be comforted. But if he was working for King she couldn't do that. She couldn't hope to do anything with him, not even try to match their price, until she knew exactly what it was that he was being paid to do. And the best way to find that out was to go to the source of the whole plan. She finished her drink and went into her bedroom to pack. Outside in the street the first of Peter Mathews' watchers settled back in his car to wait. He had taken his position as soon as Mathews called; Elizabeth Cameron had only been in her apartment ten minutes before he was right in position where he could see the front entrance. He had the full description relayed over to him on a short wave; to anyone tuned in it sounded like a radio cab pick-up call. Block four, Riverway, East 59th. Blonde, five foot seven, and aren't you a lucky guy . . . A little later he got the description and number of her car the same way. He had been there under two hours when the red convertible was brought to the front entrance. It was just after two-ten when she came out, carrying a small case, and drove off. Three miles out on the Long Island express way Mathews' man radioed back that she was taking the turn off to Freemont, Huntley Cameron's fortress house.

CHAPTER FOUR

Huntley Cameron had built Freemont in the first years of the Depression. He had never been a popular figure; there was one unpleasant divorce case behind him and a reputation for sharp practice and autocratic dealings which had already soured his image. The laying of the foundation stone of Freemont caused a large-scale riot. At a time when America's economy was staggering, its unemployed numbered ten million and millions more were across the poverty line, one of the wealthiest men in the country outraged opinion everywhere by building a monument to his own extravagance.

Not even Huntley's political friends could find an excuse for Freemont; his enemies indulged in an orgy of righteous condemnation; the site was picketed; a police guard of hundreds protected the building operation from attack. Huntley Cameron was reviled, abused and lampooned. Freemont was not just a house; it wasn't even a New England mansion, elaborate enough by any standard. It was a German castle, transported stone by stone from Westphalia, bought by Huntley on his third honeymoon, and erected in the middle of the beautiful countryside twenty miles outside Boston. Thousands of tons of earth were moved to make a small mountain on which the castle could stand in lordly surveillance of the landscape, three thousand trees were planted round the estate to give privacy, and the curious were kept at bay by an electrified fence twelve feet high. Huntley's third wife was partially blamed for Freemont; she was pictured wearing his fantastic wedding gift of diamonds, accused of ordering a solid gold bath-tub, and stoned by angry crowds on a visit to inspect the progress of her new home. She and Huntley stayed in the Waldorf for the first year; there were threats made against both their lives; newspapers, not owned by Huntley, reported that she was under sedatives and afraid to leave her suite. Whether or not she was responsible for Freemont was never established; nobody dared ask Huntley, and in the event she never lived there because he divorced her before the castle was completed.

The castle was Huntley's obsession; it was also his relaxation from the labour of increasing his money and extending his power. He played with it like an enormous toy; he never denied the rumour that he had begun the whole thing to annoy William Randolph Hearst whose castle had come all the way from Spain. Unlike Hearst, with whom he had a bitter feud, Huntley didn't buy his art treasures in bulk. There were no packing cases full of Renaissance statues or Gobelin tapestries, no Leonardos crated up in the cellars. Huntley chose everything personally, supervised its arrangement and attended to the smallest detail. The three women he married during the next twenty years were not allowed to hang a picture or choose a curtain. The gardens at Freemont were as spectacular as the castle; Huntley liked variety, and everything within the compass of a vast estate was brought in miniature to Freemont. There was a glade full of rhododendrons, an artificial lake with an eighteenth-century pavilion he had travelled all the way to Florence to inspect, a hot-house full of rare orchids, a small wood with a stream, heavily stocked with trout, and hidden at the rear, protected by fifteen feet of dry wall, a huge, hot swimming pool.

Freemont was too familiar to Elizabeth to arouse the revulsion that overcame the discerning visitor; its vulgarity, it pretentiousness, its disgusting opulence, were simply part of Huntley Cameron; part, too, of her father, who lived in comparative simplicity but with a total disregard for anyone's opinion.

She had once heard her mother say that Freemont was the worst crime against good taste that Huntley had ever committed; it reminded her of being force-fed cream and chocolate cake, every time she went there. Even the lavatory chains were hand-wrought gold. Elizabeth hadn't been able to disagree; it was all true but at the time it didn't seem important. Freemont was like Huntley: larger than life, impossible by ordinary standards, detestable and irresistible at the same time. Only Huntley would have given a staid New England name to such a place. He had no wife at the moment, only a mistress who had been clinging on for the last three years in the hope that he might revert to form and

94

marry her. Her name was Dallas Jay and she had been a singer in a Los Angeles night-club. Nobody knew how or where she had met Huntley; he never went to night-clubs. But she was installed at Freemont one day, given minks, sets of jewellery and a personal maid, and summoned to Huntley's bed by an electric buzzer operating in her room. Elizabeth hadn't seen her for some weeks, she had been holidaying in Florida before Elizabeth and Eddi King went to Beirut. Huntley placed no restrictions on her; she could go where she liked, spend what she liked, but if she went with a man she'd be out on her ass. It was his choice of words and her choice of conduct. In three years, with every columnist and scandal-sheet spy watching her, Dallas had never made a single boob.

As Elizabeth approached the wrought-iron entrance gates to Freemont, she slowed down. The guard on duty recognised the car, and after a few moments' inspection operated the electrical system which opened the gates to admit visitors. There was a telephone link with the castle; nobody got in unless Huntley gave authority. She eased the car up the long drive; as the four grey turrets appeared above the trees the road developed a steep incline. Elizabeth took the last five hundred yards up the man-made prominence in second gear. The drive levelled up as suddenly as it had begun to climb. It ended in a wide gravelled sweep before the entrance to the castle. As she got out of the car and walked through the portcullis entrance, Elizabeth remembered Keller's words: 'Who is your uncle? I've never heard of him.' It was a pity Huntley Cameron would never hear that said. He assumed everybody knew of his existence, like God. It would never occur to him that the world was full of people like Keller, to whom his name meant nothing; still less would he imagine that his niece would come any closer to one of them than passing in a closed car down a poor and dirty street. But that was why she had come to Freemont; her word was given to Leary, Peter Mathews would be waiting for information, their quarry was Eddi King and she was as anxious to trap him as they were. But first she had to know how far her uncle Huntley was involved, how much he really knew, what Keller's role was going to be; only then could she decide how to protect one or both if Huntley needed protection, and still guide

Leary towards King. Above all, she needed enough information to be able to judge how best to lead them all away from Keller.

She didn't find her uncle immediately. She went up to her room first and changed out of the trouser suit she wore for driving. Huntley hated women who wore pants; he only tolerated shorts and then on condition that the women's legs were worth looking at. After she had changed Elizabeth sat down at the dressing table. Every guest room was fitted out with toilet articles for both sexes, gold and enamel brushes matched the exquisite Venetian looking-glass and the seventeenth-century Florentine table. A bed which had belonged to one of the Visconti princesses stood in the middle of the room, a towering monument of carved and gilded wood. Elizabeth began to brush her hair. It still hung loose. She closed her eyes suddenly, remembering that Keller had played with it, drawing it over her face, twisting it through his fingers. 'Oh God,' she said out loud.

'What's the matter, honey? Aren't you feeling well?'

She hadn't heard the door open; she turned round quickly and saw the woman standing there, looking at her. All Huntley's wives had been brunettes; Dallas Jay was dark too, and in a good light she looked as if her face matched her splendidly curved body.

'Hi,' she said. 'I just heard you'd arrived and came to say hallo. So hallo. It's nice to see you.'

'Nice to see you too, Dallas.' Elizabeth got up. 'I wasn't sure if you were back from Florida. You look marvellous.'

'I got a good tan,' she said. 'Hunt was pleased to see me.'

'I'm sure he was,' Elizabeth said. Across the room Dallas passed for what she had been: a pretty professional singer with more bust than talent. Close up, she was too brown, a little too lined. It occurred to Elizabeth that she must be a lot older than anyone thought. She had always got along with her, if only because Dallas wouldn't have done anything to alienate Huntley's niece and because Elizabeth was always very careful not to play on that. She couldn't have said she liked or disliked the woman. She was so pleasant and accommodating that she wasn't quite real.

'Is my uncle around?'

'He's in the music gallery, honey. He's got that nice pub-

96

lisher friend Mr King with him. Come on downstairs and we can have a drink while we're waiting. He said he didn't want to be disturbed for a while.'

'Thanks,' Elizabeth said slowly. 'I'll come with you, Dallas. You can tell me all about Florida.'

'Everything,' Eddi King said, 'is going just as we planned it. Smooth as mother's milk.' He gave Huntley Cameron his confident smile, showing his white American-capped teeth. Before he came to the States they had had an American dentist go over his entire mouth. King was not a coward, but he remembered those long visits to the clinic with real horror.

'You're certain this man knows his business?' Huntley Cameron had a way of speaking words as if they were bullets; they came out at high velocity. He was a tall man, thin and big-boned, with deep-set eyes of indeterminate grey-brown, a blunt nose and carefully combed white hair. His face was long with an angular jaw-line and a thin sanding of freckles. He dressed in immaculately cut suits and hand-made shirts. He was fond of making jokes at the expense of fellow millionaires who indulged in eccentricities like tee-shirts and dirty sneakers. Everything about him suggested power and wealth and a degree of autocracy that took itself for granted on a manic scale. He stared hard at King as he stared at everyone; most people couldn't take it and looked away.

'He knows it.' King spoke reassuringly. 'I watched him use a pistol on a very awkward target; much more awkward than the real one on March 17. The range was the top one. He got it with the first shot. Don't worry, Huntley, I've got the right man for the job.'

'You want a whisky?' Huntley said. 'Go and help yourself. Tell me more.'

'I don't want a drink,' King said. 'It's too early for me.'

'Well, it isn't for me,' he said. 'Make it three fingers high and straight. How did you get our marksman? They're not easy to come by without going to the criminal element. And I told you,' the fierce eyes swept over him, baleful and dangerous, 'I told you not to touch them.'

'I didn't.' King handed him the glass of whisky. This was one item about Huntley Cameron that the gossip columnists had never printed. He drank like a fish without any visible effect at all. 'I have friends in the Middle East—business interests. All the scum collect round there, the deserters, the mercenaries out of a job. Our man had been in the Foreign Legion. He was one of their top marksmen in Indo-China.'

'Maybe we should send him out there now,' Cameron snarled into his glass. 'Maybe he could pick off some of our fool generals out there—when I think what that bastard Hughsden did, kept us in that war—how much money did he want?'

'He agreed to fifty thousand dollars,' King explained. 'And he wanted papers for himself and a passport. I fixed it all through these friends of mine.'

'And how do you know they can be trusted?'

King smiled. 'Because they never knew who was employing them. I was very discreet, Huntley, you must believe that. After all, this is my neck as much as yours.'

'I'm not worried about my neck,' the other man said. He held out his glass. 'Fill it up. I'm worried we might not get the business through. I'm worried in case that bastard lives long enough to do any more damage to our country. When I think of a punk like that in the White House—Christ! I lie awake nights as it is!'

King decided to join Huntley; he found the old man an ordeal when he was in this sort of mood. He poured a small whisky and drank it to steady his nerve. Cameron was not a fool; he spoke in the terms of an extravagant demagogue, he gave an impression of egomania which might have fooled someone less intimate with him into neglecting details. But not King. King wasn't taken in; he knew that a mind with the keenness and speed of a laser beam was operating all the time. Cameron talked as people expected him to talk; even the deliberate glare, the staccato question suddenly fired without warning, these were part of the persona the man had created for himself. King had seen him talking business once or twice. He was as quiet and reasoned as a company accountant. One false note, one careless word, and he would seize on it. King proceeded carefully, picking his way like a man in a nettle patch.

He eased into a chair, and lit a cigarette. He loved the music gallery because it housed two of the finest Vermeers he had ever seen, and a magnificent German virginal which had been presented to one of the Emperor Charles V's wives. Once Huntley had invited him to open the instrument and try it. The delicate, silver tones were as pure as if five centuries had never passed; King's soul was stirred by the ethereal beauty which was in that narrow rectangle of marvellously decorated wood and wire and goose quills. He had always been moved by the arts.

'I don't want you to think that I'm cold-blooded about this,' he said. 'After all, it's still a man's life. But I believe there's such a thing as patriotic duty which can ask even that. I believe we have to have Jackson assassinated or leave our country at the mercy of anarchy and civil war.'

Cameron turned his head a little and looked at him. He didn't speak immediately; he just considered King as if he had grown a second nose. 'You must be out of your head,' he said at last. 'Cold-blooded? I'd shoot that son of a bitch myself if I could get away with it. Stop talking crap, Eddi. He's got to be wiped out. Now, let's get this clear. When our man does his job he gets his money and the papers—right?'

'That will be laid on,' King said. 'He'll get everything we promised.'

'I've been thinking,' Huntley said. 'Suppose we can't get him out of the country—suppose he gets picked up?'

King's expression didn't change. 'That'll be too bad for us,' he said. 'I've been wondering about that. I don't feel happy about this escape at all.'

'Then get someone to fix it,' Huntley said. 'Right after the shooting. Have someone blow a hole in him.'

'If that's okay with you,' King said. 'I'd feel a whole lot more secure. You want me to arrange it?'

'You've fixed everything so far,' Huntley said. 'You lay it on the line and let me have the bill. Let's go down now, I want to see Elizabeth.'

King hesitated. 'I'll join you in a minute,' he said. 'I won't be long.' He turned as Huntley moved away, and he went upstairs to his room. He had no real reason for not going down with Huntley, except that on an impulse he wanted to be alone, to step off the stage for a moment. Also he wanted to congratulate himself a little, while he went over every detail, making sure he had forgotten nothing.

King went over to the magnificent mirror on the wall, and pushed his thick hair back, smoothing it down. Edward Francis King. He had never seen the real King. The photograph taken after his arrest by the Gestapo had been a flat, staring likeness, full face and profile, made grotesque by the shaven haircut given to concentration-camp prisoners. The eyes remained in his memory; they were wide and fixed with fear. Edward Francis King had died before the Russians took the camp. All that was left of him was the file with his photographs and details, and a shovelful of ash in the crematorium. That file went into the K.G.B. index with all the other data captured at the same time. The death had been a useful source of cover for short-term agents, mostly used in the Western sector of Germany after the war. But the identity of King, an American citizen who had died of typhus just before the camp was overrun, was too valuable to be wasted on some small-time operator. They had chosen him to impersonate the dead American because there was a slight facial resemblance and he was one of the brightest young men in the K.G.B. It had taken nearly ten years to train him and prepare the way for his return to the States as Edward King, but with such a chance for high-level penetration Moscow was patient. King had learned to think, speak, walk and react like an American; any slight oddity could be accounted for by his experiences in the camp and having lived so long in France. He had spent three of his years of training living in Paris, playing the part of Eddi King, establishing himself with members of the post-war American colony, laying his background with meticulous care. At last he had been ready to go over to the States, where the K.G.B. were ready to finance his fantastic venture into the inner circle of American reactionary power.

His magazine provided cover for a spy network which passed top-level information about United States policies through to the East. He got to know men of influence in every sphere; he became an influence himself, a means of manipulating people of importance in the way which the Soviets intended they should go. King was one of the biggest operators in the world. In fifteen years he had never made a single mistake or incurred the slightest suspicion. After the assassination on March 17th he would go down in history as the master spy of the twentieth century, when long after, perhaps a generation after, the truth leaked through.

Clever men abounded; he could lay claim to genius. Huntley Cameron was clever, clever enough to see the catastrophic implications of a President like John Jackson. Ruthless enough to seize on King's vague hinting and agree to finance his removal. Removal was King's word; he liked to act discreetly, the intellectual who talked about a killing with becoming vagueness. Huntley Cameron called it murder, and without a qualm of conscience. And so the brilliant gamble which had its origins in the Politburo began to take its shape in the transported German castle, under the subtle auspices of Eddi King. He had to admire Cameron for his judgement; it exactly agreed with that of the political experts in the Soviet Union. If John Jackson became President, America would erupt into civil war within two years. The student riots and racial outbreaks already disturbing the country would look like a children's pillow fight compared with the chaos and bloodshed which would result from his policies. And all that stood in Jackson's way was Patrick Casey, tough, dedicated, the liberal Democratic candidate. As Druet had said that evening in the Paris brothel, his advent to power could put back the advance of communism for fifty years. That was why Cameron had backed Casey, even to the extent of having Jackson murdered, rather than let him run.

And it was why it was essential in Soviet interests that Jackson should not only run but win. King went to the bedroom window and looked out. The grounds extended as far as he could see; there was a splendid oak which gave him particular pleasure. It stood against the sky, sturdy and majestic in its mantle of green leaves, until the wind stripped it and it stood bare and black branched, as it was now. King thought suddenly that he would never see that tree again after the weekend. It would have been obvious to assassinate Casey, following the bloodstained path beaten by the killers of Jack and Robert Kennedy. Obvious and stupid. If Casey were killed, whoever the Democrats put forward would be elected on a wave of hysterical guilt. It would not be Casey who would die. The killer brought in from Beirut would gun down another national hero, the one man who had not come out in support of Casey, the champion of the coloureds and the poor, the people's Cardinal, Martino Regazzi. He would die on March 17th, watched by millions of Americans on television.

King stepped back from the window and lit a cigarette; with a movement he pulled the long curtain a little forward, hiding the beautiful old tree.

Martino Regazzi's remark about a man trying to save his soul after the first twenty million had gone round the United States. He had stayed neutral in the election campaign so far, refusing to be drawn out on behalf of the Liberal Catholic candidate. He carried the votes of millions, irrespective of their creed. It had never been intended to let the assassin get out of the cathedral alive. King had made arrangements long before Huntley Cameron suggested it. Keller would be found dead, with just enough evidence planted on his body to lead to the first of the clues King had laid so carefully against Cameron. Beginning with Elizabeth his niece, who had brought the man into the States, and by some unexpected chance involved herself and her uncle deeper still by keeping the murderer in her apartment.

That was the scorpion sting which would disable Patrick Casey and remove him from the campaign as effectively as any bullet. His most powerful sponsor would be exposed as the man behind Regazzi's murder. Who could prove that Casey hadn't suspected, or even participated in, the killing of the one man in America powerful enough to deprive him of the Presidency—if he did as many expected, and backed the Republicans at the last minute.

The death of Martino Regazzi would convulse America and horrify the Western world. The public association of Patrick Casey with the man responsible for his murder would bury Casey's political career in the Cardinal's grave. And nobody would try to blame the communists this time.

With Casey removed, a nation beset by scandal and despair would sweep John Jackson into the White House.

This was the last weekend King would stay at Freemont; the last time he would sleep in this particular room, which had always been allotted to him over the years. It was also the end of his long fifteen years of exile. At last he would be able to go home. He had bought that magnificent *bureau plat* for his new flat in Moscow. He stubbed out his cigarette in a metal ashtray, the only concession to utility in that fantastic bedroom, equipped for a sixteenth-century Venetian prince, and went down to join Huntley Cameron and his niece.

It seemed to Elizabeth that King was looking at her more intently than he usually did. There was a query in his eyes that she had never seen before. She kissed her uncle, shook hands with King, and tried to behave normally.

'You've done something to yourself,' King said suddenly. 'Hasn't she, Huntley? You've changed your hair—that's what it is.'

He laughed and Elizabeth joined in; the tension in her eased. There was nothing sinister in his examination of her; he was just a man looking at a woman who had altered her style. For the first few minutes she had felt as if she had the name 'Leary' branded on her forehead.

'It sure suits you, honey.' That was Dallas making her contribution, saying something nice as always.

'Let's go and sit in the conservatory; I've got a new species I want to take a look at.' Huntley led the way, followed by Elizabeth, King and Dallas at the rear. She heard the woman making conversation, saying what she hoped were the right things. Elizabeth supposed it was nerves that made her hypersensitive to a situation she had taken for granted before. The ignominy of Dallas Jay's position made her feel really angry with her uncle. No one had the right to suppress another human being's personality and distort it as he had done. And he was never going to marry the poor girl. Everyone knew that except Dallas. All Huntley's wives had been socialites. He was a monumental snob about marriage. The conservatory was Huntley Cameron's favourite place of retreat; he enjoyed pointing out that old men needed heat so that he might be contradicted. It was incredibly warm; it was like stepping into the tropics from the inside of the castle. It ran for sixty feet down one side, and it was fitted out with a wide recess with comfortable lounging chairs, tables and a bar. Cacti and creepers decorated this part; Huntley protected his rare orchids and lilies from changes in atmosphere and cigarette smoke by keeping them at the far end. A manservant appeared as soon as they sat down. He brought champagne for Dallas and Elizabeth, a whisky for King and a personal decanter for Huntley.

'It's good to see you,' Huntley said to her. He thought she looked prettier than usual. King was right; the hair falling naturally to her shoulders made her look younger. And she seemed thinner, more ethereal. And she was distinctly on edge about something. He glanced over at Eddi King, and there was a hostility in the look which would have surprised the other man. He knew King was attracted by his niece, and because she was his niece, Huntley didn't blame him. But though he could look, he mustn't be allowed to touch. He might be Huntley's friend, but he wasn't in the league that could get ideas about Elizabeth Cameron. When she married, and he wished she'd hurry up, it wouldn't be a middle-class Easterner old enough to be her father.

'I wondered when you were going to call or come down,' he said. 'I missed you. Dallas here was away, browning her fanny in Florida. I was lonely.'

'I'm sorry, Uncle,' Elizabeth said. 'I meant to call, but I didn't get round to it.'

'Poor sweetie,' Dallas said. She got up and came to the back of Cameron's chair, putting her arms round him. 'All alone without us. We're all here, now, honey, and I won't ever go away again if you don't want me to.'

'Finish your drink,' Huntley said. She let go of him and went back to her chair. Elizabeth turned a little away from her uncle.

'Next time you go to Florida,' she said, 'let me know, Dallas, and I'll come with you. It doesn't do any harm, Uncle Huntley, to be left to yourself now and again!'

'Let's go and look at the orchids,' King suggested. He sensed that uncle and niece were moving towards a row. He had never seen Elizabeth in such an edgy mood. Unknowing, he used the same word to describe her as Huntley had done. Edgy, sensitive, ready to flare up.

She got up and together they moved down the long glass-walled room; the scent of the tropical plants increased as they went deeper into the hottest part of the growing area. Huge multicoloured flowers climbed over their heads; the banks of lilies exuded their clinging, fetid scent until suddenly Elizabeth stopped. The damp heat circulated round them, moist and thick, opening the pores of the skin.

'Let's go back, Eddi. I can't stand the smell of this place.'

'Wait just a moment,' King said. They were close to-

104

gether, the creeping plants made a roof over their heads. He was suddenly aroused by her. Perhaps it was the heat, or the sense of isolation, falsely created; perhaps it was something about Elizabeth herself which had never been there before, but he could have taken hold of her and pulled her down among the rioting leaves. He didn't move; he just said quietly, 'Tell me about the man. I couldn't talk on the phone for long that night. Was everything really all right? He didn't give any trouble?'

'I hardly saw him,' Elizabeth said. 'He spent all day sleeping or watching the TV. He might just as well not have been there.'

'I was worried,' King said. 'I wouldn't have landed you with keeping him for a couple of hours—I could have cut my throat when you told me what had happened. I hope you're not angry with me, are you?'

'Of course not.' She tried to say it lightly. 'You couldn't help it. And he wasn't any trouble. I told you. I hardly saw him. He just kept to himself all the time.'

This was what King had been telling himself ever since he found that Keller was still with her. He hadn't talked to her; he was a professional and he knew the rules. He showed his relief when he smiled at her, and then he came to the second most important point he had to make while there was time.

'Elizabeth, there's something I want you to promise me. Something very important.'

'What is it?' She put out one hand and played with the deep yellow petals of a South American orchid; Huntley would have forbidden her the house if he had seen her twisting the delicate flesh of the flower until it bruised. Keep calm, anything to keep calm and hide the fear which was growing in her, being alone with this man, sensing that apart from what he was saying he was looking at her with desire.

'What do you want me to promise, Eddi?'

'Not to mention that you were involved in any way with bringing this man into the States,' King said. 'I asked you to help because I didn't think I could do it without you. I never told Huntley you had any part in it. If he found out I'd involved you even by accident he'd break me. And you know him, Elizabeth, he'd do just that.'

'Yes,' she said. 'I do know him. He's very powerful, and

105

he's ruthless. I think he would destroy you, Eddi, if you got on the wrong side of him. My mother used to say it was dangerous enough being his friend in case he turned into an enemy. All right, if I promise you not to let him know, you've got to tell me something.'

'Go ahead,' King said. He was prepared for the question. He was always prepared.

'Who is this man and what's he doing here?'

'He's going to be a witness,' King said. 'A witness in one of the biggest exposés your uncle's ever launched against the gangster element in the States. That's why he had to be brought in the way he was; protected by you, so the people who might be looking for him would be off guard. That's why he had to stay hidden, and thank God you hid him. At this moment his life isn't worth a dry cent if they know he's here and who's behind it.'

'You mean Uncle's gunning for the Mafia again?'

He nodded. 'That's it. Dope, prostitution, gambling, rackets. And government corruption. I'm sorry, my dear. I should have warned you how hot this thing was, but I was frightened you might back down. A lot of women would, you know.'

'Then he's a kind of gangster,' Elizabeth said. 'A racketeer who's going to squeal, or whatever they say in the movies . . .'

'That's right,' King said. 'He's getting very well paid. Now have I done what you wanted? Will you promise me never to say or do a thing that would let Huntley know you're in on this?'

'I'd better, hadn't I?' To his surprise, she laughed, and for a brief moment she looked like Huntley Cameron himself. The gene was there, King thought; in spite of the artistic well-bred mother and her careful rearing, the girl and the old man were of the same blood.

'I can just imagine what Huntley would dream up for you if he knew you'd landed me with a mess like this. I don't know what he wouldn't do, but don't worry. I won't tell him anything. You can rely on me.'

He reached out and took her hand. For a moment she felt his lips close over the skin on the back of it, and she pulled away from him.

'It's making me sick in here,' she said. 'I must go back.'

He showed no sign of rebuff; he stood aside and let her

pass him, courteous and friendly, and followed her slowly back to join her uncle.

From the moment he began telling it in the orchid house, Elizabeth knew King's story about Keller was a lie. She had known that from the first words. The Mafia, dope, prostitution, corruption in government circles; the glib stream poured out of him, cliché after cliché, lie after lie. Huntley had attacked the Mafia before; she knew all about what he had done and when, and she could only suppose that this was why King had picked upon that particular tale.

People were ready to believe something they had heard before. But he had ignored one vital point; or not ignored, but literally been in ignorance of it. He had talked about the man as if her lie had been the truth. As if he had stayed a silent presence in another room. Believing that, King had painted his incongruous picture of a defecting racketeer; he hadn't even seen her sarcasm when she likened the whole thing to something in the movies. Keller bore no possible resemblance to the type that King described. She had slept at his side, touched the battle scars on his body, felt the calloused hard hands on her own skin. Keller was no Mafioso; that kind lived well, dressed expensively, were manicured and barbered every day. They didn't pick up starving refugees and give them shelter.

Whatever the man she loved might be, he wasn't what King said. And with that lie, her uncle's part became more suspect. How much was he actually involved, and why was King so afraid of Huntley knowing—not just because he feared Huntley's vindictive reaction, but because the story would be different from the one that he had told her? This suddenly made sense; whatever he pretended, Elizabeth realised that Eddi King was not afraid of anyone, not even her uncle. The more she tried to disentangle it, the more sinister the affair became.

She didn't talk very much during dinner; she was frightened and tense, unable to eat. She played with the food and listened to King entertaining Huntley with stories about West Germany. He seemed in excellent spirits, feeding her uncle scandals about some of the better-known European politicians, making him roar with laughter. This in itself was an achievement; Huntley was dour, and difficult to amuse. She had never really appreciated King's skill before; now she could see how he had insinuated himself with Huntley and others like him; rich, tyrannical, suspicious. King amused them. He set out to charm and entertain; he sang for his supper with superb professionalism. He was witty, he was cultured, he was always in a good mood. Elizabeth realised how much she too had liked these qualities. Only a few weeks back she had gone off to Beirut with him and found him knowledgeable and excellent company. She had been taken in, just like her uncle. She would have described him as a friend, with the one reservation. That odd sense of repulsion when he sent her flowers, the claustrophobic fear in the orchid house.

The more she tried to connect Eddi King being amusing at the dinner table with the man Leary suspected of treachery, the more confusing the image became. They were two separate entities; the one clever, familiar, the other cold and sinister. And the glib intellectual couldn't be the real one. The performance was too polished, the portrait too exact. An accomplished actor in a long running part, that's what King was. Without Leary, Elizabeth would never have seen through him. But now she couldn't believe in any aspect of his reality. And that left the other King of whom she knew nothing but the single fact of that furtive meeting in Paris. That was the real man. And that must be the one of whom she was instinctively afraid.

'You're not eating!' Huntley said suddenly. 'What's the matter—you're not on some damned fool diet, are you?'

'No, of course not,' Elizabeth said. 'I'm not very hungry.'

'I wish I didn't have to weight-watch,' Dallas came in with a rush. 'But then Hunt hates fat women, don't you, honey?'

He was in a good mood; he liked having Eddi King around and he was glad to see Elizabeth. He smiled at Dallas. 'You've got a good figure; you don't have to worry. I like what you've got and that's all you have to do, my dear. Keep it as I like it.'

'I will,' she said. She had an attractive smile, and she turned it on Huntley like a searchlight beam. 'I sure will, just for you.'

After dinner they went down to the private cinema where Huntley saw the latest films. He hadn't been to a movie theatre for twenty-five years. The latest epics, comedies and the pick of the foreign films were shown at Freemont. He had a long-standing favourite which was run at least once every few months, *Gone with the Wind*. Huntley never tired of it; he pronounced the actress Vivien Leigh as the most beautiful woman in the business. He had shown the entire movie without a break when her death was announced, and Elizabeth heard that throughout the performance he was in tears. The film they watched was a French thriller, another old classic which he enjoyed. Elizabeth found herself next to King. He lit her cigarettes and made a few comments to her and to Dallas. It was certainly the tenth time he had been forced to sit through *Rififi*. Huntley Cameron was not the sort of man to think of other people's boredom. If he was enjoying it, that was the sole criterion. Luckily it was short; they were all glad, for different reasons. Huntley because it was just the stimulus he needed after dinner, and he wanted to go to bed with Dallas; Dallas because he had indicated this by putting his hand on her leg at one time in the dark; King because he was insufferably bored and wanted to get away from them all, and Elizabeth because she had made up her mind to do something and to do it that night.

She went upstairs first. She had made an excuse to her uncle that she had a headache, kissed him, said good night to King, and hurried into her room. The bed was turned down; her nightdress, dressing gown and slippers were laid out for her. She went to the dressing table and looked at herself. She looked white, and there were dark circles of strain under her eyes. King had lied to her; another proof of that lie was his fear of her going to Huntley. Not just the fear of Huntley's anger, even his vindictiveness. But fear that his story wouldn't be borne out. That was his real reason. Huntley and he were involved in something together. But one thing was certain: whatever it was they had in common, whatever had brought Keller into the States under their auspices, their motives were not the same. There was only one way to find out what was behind it all, and that was by doing exactly what she had promised not to do. She was going to her uncle, just as soon as she was sure that Eddi King had gone to bed.

In her bedroom down the corridor Dallas was stripping off her clothes; she tore at the fastenings, laddered her stockings as she pulled them off, and ran into the bathroom. There wouldn't be time to take a bath; when Huntley felt like sex he didn't expect to be kept waiting. She switched on the shower taps and stepped under the cascading water. He was a meticulous man; he demanded bodily perfection in a woman as he demanded the same standards in his businesses and his home. Dallas was massaged twice a week, manicured, pedicured, oiled and preserved like a Sultan's favourite. The only difference was that Huntley hadn't laid a hand on her for three months. She dried herself quickly, and then standing before the full-length glass in her bedroom, she dropped the towel, stretching her arms above her head to tighten her breasts. She looked good; judicious tanning had turned her body a beautiful golden brown. A white streak ran across her hips, where the narrow bikini had protected her from the Florida sun; she had browned her breasts with a lamp. She went to the table where her cosmetics were set out; the bottles and pots and sprays were arranged in militant little rows; the lights round the mirror were theatrical bulbs, casting a pitiless glare on the face. She found the scent he liked best, a strong evocative flower scent, tipped some into her right palm and began massaging it into her skin. She dusted her face with powder, bit her lips to give them colour because he disliked lipstick stains, and stepped into a vivid pucci silk house gown which zipped invisibly up the front. Huntley didn't like elaborate nightdresses or anything with hooks and buttons. He liked to undress her in one dramatic gesture, and everything she termed her sex wear was made accordingly. She brushed her hair, glancing at herself in the glass from different angles. She was as nervous as a girl on her first call; the idea made Dallas smile. Before Huntley found her she used to feel like this for a man, but for different reasons; reasons that had nothing to do with anxiety and fear of not pleasing. There was one guy who could make her jump through hoops when he wanted to; he must have been paid off because he just disappeared. Now she went through the motions and sometimes, when he took trouble with her, she enjoyed it, but it didn't motivate her any more. Nothing motivated Dallas but the single obsession of getting Huntley Cameron to marry her. It wasn't just greed; he was generous. She had enough in her bank account to keep her for life. Being married to Huntley was her justification for being born. Look, world, look where little Dallas ended up—it was such a beautiful dream that she closed her eyes for a moment and indulged in it. She had got to the newspaper pictures, including her favourite, a large front-page photograph of herself with the caption, 'Singer weds Huntley Cameron', when the buzzer sounded.

She wasn't consciously humiliated by it any more; she accepted the idea that she would be rung for service, like a maid. She opened the door and started towards Huntley's private suite on the other side of the connecting staircase.

Seven thousand miles away in the dingy little room overlooking the Zone Franche, Souha turned uneasily in her sleep. It was almost dawn and she had spent most of the night lying awake, thinking about Keller, the thoughts accompanied by fits of crying. He had been gone for more than two weeks and there was no word from him. There was nothing left of him but the shabby suit of clothes folded away in the one chest of drawers, and a packet half-full of cigarettes which she had hidden like a treasure. Every week the money arrived; she spent only enough to buy food, keeping the rest to give back to him. Nothing would persuade her that he wasn't coming back; even the waking nightmares stopped before the end, because the pain was too much for her to bear.

After he left she kept herself occupied, cleaning the room, buying a long length of cloth to make him a dressing gown. That was her only extravagance; she chose a brightly patterned pure silk, and while she was making it the time passed. It would please him; she had seen such things in the expensive shops which sold men's clothes and realised that he had never owned one. She wasn't sure when such a splendid thing was worn, but she stood outside the window studying the way the robe was made and then went home to try to copy it.

Now it was finished; it hung on the back of the chair, waiting for him to come back and put it on, and she liked to look at it before she put the light out. It was like a talisman; if love could cross oceans and wing through space, then the longing of Souha must surely reach him wherever he was and draw him back. She was uneasy in her sleep, but the

111

hours before dawn are when the body slips furthest into unconsciousness. She didn't hear the handle of the door being turned. The man outside had come up the stairs with the delicacy of a cat stalking a bird; he moved without noise, a dark shadow swallowed up in the prevailing darkness of the house. He had been given fifty Lebanese pounds on account and promised another fifty. In his right hand, coiled round the palm, he carried the thin knotted cord which was the tool of his trade. No noise, no clues, no struggle. Those were his instructions; he could steal what he liked, so that the murder would appear connected with the robbery. Outside the door he paused, listening. He had spent two days watching the house, so that he knew the girl, and knew that there was no man with her. Even so, there might be someone from the house who went to her at night. He bent his head to the door and listened for the sound of breathing. He heard nothing. If she was alone he would strangle her and be out in the street within five minutes. If there was anyone else in the room he would have to come the next night and the next till he found her alone. He pressed down on the handle and pushed. The handle gave but the door didn't move. Keller had told her to keep it locked at night; Souha had never slept behind a locked door in her life, but because he had told her to do it, she obeyed. The man on the other side of it tried once more; he pushed, hoping that it was stuck, but the door held. It was locked. He wound the strangler's cord into a neat loop and put it in his pocket. He cursed his victim in Arabic and slipped away down the stairs as quietly as he had come up. He would have to change his tactics; it was a pity and it made his job more dangerous. The sky was turning light, the horizon showing the first streaks of red and gold before the sun came up over the edge of the sea. The man loped off towards the coast road, drawing his jellaba close against the cutting breeze. He was hungry, and the squalid refugee encampment where he lived with his family was an hour's walk. He felt sour and bitter with disappointment; a dozen people depended upon him for food and the maintenance of their miserable shack against the onslaught of other refugees without even the protection of a roof. By now the woman should have been dead. He decided to wait for that day and come back early the next morning. If necessary he could go in and hide in her room while she was out.

When the knock came on Huntley's door Dallas was on his knees. He was in a very good mood; his lack of hurry indicated that. He let her kiss him and call him pet names, cuddling her on his knees with a huge glass of whisky in one hand. Then the knock came. Dallas couldn't believe it; Huntley couldn't either. It was midnight; nobody would have dared come and disturb him at that hour without first using the internal telephone system. He gave her a little push. 'Get off and see who it is.'

If it's one of those goddamned servants, Dallas swore to herself, if it's that putty-faced butler—I'll get the old man to fire the lot of them—I'll teach them not to come busting in here when everything was going right . . .

'I'm sorry to disturb you, Dallas. I must see my uncle.'

She was so surprised to see Elizabeth standing outside that she didn't try to close the door. 'He's tired,' she whispered. 'He doesn't want anyone but me tonight. Go away, honey. Please go away.'

'What the hell are you doing at that door?' Huntley called out. 'Who is it?'

Dallas didn't dare to lie. 'It's Elizabeth, sweetheart. She wants to see you.'

This was the end of her chance that night; as soon as she had let the niece in she knew what he would do, and he did it. The tears welled up in her eyes.

'Beat it,' Huntley said. That was all. It was the way men had talked to her all her life. Come here, baby, lie down, baby, open them up, baby. Okay, beat it. She didn't look at Huntley. She looked at Elizabeth, who had ruined her opportunity, maybe for months, to get near him. Then she went out and closed the door.

'I'm sorry to do this,' Elizabeth said. 'I'm sorry about poor Dallas, she looked so upset.'

'To hell with her. Come in and shut the damned door. I'm too old for draughts.'

She came towards him, moving slowly, wondering how to make the first approach. He looked an old man sitting there in his dressing gown, until she remembered what she had interrupted. And remembered that contemptuous 'Beat it'.

I'm fond of him. She had said to Eddi King. Who was she fooling—how was it that tyrants conned people into pretending that when they pandered to them out of fear it was anything to do with fondness? He was a vile old man, indulgent to her only because she was his own blood. Her mother had always loathed him, and she had been right.

'I want to talk to you about Beirut,' she said. She didn't sit down; she felt an advantage in standing a little away from him, looking down.

'What about it?'

He knew; the way the hard eyes dilated for a second betrayed that. He knew about Beirut and about Keller. That disposed of her last hope that perhaps he and King weren't really working together.

'There's a man come into this country who's been brought here to do something for you, Huntley. I want to know what it is.'

He didn't hesitate; he glared at her. 'I don't know what the hell you're talking about!' She had caught him off guard when she first said it; now he was in control of himself. There wouldn't be another betraying flicker of an eye; he hadn't got nerves of steel or any of the other clichéd attributes. He had no nerves at all. 'I was busy when you came bursting in here,' he said. 'You can tell me your fairy story in the morning.' He got up and started to move to his bedroom.

'Don't do that, Huntley,' Elizabeth said, 'or I'll take my fairy story to the police. Right now. I think they'd listen to it.'

He turned round then, swinging his tough, rangy body as if it were on ball-bearings. She was a Cameron, in spite of that overbred mother with her arts-and-crafts disdain for money. She could be tough too. He came back and sat down in his chair.

'Get me a whisky,' he said.

'No,' Elizabeth answered. 'You get it yourself. I'm not Dallas.'

He reached out and pulled the top drawer of the eighteenth-century French petit commode which was close to his chair. It opened out in a flap, disclosing a recess full of drinks. He took the whisky decanter and tipped some into a glass.

'All right,' he said. 'It's midnight or later, so let's have the fairy story. Then I can go to bed.'

'Don't try and stall me, Huntley,' Elizabeth said. 'I'm your niece. I don't know how much that means to you, but at least it ought to prove that I'm not trying to fool around. You and Eddi King are in this thing together; you've brought a man into this country on a false passport and I want to know why.'

'And what in hell gives you the right to ask—who owes you any answers?' He was snarling at her; the full force of that bullying personality with its enormous power of intimidation beat on Elizabeth like a shower of rocks, and she threw back the only one she had.

'Because King got me to bring him in,' she said. 'That's what gives me the right.'

And this he certainly had not known. So far, Eddi King had told the truth. His face changed colour; he got up and the whisky slopped on to the carpet.

'You? You brought that guy into the States!'

'Eddi asked me to do it,' she said quietly. 'He asked it as a favour to you. He also asked me not to ever tell you.'

'The bastard.' Huntley almost whispered the word. 'The lousy bastard. Tell me again. How was it? Tell me exactly.'

'I went along to see the Lebanon,' Elizabeth said. 'You knew that. It was just a trip. But Eddi King had asked me to come specially. When we got there he asked me to take a man back home with me, see him through Customs and then leave him. He told me this was being done on your behalf, but that you mustn't know I was involved in it. But it was so important that it had to be me because I was the only one who could be really trusted. I saw this man in the street once, and then I picked him up in a taxi and we flew back to New York.'

'Jesus Christ,' Huntley Cameron said, 'I'll kill him. I'll fix him so he never crosses anyone again. And you did this?'

'I did it,' she said. 'I thought you had some scheme like the ones you've pulled out against the Administration before.—I thought from what he said you were risking an awful lot, and I couldn't let you down. I brought the man through with me.'

'But nobody connected you.' His mind was racing ahead,

trying to see the consequences of this unbelievable link that King had forged between him and the assassin of Jackson. His niece. His niece had brought the killer in. Before he allowed himself to question the motive he wanted to know the extent of that involvement and the chances of its being traced.

'You travelled together but you left him at the airport . . .'

'No,' Elizabeth said. 'No, I didn't leave him there. Nobody came to meet him after all, and he had no place to go. He's been in my apartment for the last two weeks. Until King came back from Germany. Then he got him moved out.'

'You've been keeping him in Riverways for two weeks?' He couldn't believe it. He stared at her, his brain refusing to respond to the nerve impulses all screaming danger at the same second. It was impossible. Incredible.

'What's he here for, Huntley?' She spoke quietly. The moment had come; if he held out against her, and he still might, then Eddi King would be brought into it. And that really frightened her now.

'What did King tell you—he told you something, didn't he?' He was playing it along, not knowing how much she knew, whether she had even guessed. Two weeks she had been alone with the man. And in those two weeks she had picked up something. That was why she had come down to Freemont. To face him with it.

'He told me a lot of lies,' Elizabeth said. She felt strangely calm. Huntley Cameron was the one who was afraid; he really did look old as if the last few minutes had each counted as a year. 'He said the man was connected with the Mafia, dope, running girls, that sort of thing. He told the stupidest lies imaginable, right under your nose in the conservatory this evening. And he made me promise once again that I'd never let you know I'd been mixed up in it.'

'You say it was lies.' Huntley knew it wasn't much of a straw but it was floating past and he tried to grab it. 'How do you know it's not the truth?'

'Because I know the man,' she said. 'He told me a little about himself. He's a professional soldier, he's not mixed up in rackets.' She waited; he said nothing. She took a cigarette out of a gold Fabergé box and lit it.

116

'I'm going to the police, Uncle. I'm going to clear myself, so you'd better tell me the truth.'

'You were right about the man,' he said. He gave himself a second whisky and tossed it straight down his throat. 'He's not a racketeer. He's a professional killer. What's the matter—he didn't lay you in those two weeks, by any chance?' He gave a short, unpleasant laugh. He hated her at that moment; she had stood up to him and the old fable about this being the way to win a tyrant's heart was just a fable. The shot had been aimed true. It showed in her eyes. 'A killer,' Huntley repeated. 'A guy who'd shoot a man's head off for a few thousand dollars—how was it? Different to the others? Does it give you a thrill, just to think about it?'

'Who are you going to have killed?' she asked him. 'You're the killer, Huntley, not him. You and Eddi King. Who is it?'

'If you go to the police,' he said, 'you know what it will mean. Maybe you'll talk yourself out of it; I said maybe. Once they get their hooks into you, it might not be quite so easy to play innocent. But let's look at what happens. I get arrested, so does King. So does the man. And it all comes out, Elizabeth. My part in it, King's part, and your little romance with a gunman. That's what you'll achieve by going to the police.' He sat back, relaxing with yet another drink, pretending to talk seriously. She wouldn't get to the police. He had a system which he only need touch, and half a dozen security men would be up there inside a minute. If he didn't want his niece to leave Freemont there were ways to see she didn't, and he would use them. He paid very well. He would come to Eddi King later.

'I don't want to go to the police,' Elizabeth said. 'I never intended to—I had to say something to make you tell me.' Suddenly she needed to sit down; her whole body ached, her legs were trembling. A killer; a man who would shoot another man's head off for a few thousand . . . she put a hand up to her eyes, and tried to steady herself. Had it been any different? Huntley's jibe came back to her. And it had. It had been the most important thing that ever happened to her. But she didn't care what he was, she loved him. She dropped the shielding hand and looked into her uncle's hostile face. The battle was over. He wouldn't tell her who

117

the victim was, and she didn't want to know. She just wanted to convince him of the truth. She wasn't going to the police, because she couldn't. Any more than she could tell the truth to Leary. She had to find Keller first.

'You shouldn't have threatened me,' her uncle said. 'You're my niece. I thought you'd have some family loyalty.'

'I have,' she said wearily. 'You know I couldn't turn you in and have us all disgraced, whatever happened. Just promise me you'll call it off, that's all.'

'Where is the man now?' Huntley asked her.

She shook her head. 'I don't know. Please, Huntley, whatever this is, whatever Eddi King has talked you into—don't go through with it. Don't you see he's used me to frame you?'

'Of course I see it,' Huntley snapped back at her. 'What I can't see is why. But never mind that now. I'm not giving any promises, Elizabeth. I have a duty to my country.' For a moment the narrow eyes flared open. There was a fierce, fanatic light in them. 'I have a duty to protect it and I'm going to do so. If you knew what I know, you wouldn't ask for any promise.'

'Try me,' she said. 'There's nothing I can do to stop you, so you might as well. We might as well work together to protect ourselves. Your friend Eddi King is drawing some kind of noose right round us both.'

'I want Casey to win,' the old man said. 'I want this country out of Viet Nam and I want us to have peace. If we get the wrong President we'll have a war in the Far East and a civil war at home!'

'It's Jackson,' Elizabeth broke in on him. 'My God, that's who it is!'

'And you object?' the old man asked her. 'You think that crazy punk should get to the White House? You think his life is worth anything, compared to what he'll do to this country of ours?'

'He won't get in,' Elizabeth protested. 'He hasn't a chance!'

'He has a very good chance indeed.' Cameron glared at her. 'I've had it on the best authority, it'll be a straight fight between him and Casey. The President's not standing again.'

'How do you know?' Elizabeth said. 'How can you know that?'

'How do you think I use my money?' he retorted. 'What d'you think I do for information—read my own newspapers? I *know* he isn't going to stand, because he's got a cancer condition that the public hasn't even heard about. So there's nobody for people who don't want Casey, but John Jackson! Now do you see it?'

'But what about the Vice-President?' Elizabeth could see it only too well. 'Surely there's somebody the Republicans can put forward?'

'In six months? You're talking through your ass; you sound like that log-head Dallas. Six months? To groom a candidate, to get the nomination—it's too late, don't you see that? The President's got cancer of the gut and no one found it out till now. There isn't time to catch up on Casey or Jackson. We can't afford that punk,' he lowered his voice, almost as if he were talking to himself. 'What the hell else would make me throw in with Casey and his crappy socialism except I know what's the alternative . . . Jackson's not going to run, believe me.'

'You can't kill a man, no matter what he is,' she said. 'You can't do it, Uncle.'

'One life,' Huntley said coldly. 'One cheap little huckster, against civil war, black against white, absolute ruin for us all? You want to see New York burn? And not just New York but half the cities in America? You want communism in this country—because that's what Jackson will mean in the end. You think I'm a crackpot, don't you, just another rich man with a lot of Red phobias?' He laughed again, unpleasantly, as he had done when he sneered at her for sleeping with Keller. 'If that was true I wouldn't be backing Casey. *I* can see further than my ass. That's what's made me what I am. I've told you, Jackson doesn't run. We'll wash out friend Eddi King's arrangement; don't worry about that. But I've got six months to make my own deal. And you can't stop me.'

'No, I can't stop you,' she said slowly. 'If you want to commit murder, you'll do it, whatever I say. I just know it's not the answer, that's all. What are you going to do about Eddi King? Why should he want to try and connect you with the assassination?'

119

'I don't know,' Huntley said. He leaned forward, his tough old hands knotted round one knee. 'All I can think of is blackmail. He comes and tells me you're mixed up in it to the eyeballs and then he puts the pressure on. After Jackson's got it and the guy's been taken care off too. He probably thinks he could shake me for the rest of my life.'

'What do you mean, taken care of?' She tried to keep her voice from trembling. It didn't seem to matter to him; he was already thinking out how King intended using that incriminating journey, that damning stay in Elizabeth's flat. He didn't look at her when she asked the question.

'Knocked off, after he's done the job,' he said. 'King is going to fix that too. We didn't want to risk him getting caught and talking. Christ, if I'd only known what he could have talked about . . .'

'I'm going to bed,' Elizabeth said. 'I feel awful.'

'You keep your mouth closed.' Huntley Cameron looked up. He wasn't worried about her any more. She wouldn't say anything. She wouldn't ever destroy herself and him. He wondered how in hell she had tricked him into thinking that she might, even for a few minutes. 'You go and take a trip,' he said. 'A long trip. I'll tidy up this little mess.'

She went out and walked back down the corridor to her own room. They were going to kill Keller after he'd assassinated Jackson. There was a terribly familiar ring to that. She opened the door of her bedroom. The handle clicked; the small noise sounded loud out of all proportion because of the silence over the rest of Freemont.

On the stairs below, King, one arm supporting Dallas, stopped and waited. On the thick carpet he and the drunken woman made no noise. He heard the door close in the corridor above and knew that Elizabeth had gone back to her room.

Normally he slept well. Normally he would have gone to bed and perhaps read for a while before turning off the light, but for some reason he couldn't relax at all. He had undressed and wandered round his bedroom, restless and irritable. He vented it in his mind on Huntley Cameron and that so-familiar French thriller he had been forced to watch for the umpteenth time. Thank Christ it wasn't *Gone with the Wind* again. It was one in the morning and he hadn't been able to concentrate on the travel book he had begun reading—travel bored him anyway—and it was too late even by Freemont standards to ring for what he needed. He got up and went downstairs to find himself a nightcap. And in the library, with all the lights switched on, he found Dallas Jay, sitting on the floor with a glass of vodka in one hand, crying while she tried to get drunk. He had almost turned back; he wasn't a man who liked scenes. He had nothing but contempt for the woman herself, for her cringing personality, and the total lack of intelligence which was no longer compensated by her looks. Dumb blondes should never be more than twenty-five and a dumb brunette had even less margin for error. He almost turned back and crept away, and then he changed his mind. Huntley must have kicked her out. King had distinctly heard her leave her room to go to him. He came into the library and pretended to be surprised.

'Why, Dallas! What's the matter?' She was already quite high; part of it was Stolnichnaya 80% proof, the rest a violent emotional agitation.

'It was going so well,' she wept. 'He was getting all worked up, and saying nice thing to me an' all, and then—Wham! That bitch comes walking in—she just comes and bangs on the door and walks right in on us!' She sobbed, interrupting herself long enough to take a wild swallow at her drink.

King got her up from the floor and on to a couch. He gave her a cigarette, filled up the glass again, and sat beside her. She was hysterical and a lot higher than he had first judged. 'Who came in?' he said. 'Who are you talking about?' She turned her head, the eyes red, mascara ringing them in little inky streaks of tears; she looked leathery and worn, like a chair which had been sat on by too many people, careless how they scuffed and kicked.

'That fucking niece,' she said, with the clear enunciation of the drunk for angry words. 'The great God Almighty Miss Cameron. She just had to talk to Huntley. She just had to talk to him tonight. You know something, Eddi? We were going to make it tonight. We really were. He was all ready to go when she bust in.' She bent her head and the tears dribbled down and fell off her face. 'He hasn't buzzed for me in months,' she said. 'We were getting on great. Then she came knocking. Knock. Knock. The little shit. The fancy little shit-face.' King had never heard her swear; he

121

found it repulsive in a woman. But this didn't concern him. He didn't care what she was saying now; he let her cry and maunder on; when she tried to lean against him, he edged back. Elizabeth had gone to her uncle after saying she was tired and going up early. She had waited till midnight, when she thought everyone would be asleep, and then gone to Huntley's room to see him. And that could only mean one thing. She hadn't believed his story about Keller. And she had broken her promise not to tell Huntley the truth about Beirut. King looked down at the weeping woman, repeating her obscene complaints to herself. How lucky for him that she had been with Huntley. How lucky he hadn't been able to sleep and had come down to find her. How lucky everything had been, considering that one piece of fundamental bad luck, which could mean disaster. Uncle and niece might have liaised. If Elizabeth Cameron had found out what they were planning she would never stand by and let it happen. He knew the type: assassination wouldn't be excusable, no matter who the target was. And if she told Huntley of her part in it, then the sooner Eddi King got out of Freemont, the safer he would be. 'Come on,' he said. 'Come on, you can't stay here. Huntley wouldn't like it. I'll help you up and you go to bed, Dallas. There'll be another time. To-morrow night. Don't worry, just stand up, that's it.'

Dallas hadn't got into that state in a few minutes. That meant they had really been talking. How much had either told the other?—he didn't know but he was sure that it would be enough to ruin everything. He helped Dallas up the steps and guided her very quietly to her own door. He opened it and eased her inside.

'I like you,' she said. 'You know, I always thought you were a bastard, Eddi, but now I like you. How'd you like to come in for a while?' She stood supporting herself on the lintel of the door, making her defiant, tragic little gesture against Huntley Cameron.

'No thanks,' King said softly. 'You want to marry him, don't you? I wouldn't let you take the risk.'

He passed Elizabeth's door and for a moment he hesitated. For a moment red rage blazed in him; his hand reached out, the tips of his fingers brushed the gleaming handle. He could break her neck with one blow. He was fully trained in all aspects of his work. He knew how to silence, how to kill in a single movement. She was the one who would stop it if she knew. She would go to the police or the F.B.I. if Huntley Cameron had made the ultimate mistake and let her know or even guess the truth about the man she had brought in from Beirut. But going in and killing her was not the way. His hand dropped down and his feet went on, away from her door, towards his own room. First, make sure she didn't telephone. He went inside and found what he needed on his dressing chest. It was gold, like all his personal things: key ring, St Christopher medal, bought by one of his girl friends as a memento, swizzle stick for de-fizzing champagne. The penknife had sharp strong blades. He went out into the corridor again. He knew the main geography of Freemont as well as if he lived there. He also knew where the indoor security patrol operated; two men patrolled the house at night, but they had orders not to make themselves intrusive. He made his way down the enormous staircase and through the Great Hall, where centuries ago the German barons had kept their courts, watched by the ancient portraits on the walls, his shadow lost in the tapestries. In the outside passages he met one of Cameron's security guards.

'My telephone's been ringing,' King said. He sounded querulous. 'I pick it up and nobody answers. There must be a fault somewhere. It's keeping me awake.'

'I'll come and check it, sir.'

'I've already done that,' King said. 'There's nothing wrong with the instrument. Where's the internal system—that's where it's gone wrong.'

They went together, the guard leading the way. The main telephone system was linked to a separate switchboard inside the house; this connected all the extensions in the bedrooms and living rooms, including the swimming pool and the conservatory. This was one place King had never been before. Every extension was marked. There were eighteen main bedrooms, tabbed by names. His eye flicked alone the line, searching for the little plate with the name Visconti bedroom on it. He had already found his own. The Medici. The rooms were named for their furnishings. 'Okay, I can check here myself,' he said. 'You'd better get back to your patrol. Damned telephones. Lucky I know some-thing about them.' He waited for the guard to disappear. He waited two full minutes by his watch. Then he unplugged the little cable connecting the Visconti bedroom with the switchboard, and cut through one of the twin wires. He replaced the plug; nothing showed. That would stop any attempt to call tomorrow morning, from her room. Or even that night, which was the greatest danger. And the first thing in the morning he would make sure she didn't get a chance to call anyone about anything. He turned off the lights and closed the door. Everything looked normal if the guard came back. Then he went up to his room and packed his clothes. Huntley slept late at weekends. He never came down or saw anyone before eleven. And by that time King would have disappeared and there'd be no more to fear from Elizabeth Cameron.

It was all worked out; he didn't congratulate himself. He had made a monstrous mistake, and being able to correct it was no reason to be smug. All it enabled him to do was fall asleep for a few hours.

CHAPTER FIVE

The telephone woke Peter Mathews up; he never switched the extension off. At two in the morning it brought him wide awake. He had a moment of panic and reached out his other hand in the dark while he fumbled for the light and the receiver. The bed was empty. Of course, he'd been the gentleman and driven the lady home. They'd met at a private view in one of his friends' smart galleries on 23rd, gone out to dinner and come home to bed. She had short red hair, all curled and lacquered till it looked so natural he had just wanted to run his fingers through it. From such small beginnings ...

'It's Leary,' the voice said in his ear. 'Get down to the office, will you. Something's broken.' Mathews didn't even have time to answer before he hung up. How lucky the red-head hadn't wanted to stay the night. He was dressed in ten minutes and on his way down town as the clock on Times Square moved to the half-hour.

Leary was in his office, the windows shaded, the lights on, and a jug of coffee sent a little stream of heat into the air.

'Haven't you been to bed?' Mathews said.

'No. I got a message around nine this evening. Through our Middle East section. Sit down and have a cup. You're going to need it.'

'What's happened?'

'On the face of it, the first thing wasn't much. An Arab girl called Souha Mamonlian found strangled and robbed in Beirut. Nothing out of the ordinary there, except that the Bank of Lebanon had a deposit of ten thousand dollars in her name, put there by a European man she was living with. This was reported to Interpol because the bank felt it might be connected with dope running—it's a hell of a lot of money for a girl like that, and also the boy friend was a bum. No steady job, no money, and after putting the money in the bank for her he disappeared. Our friend in Interpol thought we should know because Beirut was Eddi King's last port of call before he rendezvoused with Marcel Druet in Paris. That's number one. Number two is nastier. Have your coffee, Pete. In the course of checking up on King, we found out something else. He went direct to Paris, a day later Elizabeth Cameron left for New York. Half a dozen people at the Beirut airport, the barman, the Pan Am stewardess on the flight, said she was travelling with a man. She never mentioned this to me. She talked about King and about everything else, but she never once mentioned meeting anyone else or coming on the plane with them.'

'It looks bad,' Mathews said slowly. 'You were right, weren't you? You said she was holding out—you even said there was a man in it somewhere. There was certainly somebody with her the time I called. We've got a tail on her—she went down to Freemont for the weekend.' He finished his coffee and lit a cigarette. Leary had been right and so had he. He'd made a joke, curious to know who the guy was. Stars in her eyes, that's what he'd said, and she hadn't been drawn. She had said nothing to him, either.

'And now,' Leary said, 'for the real reason I woke you up. Look at this.' He pushed over a teletyped sheet, and settled back in his chair while Mathews read it. It was a report of an interview with a member of the faculty of Wisconsin College where Eddi King had been a student in the early thirties. It was all routine stuff, chatty and inaccurate in

125

minor details; thirty years ago was a long time; the teacher had been very junior, more interested in the basketball team than in the academic records. And that was where Leary's broad pencil had scored and scored again, beside a single paragraph.

The reason Eddi King remained in the teacher's memory so vividly was because he had been so keen on basketball. But he just hadn't made the team. Used to try exercise to increase his height. But it was no good. Five foot nine was just too short. He never made it. That was where the pencil marking stopped.

Mathews looked up. 'I don't get this? What's wrong?

Leary had his eyes shut. He spoke without opening them; he looked strained and very tired. 'King was twenty-one. He'd finished growing. I've heard of people growing down as they got older, but never growing up. Our Eddi King is over six feet tall. You see what this means, Pete? You see what those three or four inches mean?'

'It's not the same man,' Mathews said slowly. 'It's not the real Eddi King.'

'I didn't just take that,' Leary went on. 'I got through to Wisconsin myself. I checked it personally. King was a small guy, slight build. Five nine was a stretch for him.'

'How could it have been done?' Peter Mathews said. He wasn't excited; he felt chilled, as if they had opened a door and seen a dead face through the crack.

'King was interned in France during the war. It's in his file. He was released in '45, and came back here in '58. That's how it happened, Pete. The real Eddi King didn't survive that death camp. The Russians took his identity for one of their people.'

'Christ Almighty,' Mathews said. 'We've got a big one, then.'

'My guess is one of the biggest. Look at the records. He's been fifteen years here, establishing himself; who do you think financed that magazine of his—and what a perfect means of passing information, with offices in Germany and half a dozen men travelling round Europe? How much do you think it costs them to get him in the Huntley Cameron group—he must be one of the most important agents in the whole service.'

'But where does Cameron fit—and Elizabeth? For

Christ's sake don't tell me they're mixed up with the K.G.B.!'

'I don't know,' Leary said. 'But King went to the Lebanon for a reason, and he liaised in Paris with Druet to report on it, leaving your girl friend Miss Cameron to come back to the States with a different travelling companion, one she didn't tell me about when there was every opportunity.'

'If it was a straight pick-up,' Mathews suggested, 'just a guy she fell for in Beirut who went to live with her when they got home—would she have told you about that? Why should it connect with King?'

'Because while your man was tailing her to Freemont another man was talking to the hall porter at her apartment block. She sure had a guy living with her, but he left the same morning she came here. The day after friend King got back from Europe.'

'What do we do next?' Mathews said. He felt uncomfortable; he was also beginning to feel angry. He had never taken Elizabeth Cameron for more than just another trophy: intelligent, beautiful, a shade inhibited compared with some, but never with any suggestion that she could move into his cold and dangerous world. But she was in it; Leary was right, as he had been right from the start when he said she was holding something back. 'I'd like to bring her in,' he said suddenly.

'That's what I woke you for,' Leary said. 'It's around three-thirty now, you can go home and freshen up and get down to Freemont for breakfast.'

'They have guards on the gate,' Mathews said. 'It's like walking into Fort Knox.'

'She'll get you in, she knows you're her contact with me. If she's playing for their side, Pete, she'll have to find out what you want. If she isn't, she'll still see you. Take her out of Freemont and bring her here.'

Mathews looked up at his chief. 'I'd like to have an hour or two alone with her first,' he said. 'I can use my place. If I can't break her by tomorrow you can take over. I'd like to try.'

'What's the motive, Pete? Sentiment?'

'You know me better than that. I feel she's crossed me up in some way, and I don't like it. Let me have her for a while.'

'Okay,' Leary said. 'Call in and let me know what progress you're making. Right now we're trying to get a lead on whoever was staying in that flat.'

'There're so many leads,' Mathews said, 'and none of them seem to tie up.'

'Oh, I wouldn't say that.' Leary stretched his arms above his head and yawned. He felt the coffee pot, it was empty. 'One or two things connect up. King goes to Beirut, taking a cover with him—Miss Cameron. When he leaves he goes to one of the top opposition men in Western Europe to make some kind of report—right so far? Okay. Let's go back to the Lebanon. Somewhere, Miss Cameron picks up a man and takes him home with her. From what we know about her, this isn't very typical. Not typical at all. So there's two of them in the Riverways, for the period King is still abroad. Miss Cameron holds out on us about this guy, even when she hears about the plane crash. And she was shaken, Pete. She offered me Eddi King's head on a plate. But she didn't mention her house guest. Let's track back again. In the two weeks since she and King and Mr X left Beirut a girl gets murdered. That's not unusual, lots of murders happen in a place like that. The only funny thing is that healthy bank account and the European boy friend. There was another coincidence too. A Lebanese working for the airlines took delivery of a new car and it blew him and his family up the first time they went for a drive. He'd just banked a lot of money too. I think he and the Arab girl are connected. I think they were killed as part of a cover-up operation. That's how the opposition works with something big. They set it up and then they wipe out all the little people, one by one, who had a part in it. It's good security.'

'Is it dope?' Mathews asked. 'That's a big weapon in their hands these days.'

Leary got up and went into the outer office, taking the coffee pot with him. His secretary kept an electric percolator there.

'An operator like King doesn't deal in narcotics,' Leary called through the open door. 'They have a completely different set-up for that. There's thirty thousand acres in the Lebanon alone, just growing hash for export. The guy who owns them is a Member of Parliament. No, Pete, this isn't that kind of thing at all. They're not bringing dope into the

States on this run. What's worrying the hell out of me is who or what King went over to set up.'

'And whether it came here with Elizabeth Cameron and hung out in her apartment for two weeks,' Pete Mathews finished for him. He got up, stretching as Leary had done. He didn't feel tired; he felt alert and eager to get moving.

'I'll get down to Freemont around eight-thirty,' he said. 'And when I'm home I'll call you.'

'Good night, Pete.' Leary came back into the office with the coffee. The door had closed behind Mathews, but he spoke out loud, continuing the conversation with himself. 'What worries me most of all,' he said, 'what really gives me wrinkles, is that this goddamned business is blowing up in time for the Presidential election. If anything happens again...' He went back to his desk.

Keller had slept badly to start the night, and then drifted into a very deep sleep which ran over into the late morning.

When he heard knocking he woke instantly with the alertness of a man who had spent years prepared to spring up at the slightest noise.

The handle was turned round and round; he could sense the frustration on the other side of the door. The super's voice came at him through the wood like a rusty saw scraping on iron.

'There's a guy here with the TV. Open up, will ya?'

There was a man behind the super, wearing dirty overalls, with a small portable TV set in his arms.

'This is for you, bud,' he said to Keller. 'I got to set it up and show you how it works.' Keller stood aside and let him come in. He kicked the door shut and turned the key again. He heard the super say something, which he couldn't understand, and then slouch off down the passage.

'Who sent this?'

'Guy who booked the room,' the man answered. He had put the set on the table near the bed; he was pulling out an indoor aerial and the set was humming, its white screen alight.

'You should get a picture okay,' he said. He turned a knob and there was a blast of music.

'That old dope has keyhole ears.' He turned to Keller and straightened up. 'I guess we can talk through this. You want

129

one?' He held out a packet of Chesterfields towards Keller, who shook his head.

He saw the tense, suspicious look and the heavy hands held ready at his sides, the fingers slightly curled, ready to bunch into fists. 'Relax,' he said. He lit his cigarette and gulped down smoke. 'Relax, you make me nervous. I got instructions for you. Here; read this.' He tossed an envelope towards Keller, who caught it. He didn't answer the man; he gave him a last look and then dropped on the bed, ripping the flap open. It was a single sheet of paper, and it consisted of a rough plan of a very big building. Keller studied it for a moment.

'What is this place?'

'St Patrick's Cathedral. Over on Madison Avenue.' He was a sturdily built man in his middle thirties, dark-eyed and coarse-featured; the face was a series of blobs, as if he were made of sloppy putty which hadn't ever set. Like so many Americans, his origins were difficult to guess. He smoked in compulsive gulps, sucking the smoke in and blowing it back like a steam engine. He watched Keller coolly, assessing him. Rough; edgy. Not the typical contract operator he was used to dealing with. He had the same taut, killer quality in the way he moved and those pale eyes could go dead like an angry snake's; but there was a hardness, a physical quality, about him which was different to the professional gunmen. Many of the pros were poor slum specimens, with greasy tenement pallor.

This man could have broken your back if he wanted to; he seemed a different species to the deadly breed which was spawned in New York's lower East Side. The TV man made these conclusions in the few seconds while Keller studied the sketch map. In his own organisation he was quite high up. A two-year stint in Viet Nam had taught him discipline and quick thinking. He was ambitious and intelligent, and when he came home he went into the criminal ranks with ambitions beyond petty theft and strong-arm jobs. He left that to the slobs. When there was something special to be organised, or a real special contract to be carried out, then he was sent in to handle it. This was a very big contract indeed. The money which had already been spent showed just how important it was. The importation of a man from outside the States removed any stain from his own professional reputation. This one was not for him. Most definitely not for him, now that he knew who the victim was.

Keller pointed to a series of dots made in red ink down one section of the map, and again at a circle drawn round something he couldn't identify because it seemed set in the side of the wall.

'Explain this to me. And turn that noise down; he can't hear us but I can't hear you. What do these marks mean?'

The man came over and sat on the bed beside him. 'Look, he said, 'this is a rough guide; just to help the memory, see. This is where you're goin' to operate, St Pat's. Now, this is the nave, see? Up the left is the side aisle. Past the high altar you go on up till you get to this bit marked with the circle. Okay?'

'What is it?'

'Confessional box. Special box for the deaf. It ain't used now, they go across to the 50th Street Annexe. Nobody uses the box, see?' Keller didn't answer. The constant use of the word, perched irrelevantly at the end of most sentences, jarred him as much as the superintendent's West Side whine.

'Those marks show where your target comes in and goes out.' Keller turned his head towards him and stared into the muddy eyes.

'Who is the target?'

'You got scruples about who you knock over?' It was a friendly question, like asking a man if he preferred a different brand of beer.

'I don't understand you,' Keller said. 'I'm getting paid, I want to know what I have to do. If you know, you tell me; that's all.'

'Okay. Monday morning is St Patrick's Day. It's a big day over here, bud. All the Micks in America dive into the Scotch bottle and don't come out till March 18th. But they like to start it off with a prayer meetin' and a parade; all you have to worry about is the prayer meetin'. It's held right in the cathedral. And that's where your target comes in. Right through that door near the confessional box. You know what a cardinal looks like?' He grinned, making a joke of it. All the time he was watching Keller's face.

'They wear red robes,' Keller said.

131

'Sure they do. All dressed up like Santa Claus—without the whiskers. That's who you got to knock over, Cardinal Regazzi. During the High Mass on Monday morning, see? He comes in where it shows on your plan and he goes out the same way. You can take him close to, or as he goes on down to the altar. From the confessional box.'

Keller looked down at the sketch map. 'How do I get out?'

'There's an exit right by the box; leads to 51st Street. Here.' He had a pencil in his hand; Keller noticed that the end was chewed to splinters. He wasn't as nerveless as he seemed. He made a short line on the sketch. 'That's where you exit. It's a door between the confessional and the way the Cardinal comes in from the rectory. For Crissake don't muddle 'em up, or you'll run through into the Rectory. And they won't be nice to you in there, not after you've made a nasty hole in the big boss!' He laughed; it was a curiously attractive sound, full of good humour.

'You like it so far?'

'So far,' Keller said. 'I've got a lot of questions.'

'I got all the answers,' the other man said. 'I got the whole thing worked right out—here.' He tapped his temple, and added the inevitable. 'See?' 'Now, the way it goes is this. Mass starts around ten-thirty. Whenever the Cardinal shows up for one of these public shenanigins the whole place is crawlin' with C.I.A. Feds and City cops. You couldn't bring in a toothpick, bud, never mind an iron. But don't let it worry you. You come in clean as a baby's ass, an' down the left-hand aisle and land up near this confessional. Now when you pick the moment to duck in is up to you. But right behind the green curtains you'll find a kind of overall. Just pull it on; it's like the guys wear who mind the collecting boxes. This part of the church is pretty dark; don't worry if one of the other guys with an overall sees you; there's always extras brought in on St Pat's to keep a check on the crowds. The place'll be crawlin' with people anyway. Then make like you're looking around; go back to the box and pull back the curtains, act it up a bit, like you were making sure it was empty—the place will've been searched inside out the night before, but the Feds and the rest of 'em keep on checking, just in case. You know they grabbed a guy who went to Bobbie Kennedy's funeral with a *ticket*, just because he was carryin' an iron—your iron is under the top of the kneelin' rail in the confessional. The top's covered in a green stuff, like satin. Just lift it straight in the middle and a piece will come up. You'll find your iron inside, fully loaded. See?'

'You have someone working from inside the cathedral?' Keller asked. It all sounded very glib, but even without seeing the church, he understood why they had offered so much money. Not just for killing a priest, but for doing it inside a building closed and guarded by security men.

'Don't let it bother you, bud. When we organise we organise. You'll find the robe and the iron right where I said. It ain't none of your business how they got there.'

'You say I get out through this exit.' Keller referred to the pencilled line. 'How do you know it will be open, or isn't that any of my business either?'

The man held up one hand, half fooling, half conciliatory.

'Now don't get mad! Sure it's open, but it's guarded. There'll be one man on it inside the door and another guy hanging around outside. It's right by the way the Cardinal comes through.' He lit another cigarette and began to eat through it at the same hungry rate; he didn't bother to offer one to Keller a second time. 'All you have to worry about is the guy on the outside of the door,' he said. 'The way I'm told it's gotta be is pretty simple: he comes in, you knock him over just after he's passed you, you make a run for that door and get the hell out and come back here, see?'

'What about the gun—what do I do with that?'

'Just drop it, bud. You wear gloves for this kind of thing, don't you? Anyways, I brought some. They'll fit most sizes.' He pulled a pair of white cotton gloves from an inside pocket and dropped them on Keller's knee. They were loose and when he pulled one on, it covered his hand without restricting the finger movement. The gloves gave him confidence, and by this time he was in need of something to convince him that he might live to spend the money. His employers organised with more than efficiency. The attention to such detail was perfectionist. It gave Keller the feeling that however impossible the project sounded, it must still be possible. Nothing would be allowed to go wrong from their side. He had to make the change, get the pistol out of its hiding place, shoot his man and get out. That was

133

what he was being paid his enormous fee to do. And it made sense the more he thought of the circumstances of this particular killing. Anyone can shoot a pistol at point-blank range, and provided they get their victim through the head, they will probably finish him. But to be sure of killing at anything like a distance they needed an expert. Not just an expert marksman, but someone who knew the vulnerable parts of the human body. And the most difficult was a moving head among other moving heads. But if they didn't fail he wouldn't either. And he wouldn't allow himself to see the target in terms of a human being, or think of it as connected with the impassioned priest of the poor he had watched on Elizabeth's television screen. He had closed his mind in advance to whoever he was told to shoot; the initial shock of finding it was Cardinal Regazzi had been concealed from the gangster sitting beside him, and now it was dissipated by his attention to the mechanics of the assassination. And particularly by the details of his own escape.

'I brought somethin' for you.' The man got up and lifted a tool bag on to the bed. He opened it. There was nothing inside but a thick paper parcel. 'Here's the first half—twenty-five thousand bucks. You get the rest after you come back here on Monday.'

'When do I leave America?'

'When it's cooled down,' the man said. 'You stay right where you are till someone gives you the okay to move, see? You can count your dough if you get sick of lookin' at that.' He pointed to the TV. 'You'll get a real good reception with that model,' he went on. 'I got one at home myself. You better take a trip over to the Cathedral this morning. Get the layout clear and know where that confessional is. But don't try going inside it; just say your prayers and get the picture into focus. The box, the door through the rectory, the route the Cardinal takes comin' into the cathedral, and your door out to 51st Street. That's all you need to know, but be sure and know it good, see?'

'I see,' Keller said. He got up and ripped a corner of the paper away from the package. Hundred-dollar bills were packed in neat layers, bound with broad bands of paper.

'Didn't you trust me?' the man grinned at him.

'No,' Keller said. 'I didn't.' He undid the package and

134

began sorting the money. He looked up briefly to see the other man go.

Twenty-five thousand dollars. And that was only half. He played with the stacks of bills, riffling them through his fingers like a card-sharp dealing himself aces. More money than he had ever seen in his life. With this he could buy a new identity, a new existence for himself. And for Souha. He remembered her with a shock. She was part of the deal tied in with the killing and the money. A new start for her as much as for him. He wouldn't let himself think of that other woman any more than he would visualise the man whose death was to pay for these dreams of the future. He closed his mind's eye to the face of Elizabeth Cameron, and smashed a fist into the mouth of his own conscience before it could make the name Regazzi into a reproach. He hid the money in his drawer under some shirts, switched off the TV set, and went out, locking the room behind him. The superintendent was in the downstairs passage, reluctantly sweeping the dirty floor. He looked up at him, and then away, wetting his lips.

'You goin' out?'

Keller decided to make use of him. 'How do I get to St Patrick's Cathedral from this part?'

The moist mouth sagged open; there was a hairline crack between his upper dentures and the gum, it showed black as the jaw gaped. 'You goin' to *church*?'

'All Catholics,' Keller said, 'go to Mass on Sundays.'

'You take a cab—get out at Madison Avenue . . .' He stared after him, even when Keller had opened the front door and disappeared into the street; the broom supported him like a crutch. He said some obscenity under his breath and propped it against the wall. It was still there when Keller came back nearly two hours later

Dallas woke with a cramp pain in her right arm. She had fallen across the bed, face down, with her arm doubled up underneath her. The muscular contraction brought her back to consciousness; it was immediately joined by a throbbing headache which pounded inside her skull as she pulled herself up.

She wore no watch; the light by her bed made her cringe for a moment, but it showed the clock face on her dressing

135

table : six-thirty. She went to the bathroom, one hand to her forehead, her feet dragging as depression over last night's fiasco joined forces with the hangover. She peered at herself in the glass; three pain-killing tablets dissolved in her tooth mug. 'Christ,' she muttered at the bleared, ravaged face, and it grimaced in sympathy. 'You sure look like hell this morning.' She had a habit of talking to herself out loud; it was the result of being long periods without anyone else to talk to, when Huntley was busy. It was also the result of watching every word when she did speak. There had to be a safety valve, and it took the form of long, candid, often obscene monologues in private. Everything had got screwed up last night. She drank the aspirin down, and shuddered. She had got stoned, and said a lot of things to Eddi King— Christ Almighty, she remembered inviting him in—she stumbled back to the bedroom and sank down on the bed. If he ever told Huntley about that . . . If anyone saw her in the library with King and told Huntley she was drunk and calling that bitch niece names. It was all too much for Dallas. She rushed back to the bathroom and was sick. It made her headache worse, but it settled her nerves. Huntley mustn't know; the niece mustn't find out what Dallas had said about her; King must be persuaded to keep quiet. How the hell did she do that? How the hell did she shut his mouth? She cursed herself for letting go, for giving way; she cried a little and then stopped, remembering how awful she already looked. What could she do about King—the question chased round and round in her brain like a panic-stricken rat. The solution which occurred to her first was to renew the offer of the previous night. But he had turned her down. He had turned her down drunk and loused up with crying; maybe sober and looking right, he'd change his mind. It was a ghastly risk, but her own body was the only coin of exchange Dallas had ever possessed. That she knew how to use. Then he could hardly go to Huntley and say he'd cheated with his girl friend; it wasn't the same as saying he'd been pro-positioned and refused.

She went back to the bathroom and washed under the shower. She took more pain-relievers; the others had gone down the pan, and then very carefully she began to make her face up. She changed her Pucci one-piece gown for the see-through, frothy nightdress she wore to please herself.

Most men liked that kind of thing. She put on body scent and sprayed her hair and neck, and looked at herself. The face was disappointing but at seven in the morning he wouldn't be worried about that. The rest was as good as it had ever been. It was a terrible gamble, but despair made light of the odds. She had opened her mouth too wide last night, and she was completely in King's power. Trusting to the kindness of discretion of men was something Dallas Jay was not encouraged to do by past experience. They were all bastards. All any of them wanted with a girl was a screw. Well, that was something she could give, and give with the best. On her way through the bedroom door it struck her that she was being rather clever, involving Eddi King. The real gamble was whether he would pass up a second opportunity; he'd be sleepy, and the morning was a good time to catch a man in that kind of mood. She went on tiptoe down the corridor and slipped into his room.

King woke immediately at the sound of the door opening. He was sitting up with the light switched on before she had taken three steps towards him.

'Dallas! What the hell are you doing?'

She came and sat on the edge of the bed. 'I wanted to say thanks for last night. You were real good to me.' She bent over and kissed him on the mouth; her fingers began unbuttoning his pyjamas. King let her go on; he let his body respond, it would have been difficult not to without throwing the woman off. She was very skilful; she worked in silence, like the professional she was, until he'd pulled her into the bed with him. He knew now why Huntley put up with that vapid mind and gushing tongue, for ever saying what she supposed to be the right thing. In this context the woman was superb. He let himself go and climbed on the undulating body, determined to show that he had something to offer on his own account. When they had finished he began to carry out his original plan, formulated after cutting Elizabeth's telephone wire a few hours earlier. It had been a good plan then; now, with Dallas in complete alliance with him, it was a certainty.

'Jesus,' she whispered to him, 'I haven't had anything like that in years. You're an atom bomb, honey . . .'

'You're a crazy girl,' King said, 'but sweet. I like you, Dallas. I've always liked you; I just couldn't show it.'

'I know,' she said. 'I felt the same about you.' It seemed like the truth now. He had a lot of power; she felt like a racing car that had been given a run at full throttle after choking and stalling through traffic. 'Hunt would kill me,' she went on. 'He'd kill both of us.'

In the semi-dark King smiled. That was it. She had involved him to keep him quiet about last night. She wasn't as stupid as she seemed. This was going to work out perfectly. He was even a little irritated that he hadn't thought of it himself.

'You took quite a chance coming to me,' he said. He rubbed her big breast with his left hand, his voice soothing, intimate. 'But I'm glad you did.'

'So'm I,' she murmured. 'It was worth it. You're quite a lover, you know that?'

'You really want to marry Huntley, don't you?' She wasn't expecting that question, and for a while she didn't answer. She wished he'd stop caressing her while they talked; it made it harder for her to concentrate.

'I want it,' she said at last. 'I want to marry him more than anything.'

'Then what has Elizabeth got against you?'

'Against me?' She pulled his hand away and sat up, surprise ringing in her voice. 'What are you saying, Eddi? What *could* she have against me?'

'I'm not sure,' he said. 'But she broke you two up deliberately last night. She thinks you're after his money, Dallas. And she's his only relative, remember that.'

'For Christ's sake . . .' she said. 'You mean she wants the dough for herself!'

'Why not? A couple of hundred million dollars. She wouldn't approve of any marriage, I know that for sure. She's made that clear to me several times. Oh, it's not that she doesn't like you, Dallas, she's never said *that*. So long as he goes on keeping you, and doesn't make it legal, Elizabeth won't mind. It's nothing personal, don't think that. I guess it's just the money.'

'Oh sure,' Dallas sat up, both arms round her knees. Her mind was seething with thoughts, obscene names for Huntley, Elizabeth, even for herself, for being fooled by the girl, thinking she was at least a neutral in the long weary war to win a marriage certificate out of the old bastard. 'But the

138

money's enough.' She turned to King. 'What am I going to do, Eddi? If she's against me, I haven't a prayer.'

'Would you like to let me help you,' he asked her. He reached up and pulled her down to him. He didn't want her sexually at that moment, but he judged the type. Being made love to was a necessity to Dallas; it seemed to bolster her self-confidence. It dulled the anxieties in her kind of personality, like stroking a nervous animal. He caressed her as he talked; his own body cold and detached from what was happening. 'I have a lot of influence with Huntley. I don't know what Elizabeth said to him last night, but if it was anything about you, I can find out. I can maybe put it right.'

'Oh, Eddi,' she sighed, 'Eddi, if only you could do that. I'd be so grateful. I'd give you the best time you've ever had.'

'You do what I tell you.' King's voice altered; there was a tone of authority in it. 'You get her to take an early swim in the pool this morning; and you keep her there, till I've seen Huntley. Okay?'

'Okay,' she whispered, looking up, trying to see him in the dark. 'I'll try.'

'You better do more than try,' King said. 'You better succeed, unless you want to risk Huntley throwing you out. She could have said anything against you last night.' He reached out and switched on the light. 'It's seven-forty-five,' he said. 'Get up and get out of here. Go to her room by eight o'clock, Dallas, and, remember, everything depends on you now. You get her out of the house and down to that pool while I see Huntley!'

'I'll do it, Eddi,' she said. 'Why should she screw up my chances—I've worked hard to get settled. With you rooting for me, I'll make it. I know that.' She got up, paused at the door and smiled at him. The body and the technique were superb, he thought, but even in that light the face was fraying round the edges.

'We can still have fun together,' she said softly. 'I'll be good to you, Eddi.'

He went under the shower and made his plans, calmly and with his usual attention to the smallest detail. Dallas would get the girl down to the pool; he wouldn't go near Huntley, that was the last thing he intended doing. He would follow the two women down after a short interval, and then join them. In the water he would be able to deal with Elizabeth Cameron.

Elizabeth was awake when Dallas came into her room. She hadn't been able to sleep through the few hours that were left of the night. A murder was going to be committed, one of those grim political killings that had suddenly stained the great American nation with innocent blood; that was horrifying enough. The life of one cheap huckster. That was how her uncle had described the assassination of a human being, however contemptible, and there was nothing she could do to stop him. Except tell Peter Mathews what was being planned. And if she did that Keller was immediately involved. If they investigated Cameron's and King's conspiracy they must uncover the man she loved. If she did nothing, and she could get to Keller first, help him to get out of the country, then she could tell Mathews what her uncle was going to do. There wasn't any doubt in Elizabeth's mind. Everything her uncle said was true about the consequences of Jackson's being elected. But killing him was not the way to stop it. Using violence was the easy solution, but the wrong one. Whatever Jackson was, coming down to his level was not the way to beat him, or the forces which he represented. She had forgotten about Dallas; when the woman came in, smiling in her usual ingratiating way, she noticed suddenly that she looked haggard and as if she had been crying. 'Hello,' Elizabeth said. 'Come in; I'm just having my coffee. Join me?'

'No thanks, honey.' Dallas kept the hatred out of her eyes, she made her voice sweeter than normal. She sat on the edge of the bed while Elizabeth poured coffee from her breakfast tray, and ate a piece of toast. Women never came down for breakfast at Freemont. It was Huntley's directive that women should keep out of the way until he'd had time to get up himself and organise his day.

'I'll get another cup,' Elizabeth said. She realised what that intrusion last night must have meant to the unhappy woman. She picked up the telephone to ring down. 'It doesn't work,' she said. 'Must be a fault somewhere. I'll report it when I go downstairs.'

'I'm sorry to bust in on you,' Dallas said, 'but I want to

140

talk to you, Elizabeth. I've got to talk to you about last night.'

'I'm sorry.' She reached out on an impulse and touched the older woman's hand. 'I'm so terribly sorry I disturbed you and Huntley, Dallas, but I had to do it, I just had to. Please believe me.'

'Oh, sure.' There was nothing in Dallas' eyes or face to suggest that she didn't accept the apology. Sure, she said, in her silent conversation with herself, sure you had to; you just had to stop him laying me, and getting all cosy again, because you want the money for yourself. And you're so sorry, aren't you, honey? . . . 'Sure I believe you,' Dallas said. 'But I'm in trouble. I'm in real trouble and I thought . . .' She hesitated, acting the part for an Academy Award. 'I hoped maybe you'd be able to help—you wouldn't mind, would you, Elizabeth, letting me talk to you about it?'

'Of course I wouldn't.' Elizabeth had never felt more sorry for her. Living under the whims of a man like Huntley was bad enough; suffering the snubs and humiliations which he inflicted on her without thinking had made Dallas into the cringing travesty of a rich man's mistress. Elizabeth actually took hold of her hand and held it. 'I'll do anything I can to help you,' she said. 'I know my uncle; if you need a friend, Dallas, I'm right with you.'

For a moment Dallas was shaken. It seemed so genuine; there were even tears in the girl's eyes. But it couldn't be; she was just a clever bitch, playing for first prize in the money stakes. Eddi King had said she was an enemy; he must know. 'Look,' she said, 'I can't talk here. Come down to the pool with me. We can be private there. We can have a swim and I can tell you what it's all about—please, honey, come on down as soon as you've finished your breakfast?'

'I have finished,' Elizabeth said. 'I could do with a swim; I didn't sleep well last night. I guess you didn't either. Poor Dallas. Don't worry, whatever it is, we'll think of something.'

'I'll come back in five minutes,' Dallas said. She wasn't leaving anything to chance. 'We can go to the pool together.'

The pool was open-air; Huntley disliked swimming indoors, and he solved the problem by having the pool heated to a temperature of 82° and surrounding it with a fifteen-foot dry wall. A heating system operated within the area from a

141

generator built into the foundations, so that the atmosphere was mild in winter, and an electrically operated glass roof in two sections could slide over the pool area to protect it from rain. There were the usual changing rooms, a bar, an elaborate barbecue, and his latest addition—a sauna bath, with a small separate pool of ice-cold water. The sun was shining, and within the sheltered, artificially warmed patio it was hot enough to lie out in a swimming suit. Elizabeth and Dallas had walked down together, and when they reached the patio Dallas still hadn't pieced together a story which justified the drama with which she had invested the morning swim. She decided to play for time. 'Let's swim first,' she said. 'Then we can have something hot, like coffee and rum or something, and we can talk. I'll go order it now.' She went into the bar and picked up the house telephone. When Huntley visited the pool there was a barman on duty; otherwise guests phoned through for what they wanted if it wasn't available and it was sent down from the castle.

'Two large Jamaican coffees,' Dallas ordered. 'In about ten minutes. And brings some cookies, okay? Thanks.' She called to Elizabeth, who was stretched out on a canvas chaise-longue.

'I'm going to get changed, honey. Coffee's coming.'

As Elizabeth got up the telephone buzzed in the bar; she went over and picked it up. It was the guard on duty at the front gate. 'Sorry to disturb you, Miss Cameron. There's a man here says he's a friend of yours. A Mr Peter Mathews. Is it all right if he comes through? Will you authorise entry?' Elizabeth put a hand over the mouthpiece for a second. Pete Mathews. Of course, Leary wanted a report. In the few seconds she controlled a panic impulse to refuse him entry, to tell the guard she'd never heard of him, to do anything to stall the questions which she couldn't answer. Not before seeing Keller. But that wasn't the way. That wouldn't gain anything. She had better see him, find out what he wanted. But not there, not with Dallas listening.

'Miss Cameron? You still there?' The man's voice came through the mouthpiece on a louder note; she spoke back quickly.

'Yes, I'm here. I know Mr Mathews. You can let him in, and ask him to wait in the front courtyard. I'll be right over.' She put the phone down, and as she did so, Dallas came out of the changing cubicle. She had heard the phone ring, and struggled into her bathing suit in a panic, thinking that it might be Huntley. 'A friend of mine's come down,' Elizabeth explained. 'That was the man on the gate.'

'Oh.' Dallas made it bright and casual. It wasn't Huntley, that was all she cared about. 'Anyone I know?'

'I don't think so,' Elizabeth said. 'Peter Mathews; he was a boy friend of mine a long time ago. But you'll like him. He's very amusing; I'll bring him down here. And don't worry,' she said gently. 'We'll have our talk a little later.'

'Hurry back,' Dallas said. It didn't matter where Elizabeth went so long as she kept out of Huntley's way and left Eddi King time to find out the score on Dallas' behalf. 'Hey,' she called out, 'I left my cap behind, can I borrow yours? My hair gets in such a mess . . .' She went back to the pool; Elizabeth's suit and cap were rolled up beside the chair. She picked up the swimming cap; it was a plain white helmet, not pretty, with plastic flowers like her own cap, which she had forgotten in the rush. It had a broad black stripe running down the middle and at least it would keep her hair properly dry. She pulled it on, tucked her hair tightly underneath and dived into the steaming water.

She was a good swimmer; the exercise kept her figure in shape. Her family came from the Eastern seaboard; her father kept a small grocery store, and Dallas played on the beaches and learned to swim from the time she could walk. She turned on her back, easing along through the water in a backstroke; she saw a maid bring the coffee and go away again. She swam the length of the pool lying deep in the water. Then she turned over and began the strenuous butterfly stroke for the return length. And that was when King slipped out of the changing room where he had hidden as the maid rounded the path with the tray of coffee. He saw the half-submerged figure in the water, the distinctive Olympic style cap that Elizabeth Cameron always wore; the last time they had swum in that pool, before going to Beirut together, he had teased her about wearing it. Dallas wasn't there. This was lucky, but it wouldn't have mattered if she had been. She must be in a changing room; the two cups of laced coffee were untouched in the bar. He didn't dive into the pool; he slipped in off the edge on the opposite side to the swimmer, a little behind and out of sight. He came up behind her on a silent, powerful breast stroke. And then he leapt. He came down on her back, his legs gripping her middle, his weight plunging her under the surface. There mustn't be a struggle, because this would mean bruises; she swam too well to try to hold under water. He found the carotid artery on the side of her neck, and pressed hard with his thumb, not touching her throat. A second later the threshing body slackened; he opened his legs and floated away from her, watching the bubbles rise in a froth as the mouth, opening in unconsciousness, sucked in water and expelled air. He didn't wait to see her drown. Pressure on that artery knocked a man out for several minutes; a direct blow could kill. He climbed out and ran to where he had left his clothes. There was no sign of Dallas. He was having all the luck. Nobody need ever know he had been there at all. Elizabeth had been swimming when she drowned. He turned for a second look at the pool. There was nothing on the surface and the air bubbles had stopped bursting.

'I'm sorry about dragging you away like this, Liz, but Schloss Freemont always did give me the hives. I guess I'm just a serf at heart.'

'I'm glad to get away,' Elizabeth answered. Mathews had suggested a drive out immediately. He had been insistent in his charming way, and she had got a coat and come with him, realising that she too felt safer when they were outside the wall.

'Leary wanted to know if you had any news,' he said. He was driving slowly, taking his time on the sunny morning drive back to the city. He had been thinking on his way down, and taking her back to his apartment and putting pressure on her seemed the last resort. First, he had to decide if she were working actively with Eddi King; if this was so, then Leary's expert interrogators were the right people to deal with her. If she were protecting the mysterious man for personal motives, then perhaps the soft approach was the wiser one. He had been angry in Leary's office; part of that anger was injured pride, he recognised that now. Elizabeth had found someone else; but not someone from their own milieu, a husband, a lover, he wouldn't have minded about that. But a stranger, capable of giving her what he, so obviously, had not; this had made him angry.

If he took Elizabeth home and began trying to beat the information out of her it wouldn't be impersonal. And being impersonal was the prerequisite for this kind of questioning. If it came to that level, then it was better for someone else to do it. He glanced at her sideways; she seemed tired and nervous, smoking continuously.

'Eddi King is there,' she said. 'Staying the weekend. I have a feeling he's got my uncle mixed up in something.' She lit another cigarette and her hand was shaking.

Mathews noticed it; she was under a strain, and she wasn't good at hiding it. At that moment he would have staked his job that whatever she had hidden from Leary, Elizabeth was no professional. 'Any idea what it could be?'

'I don't know,' she went on slowly, trying to be careful, not to say too much. 'But it must be political. They're always talking politics.'

'What are King's politics?' Mathews said. 'I mean what does he pretend they are?'

'Very right wing,' she answered. 'The absolute opposite of the Democrats. When you say pretend—you're pretty sure he's a traitor, aren't you?'

'Absolutely certain.' Mathews did a racing change as he answered and for a moment the car gathered speed. It was a Jensen; he had always driven a fast, expensive foreign car. It was what he described as part of his charm.

'He's working for the Reds,' he said. 'That's the funny thing about this business, Liz. You get one lead, that meeting with Marcel Druet in Paris, for example, and then all of a sudden other bits and pieces start fitting into the one piece until you start to see a pattern. We've had quite a few extras to build up in the last couple of days.' Including the evidence about you, he said to himself, easing his foot off the accelerator, slowing down. He didn't want to get back too quickly. He wanted to draw her out more if he could.

'What have you found out?' The fear was in her voice; she was so obvious that he wondered who it was for; he knew the answer to that; she had never been a coward. She was scared to death, but not for herself.

'King went to the Lebanon for a reason, he took you along as a blind. He fixed up something while he was there. That's what he reported to Druet—whatever it was.' He knew without looking at her that she had tensed visibly while

145

he was talking. He heard the click of the handbag she carried being opened and closed and then opened again. It gave her trembling hands something to do. He was certain she knew what King went to Beirut to arrange. She knew all about it, and he was equally sure she had only just found out, during the weekend at Freemont.

'You don't know what it was? You've no clue?'

'We're getting an idea,' Mathews said. 'And it looks very nasty. Very nasty indeed. It must be, because a couple of people in Beirut have already been murdered, and we think they were connected with it.'

'Why? Who were they?'

'Oh,—just small fry—an airport tout buys a new car that blows him and his wife and kids sky high, and an Arab girl gets strangled. Both had suddenly got money, big money. They'd been paid off, and then our friends paid them off properly, just to make sure they didn't talk. It's the usual pattern when there's something big. They wipe out the little people first. The girl had a European boy friend, he's disappeared too. Her name was Souha—in Arabic it means "little star".'

Elizabeth needed fresh air; the feeling of claustrophobia came on her so quickly, that she felt physically sick. The dreadful, sinister echo of those words wouldn't stop repeating in her head. An Arab girl was strangled. She had a European boy friend, he's disappeared . . . her name was Souha . . . If she could only get the window open.

'Press the button on the right,' Mathews said. 'Here,' he reached over and did it for her; the window whined down. 'Leary believes King had someone smuggled into the States,' he said. She was taking in the air, fighting to get hold of herself. He pulled the car over to the side of the road; luckily they were off the main highway and he was able to stop. 'What's the matter, Liz? Don't you feel well?'

'It was hot,' she said. 'I felt terribly hot, that's all.' She leaned back, closing her eyes for a moment. She had never fainted or lost control of herself in her life, but in the last few minutes she had come very close.

'You didn't travel back with anyone, did you, Liz?'

'I don't know what you're talking about.' She turned her head away from him. 'I came home alone.'

'Okay.' Mathews started the car up, and nosed the long

bonnet out on to the road. 'I just wanted to be sure. You feeling better now?'

'I'm all right,' Elizabeth said. 'The weekend has been a strain; I didn't get much sleep last night.'

Until he had asked her the question, precipitated the moment of truth and been met by a lie, Mathews hadn't been certain how to proceed. Now he saw a way; not the way Leary had suggested, but a better one, which would lead to the destination faster than hours of interrogating a stubborn girl. If he was wrong, he could switch back to Leary's original instructions and no harm would be done. 'Do you want me to take you back to Freemont, Liz? Maybe you ought to lie down. I won't stay for lunch, I'll tool on home.'

'No,' she spoke too quickly. 'No, I don't want to go back there. I can get my things sent up. I'd like to go home, Pete. Will you take me home?'

She looked white and sick. His plan was going to work. He had been sure it would. 'Sure I'll take you back to your apartment. Maybe if you're up to it we could have dinner tonight.'

'Maybe,' Elizabeth said. 'Yes, if I feel better, if I get a rest—that would be nice, Pete.'

She had the door open and was out before he had time to get out of his seat. She leaned through the open window, her long hair hanging on either side of her face; there was a little colour in it now. 'Thanks,' she said. 'Don't bother to see me up, I'm fine now. I'll call you after I've had a rest.' Mathews watched her disappear inside the entrance; he slipped the car into gear and moved off. In the driving mirror he noticed the blue Chev which had picked them up outside Freemont park on the opposite side of the street. His man would take over now. He had better put in a call to Leary and tell him what he had done. If his guess was right, Elizabeth Cameron would leave the apartment just as soon as she was sure he had gone. The tail in the Chev would pick her up. Mathews had taken a risk, but in every aspect it was calculated. He had asked her the primary question, and she had lied; he expected that. She hadn't been caught off guard because subconsciously this was the one question she was determined not to answer. This was what would have caused so much delay in Leary's original plan. He had told her enough to frighten her, to make it seem that

147

they knew more than they did, or were certain to find out the rest in a matter of hours. He had told her just enough to panic her. When she came out she would be on her way to warn the man. And she would lead Mathews' people straight to him.

CHAPTER SIX

It was the maid who came to take the coffee cups away who saw the body lying at the bottom of the pool. By the time Huntley got down from the castle, Dallas had been brought up and laid out on the terrace. One of his security guards was straddled over her, trying resuscitation. She lay face down, her arms outspread, a pool of water by her head; more water flowed out of the open mouth with the rhythmic movements of the man pressing against her flooded lungs.

When Huntley first saw her, he thought it was Elizabeth. She still wore the distinctive swimming cap.

The maid had been having hysterics in a corner by the bar; now she was hustled out of the way. The place was surrounded by Huntley's security guards; an immediate order had been issued to the telephone operator not to put through any outgoing calls. From the moment the body was brought to the surface, Freemont was sealed off from the world, until Huntley Cameron had decided what to do.

'It's no good, Mr Cameron, she's dead. She's quite cold.' The guard got up, wiping his wet hands on the seat of his pants.

'How could it happen?' Huntley's voice was thick. It was shock as much as emotion. She was his niece, the only living relative he had. There was something obscene about the wet body, gurgling water on to the terrazzo floor.

'I don't know, sir. Miss Jay was a very strong swimmer. She must have had a heart attack or something.'

Miss Jay. Huntley straightened up; the sagging jaw snapped shut. 'It's not my niece? For Christ's sake, why didn't you say so. Turn her over!'

He bent and looked, satisfying himself that it was Dallas. Of course; the bathing cap had fooled him. How could she have drowned; she swam like an eel . . . He hesitated; this would be a page one accident. Nation-wide coverage. Scan-

148

dal, suggestions of suicide. But he still had time to present it his way, to slant the facts from his angle. 'Get Dr Harper up here; don't phone, take a car and get him. And don't say anything, just bring him here!'

One of the guards disappeared. Harper was Huntley's personal doctor. He lived in Freemont because Huntley had bought him the house and established him within half a mile. He attended a children's clinic twice a week for appearance's sake, but he had no private patients except the staff at Freemont. His retainer was enormous.

An hour later he was shown into Huntley's private office on the first floor of the east turret. He was a big man, heavily built, dressed incongruously in city clothes on the weekend.

'What did you find?'

'Death by drowning, Mr Cameron. I'd say the poor girl had been dead around an hour and a half, maybe more.'

'How could she have drowned?' Huntley glared at him. 'She was as strong as a goddamned bull; you checked her health every six months—what did you miss?'

'I didn't miss anything,' the doctor explained. 'She was in perfect health then and there's nothing to suggest any physical malfunction now.' He set his mouth in professional obduracy. He hadn't made any mistake with her and he wouldn't let Huntley infer that he had. What he was prepared to say in public as part of his personal service to Cameron was something different.

'Then how did it happen? You trying to tell me she just opened her mouth and swallowed water?' While he waited for the doctor's report Huntley had been going through every detail of the previous day, particularly the abrupt end of their night together. It couldn't be suicide. She was stupid and a gabber, but there had never been any sign of unbalance. Only a nut would have got so upset by being sent away that they'd have drowned themselves next morning.

But being Huntley, he hadn't just sat in his office and thought it out. He had personally questioned his staff and three disquieting facts had emerged out of the mass of unimportant details. Eddi King had been seen helping Dallas up the stairs by a patrolling guard; the same guard had found evidence in the library that she had got drunk. He had kept the empty vodka bottle to show his employer.

Within minutes King had come down and complained to another guard that his telephone was making noises, and when the phones were checked that morning, nothing was found to be wrong with his set. On the other hand the wire connecting Elizabeth's room phone to the switchboard had been cut through. His niece had gone to the pool with Dallas that morning, and then left with a man who had come down soon after nine o'clock, giving the name of Peter Mathews. This satisfied Huntley, who remembered an old boy friend of Elizabeth's who used to visit Freemont some years back. There was nothing wrong with her taking off with an old beau. It was probably just what she needed to steady her after their talk last night. The absence of Eddi King was very different. He had checked out of the castle twenty minutes after Elizabeth and Mathews left, and he had gone without a word. The gate guard timed his car out at nine-forty. The maid who had brought coffee down to the pool had reported seeing what she thought to be Elizabeth swimming alone at around nine-fifteen. So Dallas was alive when Elizabeth left. The maid's mistake had struck him because it was the same as he had made when he first saw the body. She too had seen that distinctive black and white cap and made the wrong identification.

'You can see how this is going to look!' Huntley barked at the doctor: 'Nothing wrong with her, just found drowned? It's going to look like the tramp committed suicide! There'll be an inquest, an enquiry—for Christ's sake, this could be used against the Democrats! The last thing we can afford is a scandal, and boy, would my enemies make a Roman holiday out of this!' He paused, considering Harper carefully. He paid him twenty-five thousand dollars a year just to be within call. Fees were extra. This might be the one time when he would really earn that massive retainer.

'You don't think she killed herself?'

'No.' Harper shook his big head. Of necessity, he was a very good doctor, and in his professional capacity he overlooked nothing.

'I did find something which might account for it. I made a very thorough examination. There is absolutely nothing I can find without an autopsy, but I did notice one small thing.' He took his time deliberately. The rich expected value for their money and he was going to give Huntley Cameron full value. He was also going to give him an unpleasant shock and this he wanted to prolong on his own account. He disliked being bullied, but he was too lazy to earn his money the regular way.

'I found a tiny bruise on the side of her neck, near the collar bone.'

'So?'

'So it seems pressure was applied to the carotid artery before death,' Harper said. 'This is one of the nerve centres of the body, Mr Cameron. A blow on that nerve can paralyse or even kill. Quick pressure on the same spot, applied by someone who knew where to locate the nerve, would cause the person to lose consciousness for some minutes.' He cleared his throat; the look on Huntley's face delighted him. 'It would be very difficult to prove, because a bruise isn't evidence, not just one little mark. But I think Miss Jay was murdered. Somebody with considerable knowledge of such things blacked her out while she was swimming, and left her to drown. Now that,' he cleared his throat a second time, so he could repeat it, 'that would certainly make a nasty scandal.'

Huntley didn't answer. He had been sitting down behind his desk. Now he got up and went to the cabinet built into the stone wall of the turret room, opened it and drank down one of the largest straight whiskies Harper had ever seen poured out. He knew Huntley drank; he had spent five years watching that cast-iron body for any sign of deterioration due to alcohol, but never found a symptom. Huntley spoke more quietly, almost casually.

'This mustn't come out,' he said. He refilled the glass. 'You realise this, Harper. Suicide, murder, whatever the hell really happened, it mustn't make the papers. How much do I pay you every year?'

Harper stiffened. 'Twenty-five thousand. But you understand I can't possibly cover up anything...'

'I think it should be forty thousand,' Huntley said. 'A man's health is the most valuable possession he's got. You're a good doctor. You're worth forty thousand dollars a year to me.'

Harper opened his mouth and then very slowly it began to shut again. Forty thousand dollars. For that much money he'd be worked off his feet in ordinary practice; answering every call, dancing attendance on rich women with nothing but hypochondria to shield them from old age; travelling, consulting, running at full pressure. And of course he'd have to buy a new house for the family. They liked living where they were. His wife had just installed a sauna bath next to their pool; this was the ultimate status symbol and it had cost a lot of money. He looked at Huntley Cameron, but the old man was tossing back his whisky and paid him no attention.

'What would you like me to put on the death certificate?'

'The truth, of course.' Huntley looked at him that time, with surprise. 'What else? Whatever caused the poor kid's death.'

'Heart failure,' Dr Harper said. He mumbled the words slightly. 'She'd been on the pill for the last couple of years. I prescribed them myself. In my findings she suffered a cardiac failure which may or may not be a result of using this form of contraception. I shall make it clear in my statement that I don't approve of this method until it's been further investigated.'

'You do that,' Huntley said. 'Now I guess we'd better call the police. You talk to them, Harper. I'm too upset.'

By lunchtime Freemont was under siege. Reporters, photographers, TV cameras and sightseers were camped round the walls like an army. Police were on duty outside, co-operating with the Cameron security force, to control the traffic and prevent any attempt to climb into the grounds. Immediately the police were notified, Huntley's own news service broke the story; he himself had stayed in his office, giving one short interview to the local police captain who got his picture in the papers and appeared on television, saying the millionaire was broken-hearted at the death of his fiancée. They had been planning to get married after the Presidential election. Huntley had played his part well; he didn't underestimate his own power, nor did he use it unnecessarily, except with someone like Harper who he knew could be bought. It was wise to have the local police on his side; he filled the captain up with whisky, and lies about himself and Dallas, and sent him away as his friend. The captain proved to be a better guardian of Huntley's wish for privacy than any of the men on his private payroll. Huntley turned on the TV in his office and watched for the first news reports to come in. And while he listened and watched he was following the three unanswered questions through, like a man reeling up a cotton thread through a maze. Why had someone cut the telephone wire to Elizabeth's room? Why had Eddi King disappeared? Why should anyone want to murder Dallas? The fourth question was answered only in conjunction with the other three. Who had killed her? And when he came to the end of the cotton he was also out of the maze; he could see clearly.

Nobody had wanted to kill Dallas. But somebody had wanted to keep Elizabeth from making contact with the outside world. Somebody had tampered with her phone to make certain she was incommunicado for the night. And the same person had made the error into which both he and the maid at the pool had fallen. They had mistaken the swimmer for Elizabeth Cameron because of the cap.

Whoever had killed Dallas had done so thinking that their victim was his niece. And then they had run for it. As Eddi King had run, leaving what he hoped would seem an accident lying at the bottom of the swimming pool.

There was only one reason why King should fear Elizabeth enough to need to murder her. Somehow, probably through Dallas' drunken maunderings, he had discovered that she had liaised with him, Huntley, and guessed that she was in possession of the assassination plan. So he had tried to kill her to protect herself. Huntley was safe because he was an equal accomplice. But King had feared Elizabeth might talk. He had feared that she might betray both him and her uncle.

And so he had cut her telephone and sneaked down to the pool that morning. Huntley wondered exactly how he would feel when he discovered he had killed the wrong girl. There were two things he had to do. First he had to find Elizabeth and tell her to come back to Freemont, where she could be protected. Second, he had to think how to settle with his good friend Eddi King. He owed that to Dallas, anyway.

New York on a Sunday was like a city struck by plague. The streets were almost empty of traffic; the absence of noise in its human and mechanical variations was almost sinister. Elizabeth sat back in the cab and looked out at the clear streets and vacant sidewalks. The morning was chill, and clouds were gathering. The brief sunshine at Freemont had gone and the March day would be damp and depressing. She had forgotten that her car was still at Freemont; as soon as she was inside her apartment, she called down for a cab, checking that the slip of paper with Keller's address on it was still in her handbag, and then come out again, only ten minutes after Peter Mathews had driven away. She had to get to Keller. Leary's people were getting very close. That single question, 'Did you travel back with anyone?' . . . that had shown how near they were to the truth.

And the two murders in Beirut; Souha, the Arab girl who had been strangled. It was beyond coincidence; the money, the European she had been living with, since disappeared. As soon as Mathews told her the name she had known it must be Keller's girl.

'Lady, you know anyone owns a blue Chev?' It was the first time the driver had spoken; she had thanked God not to have drawn a garrulous type. Some of them talked from the start to the finish of the trip.

'No, I guess not. Why?'

The man glanced back over his shoulder at her. He had a heavy, dark face and a bristled jaw in need of shaving.

'Because there's a blue Chev tailing us,' he said. 'He's been right with us since I picked you up.'

'You're sure? You're sure he's following us?'

'Sure I'm sure. Look, lady, there's no traffic around. I noticed him way back in the mirror. I don't want trouble. You better get out.'

'No, please,' Elizabeth said quickly. 'Here's ten dollars; just go on for a while.' She looked back and through the rear window she saw the car, just rounding a corner after them. What a fool not to have thought of this. Of course Mathews was having her followed. And she had been just about to do what he expected and show them the way to Keller. Suddenly she found herself shaking with anger. He had been playing her along deliberately; he was no more honest in his professional dealings than he had been as a lover. She called through to the driver.

'Drop me at Lexington Avenue.'

'Okay.'

The driver of the Chev was doing thirty miles an hour, a steady cruising speed which kept the cab in view. When it stopped at a traffic light it was six cars ahead of him. Elizabeth looked back through the rear window; the Chev was hidden in a solid wedge of other cars. She didn't wait, or say anything to the cab driver. She opened the offside door, bending a little, and ran for the sidewalk. Then she stopped, staring into a shop window, until she saw the traffic move and the Chev reflected in the plate glass as it drove past her in pursuit of the cab.

She undid her silk scarf and tied it over her head; rain had begun to fall in a thin, chilly drizzle. She started to walk, watching for an empty cab. The rain fell harder, turning the sidewalks greasy, driving against her in the wind. There were no cabs visible; the cars were multiplying and they congealed at each traffic light before spreading out again, their wipers whirring; Elizabeth walked slowly, keeping near the kerb. She had reached the middle of Lexington and she was wet through before she saw a cab going at cruising speed. It pulled in for her and she jumped in.

'Morries Hotel. West 39th.'

The Chev had followed her original cab to the end of the avenue; it suddenly occurred to the driver that it was going at a dawdling pace, as if looking for a fare. When he finally drew up alongside and passed, he saw that it was empty. He swore, picked up his radio phone and called in. 'Red Charlie to switchboard. I lost the fare. She slipped me. No, no possibility now.' She had shaken him off with the skill of a professional. He got instructions to go back to his post outside her apartment and wait.

When Elizabeth stepped out of the cab, she hesitated. The driver took the fare and a tip, and then looked at her for the first time. His expression told her more about Morries Hotel than the shabby entrance.

'Have a good time,' he said, and drove off. She had never been in such a place in her life. She walked through the door, past the nudie magazines and the smutty art books, determined to keep looking straight ahead. At the top of the dirty stairway she came to the superintendent. He was reading one of the tabloids, worrying his bad teeth with a split match, a cigarette burning away in a saucer beside him. An empty coffee cup was by his elbow, and there were wet

155

rings on the table. He hadn't washed or shaved, and he looked as if he had slept in his shirt. He had heard her come up the stairs and had seen her quickly from behind the paper. He went on reading.

'I'm looking for a Mr Keller,' Elizabeth said. She was surprised at the speed with which her heart was beating. She had never appreciated the risk of being assaulted or robbed in a place like this until she actually stood there. The paper, with its lurid black headlines, lowered a little, and the smudged glasses peered at her.

'Beat it,' the mouth opened and shut. 'We don't run no cat house!'

'Keller,' Elizabeth repeated. 'He came here on Friday. Please, it's terribly important. I know he's here.'

Again the paper went down, lower still this time, and the little eyes sneered at her through the prismatic lenses. But he said nothing. She had got the message. She was opening her purse. Elizabeth didn't know how much to give him; she gave the biggest note she could find loose.

'Here,' she said. 'Here's ten dollars. Now take me to him, please.'

'What's he look like?' the super said. 'We got two or three guys come in for rooms. Nobody with that name.'

Of course, Elizabeth realized her own naïveté; of course he wouldn't use his own name.

'He's big,' she said. 'Not tall, but well built. Fair, blue eyes. Not American . . .' She trailed off, suddenly losing hope. Her eyes filled with tears; she felt like turning and running down the stairs and out into the street. The super scraped back his chair. 'I'll take you up.'

Keller's portable TV set was tuned in to a news programme; the main item was the St Patrick's Day Parade the next day. Keller was sitting in front of it watching intently. The announcer was giving details of the service in the cathedral; a list of guests followed, with a commentary on each. The Mayor of New York. The Governor. The Presidential candidate John Jackson. The Vice-President, who was a Catholic. The list went on and on. The Democrat candidate, Patrick Casey, would miss the High Mass for the first time in his political career; he was away on a fact-finding mission in strife-ridden central America . . . The announcer returned to Jackson. As a chosen spokesman for the white Anglo-Saxon element in the South, where Roman Catholicism was regarded with the same superstitious horror as witchcraft, Jackson's attendance at a High Mass was an obvious bid for popularity with the hostile Irish, Polish and Italian elements in the electorate. The still photograph of Jackson was replaced by shots of Jackson taken from newsreels, during the commentary. Jackson speaking at rallies, glad-handling at conventions, posing with his wife and four children for publicity shots.

Keller disliked his face. It was thin, with a pinched mouth, and the grey hair was brushed up into a halo round the skull. His tight little eyes, falsely smiling, peered out from behind steel-rimmed glasses. Then the scene changed, and it was the Cardinal's image he saw projected on the screen. He switched off the set immediately. He didn't want to hear about Regazzi, or see his face. It wouldn't help tomorrow.

When he heard Elizabeth's knock he thought it must be the superintendent again, pestering him for the night's rent. 'What do you want?' he called out, but there was no answer, only another knock. He went to the door.

'Who's there?'

'It's me, Bruno. Please let me in.'

He opened the door slowly and stepped back. She didn't wait for him to speak. She came in and went straight into his arms.

'Thank God I found you,' was all she said.

For a moment Keller didn't move; one hand went up to stroke her hair as he had always done when they embraced. He forced it down, and made himself put her away from him. He could hardly believe that she was there.

'How did you find me?' he said. 'Why did you come here?'

She took off her wet coat and paused, looking round the room. 'You wrote this address down. I found the pad afterwards. But it doesn't matter how, it only matters why.'

'Then why?' Keller asked. 'It's finished between us. I sent you roses just to say goodbye. I don't want you here, Elizabeth. Put your coat back on and go home.' He walked away from her towards the door.

'It's no good trying to throw me out.' She said it quietly. The rain glistened on her face and hair. 'It's no good trying to lie to me any more either. I know what you've come to do. You've come to assassinate John Jackson for my uncle and for the man who hired you, Eddi King. I've come to offer you double what they're paying not to do it.'

For some moments there was silence in the room. A car passed outside, its engine throbbing and then dying out. Keller waited. His heart was pounding in his chest.

'Why haven't you gone to the police?'

'Because I've been trying to find you first,' she said. 'I couldn't lead them to you, Bruno—don't you know I love you?'

'This is none of your business.' He said it angrily. 'I told you before, stay out of it. Now for the last time go home!'

'It is my business,' she said. She lit a cigarette and sat down on the one chair. 'Our Intelligence people are on to the whole thing. They know Eddi King is a communist agent. That's who you're working for—the communists.'

'And your uncle,' Keller asked. 'What about him?'

'He's being used by them, he doesn't know the truth. But he's no better. He's paying you to do this, Bruno. Murder means nothing to him either.' She got up and held out both hands to him. He didn't move.

'All right, I'll have to tell you then,' she said. 'If the money won't change you perhaps this will. You're never going to collect it. Immediately you've killed Jackson you'll be killed yourself, to keep you from being arrested and talking. And that's not all. I'm afraid they've murdered your girl in Beirut.'

He reached her with the speed of an animal springing on its prey. His fingers drove into her arms, he shook her.

'Souha! What do you mean, what's happened to Souha!'

'Don't hurt me,' Elizabeth said quietly. 'Let me tell you how it happened. She was strangled; another man was dynamited in his car, with his whole family. He worked for the airport as a kind of guide.'

'Fuad,' Keller said. 'Fuad Hamedin. How do you know it was Souha—who told you this?'

'My old lover, Peter Mathews. He's with American Intelligence, the C.I.A. He only contacted me to find out about this man Eddi King. I promised to watch him and report. I saw Mathews this morning and he told me about the murders. He said her name was Souha. She had a big bank account, so had the guide. Mathews said this is what

158

always happens; they pay off the little people first to wipe out any clues. Just as they were going to do with you.'

'The guide was Fuad,' Keller muttered. 'That makes the girl my Souha. I gave her ten thousand dollars before I left. I thought she'd be safe if I didn't get back.' He sat down on the bed, his hands clenching between his knees. 'I'll get whoever did it,' he said. 'I'll kill them.'

'You won't get the chance,' Elizabeth said. 'This whole plan is about to blow up. I've only got to tell Peter Mathews what I know and everyone will be arrested. I can do that tomorrow, after you've gone.'

Keller wasn't listening. Souha was dead. Strangled, that's what she had said. He could imagine it; he knew the professional Arab killers, with their lengths of knotted cord. He hadn't cried since he was a child in the orphanage. He wanted to get his hands on somebody and squeeze and squeeze them round the throat as the murderer's cord had squeezed Souha's little neck. They had killed her, and Fuad too; he had seen the wife once and the fat, over-indulged little children. The car had blown up under them like a firework. Very clever. Real professional work. He would have been paid the last part of his price, in the same efficient way, after he had left the cathedral. Maybe even before . . .

'You can get on a plane tonight,' Elizabeth said. She had kept control very well until then; she had been calm and gentle and determined. But all her bolts were shot and none seemed to have penetrated. He hardly seemed to hear what she was saying.

'You say you know all about it?' He looked up at her, his eyes sunk deep in their sockets. 'You're wrong about one thing. Two things. The plan isn't going to blow up because it's timed for tomorrow morning. And the target isn't this Jackson you keep talking about, it's Cardinal Regazzi.'

'It's not possible!' Elizabeth cried out. 'My uncle told me it was Jackson! He wouldn't want to kill the Cardinal! He doesn't want Jackson running for President . . .'

'Then this Mr King is making him pay for the wrong killing,' Keller said slowly. 'Here, look at this.' He gave her the plan. 'The Cardinal is the one your communists want put out of the way. He seemed a good man to me. Maybe that's

159

why they don't like him.' He put his head down suddenly and she heard a strange sound.

'Why did they have to hurt her?' he said. 'She knew nothing; she couldn't have talked to anyone. Why did she have to die like that?'

Elizabeth got up and came to him; she sat beside him on the bed and put her arms around him. 'I didn't know you loved her,' she said slowly. She felt sick and stricken inside, for her own selfish reasons. 'I'm so sorry I had to tell you. Please let me comfort you, turn to me a little.'

'I was sorry for her,' Keller said at last. He had let Elizabeth hold him. 'I wanted to take care of her because she trusted me. She'd been kicked and pushed around by everyone. I thought I was doing something good for her, giving her some money, and a passport. But I brought her bad luck. She never had anything in her life.'

'She had you,' Elizabeth said slowly. 'I believe that's all she could have wanted. I know it's all I want.'

He looked at her then; he seemed older, the lines by the eyes and mouth scored deeper since she had come into the room.

'You? What could I give a woman like you? I gave Souha things she'd never had, things you were born with.' It wasn't a reproach, it was a statement of fact. Tears came into Elizabeth's eyes.

'I said I loved you. You talk about giving me nothing; don't you know what it means to be fulfilled—to be loved and able to love the way you've taught me? Bruno, please look at me, listen to me! I can't tell you the difference between your girl Souha and me, maybe it's not so much as you think. I only know you mean more to me than anything in the world. I don't want to live without you!' She found her bag and riffled through it with shaking hands; when she took out the cigarette he had to light it for her.

'Even when I knew you'd come over here to kill a man for money it didn't make any difference to the way I felt. I didn't care, darling. I didn't give a damn. All I want is for you to be safe and for us to be together.'

'That isn't possible,' Keller said. 'You ought to know that. If I don't do what I'm told I swear they'll kill me. If I do do it—you know the answer to that better than I do. There's no way out for us.' He tightened his arm around her. 'There

160

never is in this kind of dirty mess. I should have stayed where I belonged—in the gutter, looking up.'

'You belong with me,' Elizabeth said fiercely. 'You never had a chance in your life—you told me that. Now you're going to get one. We can leave here now, my darling. We can walk out and go to Kennedy and be on a plane for anywhere in the world in two hours. You've committed no crime—you've got a passport. I've got money. Bruno, please! Come away with me!'

He didn't answer her; he only held her closer. He had never believed that she loved him before. She had said so, but he had never been able to accept it. There was nothing to love for a rich woman who had everything and could have taken any man she chose. The wretched stray fainting with hunger in the gutter at Beirut was different; she had reason to love the man who fed and housed her, and treated her with gentleness. Elizabeth was crying. He had seen a lot of women cry; women in villages weeping over their dead, victims of the brutality and waste of war, prostitutes afraid of being beaten up because they'd robbed their customers—tears had never moved Keller. But he couldn't bear to see Elizabeth cry. Now he turned her to him and threw the half-smoked cigarette away.

He kissed her and his powerful hand gently stroked her hair.

'Don't do that; I don't like to see it. Don't cry for me.'

'Come with me,' Elizabeth begged him. 'Don't you see they can't have their killing without you?'

'Somebody else will do it if I don't,' Keller said. 'The world is full of men who'll kill anyone for fifty thousand dollars. My running away won't stop them. And it won't bring back Souha or Fuad's children.'

'Nothing will do that,' she whispered. She was keeping control of herself with difficulty. She hadn't been able to move him, to persuade him. Why not—why, why, wouldn't he give up the whole horrific venture and just go away with her? Then, when he was safely out of reach, she could tell Leary everything. Then the Cardinal could be protected, King arrested—even her uncle. She didn't care what happened to anyone now if only she could keep Keller alive. If this was what being in love really meant, how lucky it happened only once in a whole lifetime's span . . .

161

'You're not going to kill the Cardinal?'

He looked into the desperate face, so distraught with tears. 'No,' Keller said. 'I promise you that. Not the Cardinal. They paid me half the money. It came this morning. Why did your uncle want this man Jackson dead?

'Oh, darling, I don't know—what does it matter? Oh, because he said he'd destroy America if he was President. There'd be race riots, and terrible strikes—all the trouble you can think of—it isn't important to us. It's none of our business.'

'That would please your friend King, wouldn't it—to see your country torn to pieces from inside?'

'Bruno, what are you thinking? Bruno . . .' She saw the direction of his thoughts and cried out to him in despair. 'Leave it alone—what do you care about American politics —none of this is anything to do with you. Or us,' she went on. 'The C.I.A., the police—they're the people to deal with all this. Not you, going on some crazy crusade you don't even understand.'

'I understand a bad bargain,' Keller said quietly. 'You hire someone and then you kill his girl and plan to murder him after he's done the job for you. I understand that very well. It's not difficult.'

'I won't let you.' She twisted round and began to kiss him; he could taste the salt of tears on her mouth. 'I won't let you try it, Bruno. You're coming away with me—we're going to be happy together . . .'

He had never intended making love to her; at one point he tried to stop, but she cried and clung, and he couldn't control himself. The sleazy room began to blur around them, the background fading as the sense of time and place receded. They might have been back in Elizabeth's apartment the first time they had come together. But then she had been nervous; shy of her own passion and dominated by the force of his. Now she met him equally, fired by more than a physical need, impelled by the female belief that through this medium it was possible to change the purpose of a man.

When it was over they didn't speak for some moments; he seemed more exhausted than she, as if for some reason his enormous strength had failed him.

'Will you come away with me? I have a house in Mexico;

162

its a place called Cuernavaca. It's very beautiful, Bruno. It belonged to my mother. We'll be safe there. It's tucked away below the Empress Carlotta's gardens. She loved it so, and she left it to me. We'll be happy there—we can start a new life. Nobody will ever find us.'

Keller didn't answer her.

'Come with me, darling. Please.'

If he ran and tried to cheat them, the organisation which had taken the trouble to blow up Fuad Hamedin and have Souha murdered would see he didn't get very far with twenty-five thousand dollars of their money. Even if he left Souha to lie in her grave unrevenged he couldn't risk involving Elizabeth in what must end as a sentence of death passed against him.

'Someone would find us,' he said. 'Mr King's friends. It wouldn't work.'

'Yes it would,' Elizabeth said fiercely. 'Nobody knows about my house, I've never been to Mexico—my mother bought and furnished it but she never lived there! All we have to do is take a plane tomorrow and just disappear! You might even marry me one day,' she said, and tried to smile at him.

He reached up for her and kissed her. Mexico. It might be possible; it just might be possible to get away with it. But not on her terms. Not as a coward running away, leaving the way open for them to try again with someone else. He couldn't live in Mexico or anywhere else with that on his mind.

'I'll come with you,' he said. 'I'll meet you at the airport. Where do I wait, and what time?'

'The Eastern Airlines building, Mexico flight counter.' She clung to him for a moment, trying to keep calm. Relief made her want to laugh and weep at once. 'Say eleven o'clock, darling. I'm so happy, Bruno. I'm so terribly happy you've said yes. And don't worry about King. I'll fix him after we've gone. I've been holding out on our C.I.A. because I couldn't tell the truth without leading them to you. But when we're in Cuernavaca they can pull them all in; my uncle included.'

'And you said nobody would know where we were,' Keller said.

'A letter, posted here tomorrow morning before we go— that's all I have to do.'

'You'd better go home,' Keller said. 'It's getting dark and this is a bad area. It's not safe for you to go through the streets.' He helped her with her coat and for a moment held her close to him.

At the door of his room she turned to him.

'You'll come to the airport—you won't go back on this and do anything crazy? Promise me?'

'I'll come,' Keller said. 'Whoever is first will wait for the other. I promise you I'll come.'

He went down the grimy stairs with her to the front door. For the last time, sensing that the superintendent was spying on them from the upstairs landing, he kissed her.

'Goodbye; take care.'

'I'm going to pack, my darling,' Elizabeth said. 'Eleven tomorrow, the Eastern Airlines building. I'm not even going to say goodbye.'

Keller closed the front door and started back up the stairs. The sketch of the cathedral lay on the floor of his room. He picked it up and set light to it with a match. He crumbled the black wisps of paper into dust between his fingers. He had spent the morning at St Patrick's, at his first Mass since he left the orphanage. He knew exactly where to go next morning.

In his apartment on Park Avenue, Eddi King had been making preparations for a journey. His bags were packed, his papers had been put through a shredder which he kept specially for this purpose, and the remains flushed down the lavatory.

He looked round the apartment with some regret. He had lived there nearly seven years. There was a beautiful seventeenth-century Italian Nativity, bought for its exquisite use of form and colour and the serenity of its composition; the religious significance offended him no more than any other allegorical subject. He had been tempted to cut the painting out of its frame and take it with him, but he decided it was a foolish thing to do. If his bags were opened, and in Argentina they probably would be, the canvas would only call attention to him. It would have to stay behind, with the rest of his possessions, to be photographed and pawed over by the authorities after he had gone. It was five o'clock. His plane left for Buenos Aires in two hours. It seemed extraordinary that after all the years of exile he was really going home. His memories of Russia were dim and even distorted by time. He had left a country blasted by war and ruled by the Stalinist terror which was now officially denounced. He would find many changes; no familiar faces. It was a daunting prospect in one sense but an immense relief in every other. His time had run out; his luck was about to follow. Killing Cameron's niece was the signal. When a man in his position had to resort to the methods of the petty cut-throat, it was time he headed home. His nerves had been shaken by that incident. He hadn't realised until he was on the way back from Freemont, and he found his hands sticking to the steering wheel with sweat, and his limbs shaking.

He hadn't used violence since his training days. There was no element of scruple or distaste in his reaction. It was simply fear of having messed it up, of being seen leaving the pool, naked and dripping, after blacking Elizabeth Cameron out. He wasn't as young as he thought; age told on the nerves, and not age alone, but soft living and lack of practice. He was due to leave that night and he had driven home at a wild speed to clear everything up and get on his way.

He deserved his reward, and the reward might not be generous by American standards but in terms of life in the Soviet Union he would enjoy the privilege of the new élite. The scientists, the administrators, the politicians, the faithful servants of the K.G.B. He would live in a comfortable flat and have a dacha in the country, and work with the Ministry of the Interior. He poured himself a Bourbon and dropped in two cubes of ice. He wouldn't be there to see his great coup the next morning; the killer would gun down the people's Prince of the Catholic Church and die within minutes himself. King's man had reported back after Keller's visit to the cathedral. He would shoot him dead as he tried to escape. The inevitable process of checking up on the dead man would nail Huntley Cameron and with him the hopes of a Democrat President of the United States. From the vantage-point of Moscow, King would be able to watch the advent of John Jackson to political supremacy, surveying the chaos which must follow like an observer watching a volcano in eruption. That moment would begin tomorrow, with the death of Martino Regazzi. He looked at his watch; it was still too early to drive to Kennedy. He switched on the TV set and sat down with the Bourbon to take his last sample of the American way of life.

He was in time for the last part of the programme Keller had been watching; unlike Keller he didn't cut out when Regazzi came on. He watched with interest, and reached out to pour himself another drink. That was when the news item about the death of Huntley Cameron's fiancée hit him. He didn't drop the bottle; he went on holding it poised in the air, the sweat coming out cold all over his back and under his collar. Heart failure while swimming in the multi-millionaire's luxury pool at Freemont. King inched forward, staring at the set, refusing to accept the words coming out of that photoelectric projection's mouth.

Dallas. Dallas Jay was dead in the pool. Not Elizabeth Cameron, but Dallas. He had killed the wrong woman. And the other one, the one who had gone to her uncle and could have the power to destroy his entire operation—she was still alive. He got up from his chair and punched the set button to 'off'. He had made a mess of the job; that nervous *crise* on the way back to New York was justified. Huntley might not have talked, but the risk was too great to contemplate even for a moment. He had committed murder to obviate that risk, but he had bungled it. He was so angry he fumbled, getting the phone off the hook. He cursed her as he dialled the Washington number of his emergency contact. He spoke quickly after using his identification name. The plan was set; everything would go through tomorrow. While he was waiting for the number to answer, King's brain had hurtled forward beyond the immediate danger of her contacting the police before the morning, warning them that Jackson was in peril. Even if she didn't, her foreknowledge of the plan, her ability to swear that Regazzi had never been her uncle's target—this alone made it imperative for her to be silenced as soon as possible. He gave her name and apartment address to Washington. Urgent, urgent, he barked down the telephone. If they didn't settle it quickly, it would be their responsibility; in two hours he would have left the country. He had just hung up when the doorbell rang. For a moment he hesitated; he wasn't expecting any caller;

166

nobody even knew he was in New York. The bell sounded again, longer, more determined. He went into the hall, frowning, ready to be rude, and opened the door.

Two men were standing outside; both were plainly dressed and wore hats; the taller took his off.

'Mr King?'

'What do you want—I'm just going out,' King said. He was ready to slam the door on them. The same man held out his hand; there was a case with a badge in the palm.

'We're from the F.B.I. We want you to come with us, please.'

It was Leary's decision to arrest King; having lost Elizabeth and the chance of picking up her companion from Beirut, he felt it was imperative to grab the main suspect and see what could be got out of him. Even if he yielded nothing, and Leary doubted the success of interrogation with an agent of King's calibre, it might scare his associates into abandoning their plan. As Leary had reminded Mathews, the next day was St Patrick's and half the political targets in New York State would be gathered in one place. His error of judgement had probably cost him the assassin himself; at the worst he had been left loose to carry out his job.

When Mathews suggested going back to bring Elizabeth in, Leary actually snarled at him. 'And what the hell good would that do, you stupid bastard! She's had time to warn the guy off by now! Her only use was to lead us to this man, whoever he is. But you balled that up—you just disregarded my orders and followed your own bloody stupid nose and balled it up!'

For once there was no ready answer from Peter Mathews; he stood in front of Leary's desk and let the Irish invective flow over him. When Leary wanted to point out a mistake he knew how to do it.

'I'll tell you what you'll do,' he said to Mathews. He had exhausted his anger, and now he was just cold and furious. 'You'll do what that knuckle-head Ford should have done —losing the girl like that—Christ, it's the oldest trick in the game! You'll keep a tail on her day and night yourself. You'll sit outside her apartment in a car and you'll stay awake, buddy, or else . . . If she's so involved with this guy that she'd go this far to protect him, then my guess is when he decides to go she'll try to make a run for it with him. Of course . . .' he paused and refreshed himself with the inevitable cup of coffee, 'of course, thanks to your mishandling, they may have gotten out already—but only time will show that. If she comes back to her apartment there's some hope. You stick with her, and you'd better draw yourself a gun. If the lover boy shows up, you're going to need it. Now get to hell out of here!'

Mathews hesitated. 'I'm sorry, sir.'

Leary's eyes flickered towards him with dislike. 'Screw up anything else and you will be,' he said.

Mathews went out, passed through the outer office where Leary's secretary was typing, and grimaced. She smiled at him in sympathy and shook her head. There were no Sundays as far as her job was concerned. When the decision was made to arrest King the staff had been called back to work through the night. The F.B.I. had delivered him to Leary's building through the back entrance and driven off. When the C.I.A. were finished with him he would be sent back to them and officially charged. But that might not be for many weeks. Mathews took out one of the cars equipped with two-way radio telephone and drove back up town to East 59th. Elizabeth had given his man the slip. All that afternoon he had been trying to figure out his mistake with her. She wasn't a professional agent, working for anybody. He had staked his career on that, and it seemed he had lost. But he still wouldn't accept it. She had shaken off his tail in a way Leary considered showed some sinister expertise; but though he hadn't dared to say so, Mathews disagreed. He knew less about most things than Leary, but he reckoned on knowing a bookful about women. When it meant protecting a man she loved, a stupid woman could behave very cleverly. And Elizabeth wasn't stupid by any standard. She had discovered she was being followed—maybe the cab driver had noticed—and just lost herself. It showed she was quick and resourceful, but it didn't prove she was a traitor. He wasn't angry with her any more. He didn't even resent her for outwitting him. He respected her for it. It made her into an opponent instead of a pawn; the one he was out to get was the man she was protecting. He stopped outside her apartment and went in.

168

The hall porter saluted him. ''Evening, Mr Mathews. Shall I take you up?'

'No thanks,' Mathews said. 'I just came round to see if Miss Cameron had left my brief-case for me.'

'No, nothing's been left with me, and there's nothing in the office. Miss Cameron's just come in, though.'

'Then I can't have left it here,' Mathews shrugged. He grinned at the porter. 'I have a couple of other places to try. Good night.'

He went back and climbed in the front seat of the car. He was over six feet and the space was cramped. The hours ahead would not be comfortable. He phoned in briefly. 'The fare's still in her apartment. Am waiting as instructed.'

It might be a very long wait indeed, or if there was an early rendezvous it could be very short.

The telephone was ringing when Elizabeth walked in; Huntley was on the other end. He didn't let her speak. He talked at speed, barking the news of Dallas' death, cutting through her exclamation with a fierce injunction to shut up for Christ's sake and listen. Dallas had been murdered in mistake for her, and King had disappeared. He was convinced that Elizabeth's life was in danger. She was to come down to Freemont immediately where she would be safe. Having told her not to answer he then waited; there was silence and he shouted, thinking they had been cut off. 'You hear me—get hold of Mathews and tell him to drive you down right away!'

The idea of asking Peter Mathews for protection made Elizabeth smile. 'I can't,' she said quietly. 'I can't come to Freemont, Uncle, I have an appointment tomorrow morning.'

'You goddamned fool,' he was yelling through the wire. 'Don't you realise this guy King knocked off Dallas this morning, thinking it was you? He may be on his way round now, to get you!'

'Don't worry about me. I'll be all right. I'm going away tomorrow anyway.' Then she hung up. Dallas was dead. She gave in to the shock of it, and shivered. Poor woman. Poor, deluded woman, hoping that a man like Huntley Cameron would prove capable of affection or reward for service. She had wanted to marry him so much. She remembered the ageing face and the voice, pitched on the same pleasing note, with the platitudes tumbling out, and the miserable irony of that useless death made Elizabeth turn away and cry. The greater irony escaped her; hers were the only tears anybody shed for Dallas Jay.

She went through to her bedroom and began to pack a single bag. She didn't want much luggage; she would certainly take her jewellery, because she might need to sell some until sufficient transfer of funds could be arranged. Choosing a few clothes, assembling what she most wanted to take with her to her new life, Elizabeth was able to close her mind to that telephone call, and the threat of a man who might at that moment be on his way up in the lift. She went to her door and bolted it. After a moment she lifted the house telephone and called through to the porter. 'I don't want to be disturbed tonight,' she said. 'If anyone calls, I've gone down to Freemont. And don't let anyone come up to the apartment.' That should throw King off the scent. Suddenly she found herself trembling.

She had always feared him; subconsciously she had felt a sinister influence behind the smiling sophisticate; it had taken the form of physical revulsion. Remembering the white roses in Beirut she felt sick; sicker still at the thought of that moment in the orchid house at Freemont when he had pressed her hand against his mouth and she had wrenched it away. Huntley said he had murdered Dallas in mistake for her. But how—and why? He had somehow guessed that she knew of the assassination; he had tried to kill her to stop her betraying it. It must be the cold that made her tremble; but the temperature in the apartment never varied; it was 75°. She went back to her room and finished packing. She checked on her money and then looked up the number of Eastern Airlines.

The only way to keep her fear under control was to keep occupied, to think of going away with Keller, so that her mind had no time to wonder what Eddi King might be doing at that moment. Nobody, she insisted, could get up to her apartment; with the doors bolted, even if they did slip past the porter, they couldn't get inside. And the twelfth floor had its obvious advantage. He could hardly climb through the window. But even the idea made her swing round, realising the windows were behind her. Eastern Airlines had a midday flight to Mexico City, it was part of the new

170

schedule which was operating from mid-March. Elizabeth booked two tickets; she gave her travel agent's number. The airline said they would check through with them and leave her tickets at their desk at the airport.

Eleven would give her and Keller just enough time to catch the plane. She went into the kitchen and made coffee; she hadn't touched food since breakfast and yet she didn't feel like eating. But perhaps if she made herself take something it might stop the persistent trembling of her body. Fatigue and emptiness. That was the cause; Elizabeth said it to herself out loud. She was safe; nobody could get to her. She had nothing to fear. She made herself an omelette and managed to get most of it down. She insisted that she felt better.

Sitting in the breakfast area in the kitchen, drinking coffee, reminded her of that first morning, when she made Keller breakfast. He hadn't liked the waffles. The night before she hadn't been able to sleep; too shaken and confused by what had happened to her, roused by an instinct as accurate as her dread of Eddi King. The moment of truth had come into her life when an angry man kissed her, to insult, not seduce; to punish her arrogance and put the situation in perspective. Her money, her sophistication were no match for a man who really was a man. He had shown her the consequences of trying to treat him as anything less. And he had made her love him from that first moment. Perhaps even before, when they were on the plane together. Long before the night they became lovers.

They had come halfway across the world together to America, and tomorrow they would leave together. Probably for ever. She couldn't imagine what her new life would be like; she could only judge in terms of him and the time they had been together in her flat. That was the only happiness she had ever experienced. Making love was wonderful; it had been wonderful that afternoon, lying together in the shabby bedroom, with the news of death just spoken between them. He had given her freedom in the only sense that mattered. Freedom to be herself, to give herself in love without shame or reservation. This was the true emancipation for her sex. The equality, the bank accounts, the tedious in-fighting of the so-called sex war . . . they were sham, hers the reality. Love was a coin which society had debased; it

171

meant so much more than the physical act; it was talked about in terms of performance, like an automobile. What she felt for Keller and he for her could never be measured in any known terms or even accurately described. It was unique to them. It gave her the courage to sit in her apartment, knowing that one woman had already been killed in mistake for her and the murderer was still unsatisfied. It gave her the impetus to tear up her roots from the safe soil of America and go into exile with the man she loved.

It was stronger than all the conventions of her upbringing, which had never permitted a man prepared to kill for money to be a human being worthy of another human being's love. She had said it to him that afternoon, weeping and desperate in her fear of losing him. She didn't care what he was or what he had done.

If he went ahead and pulled the trigger tomorrow and still found a way to join her at the airport, she'd go with him.

It was as simple as that. As primeval and inevitable as the meeting of the first man and woman who loved each other in defiance of the law.

St Patrick's Cathedral was closed at ten o'clock at night; it was nine-fifty and little knots of worshippers were still inside the building, resisting the efforts of the vergers to get rid of them. The lights above the main nave were being switched out; the side doors were already locked with the exception of the exit leading into Madison Avenue. Monsignor Jameson had been on his feet since 6 a.m.; there had been no time for the afternoon doze which he felt was such a necessity at his age. He had been with the Cardinal most of the afternoon, making the final draft of his sermon for next day. Patrick Jameson was not an excitable man, but he attributed his splitting headache more to his anxiety over that speech than to his lack of sleep and general fatigue. Every time the Cardinal revised it, it came out more controversial, more fiercely uncompromising, than before. Jameson had given up trying to get it watered down; he had thrown his hands in the air, which wrung a smile out of the Cardinal, and said simply, 'God help us, your Eminence, I'll get it typed by this evening.'

It was one of the most scathing attacks upon a political

ideology that Jameson had ever heard, not even excepting the thunderbolts of abuse hurled at Nazi Germany during the war. As a cautious man, with a dislike of politics and politicians, the Monsignor cringed at the verbal grenades his Cardinal intended to fling at John Jackson the next morning. But there was a ringing splendour about the denunciations which found a response in his Celtic spirit, never quite proof against the power of a great phrase. While he typed the speech that evening, eating a sandwich instead of the substantial dinner he needed, and upsetting his digestion with cups of coffee, Jameson deplored what the Cardinal was doing, and fought down his pride in being part of it at the same time. He didn't resent the long hours now; he worked them without grumbling to himself and found them less burdensome than they once were. He would never understand Regazzi; it was like watching lightning. You could see the flash but you couldn't hope to catch it for analysis. But before he had misunderstood him. Perhaps, Jameson wondered, perhaps all saints were as difficult as this man; perhaps those who loved God and humanity in the mass were as remote and lonely as his Cardinal.

With that great burden of love upon his shoulders for those who had no other advocate in the courts of power, perhaps it was natural for him to forget the comfort of those working with him. Now, he embarrassed Jameson by sometimes telling him to go to bed. But not often, and then the Monsignor suspected it was because he made a special effort to remember. The Cardinal too was anxious about his sermon, but his fear was that it said too little, rather than the worry of his secretary that it said far too much. Jameson had finished typing, and he was making his last round of the cathedral for the night. One of the worshippers got out of his pew and pushed hard against him as he hurried down the aisle. Jameson suppressed the unchristian impulse to call him a rude sonofabitch and walked back down the central nave. St Patrick's was his favourite day in the Church's calendar; he hardly dared admit it, but he liked it more than Christmas. His parents were first generation immigrants from County Kerry; he, like Cardinal Regazzi, was one of a large, poor family. But the expatriate Irish were ambitious; they worked hard to evolve from the poverty which had driven them from their homes. America

173

was said to be the land of opportunity. Whether this was true or not, they set about to make it so.

Jameson's father was a hard man; he disciplined his children with his fists and a strap, but he worked for them all, and three out of his four sons went to college. The fourth, and two of his sisters, died in early adolescence from the Celtic scourge, T.B. It was his brother's death which brought Pat Jameson to the priesthood. They had been very close as boys, and the younger had always wished to be a priest. At his death, it seemed as if the desire had passed directly to his brother Patrick. For his father he had respect but no affection—he was an impossible man to love; bitter, ignorant and autocratic. His mother, Patrick Jameson spoke of as a saint. She was gentle, simple, obedient to the dictates of her religion and her husband. She made a strength out of submission, and her children literally confused her in their minds with the image of the tender Virgin whose picture was above every child's bed. Later, long after her death, when the confessional had educated him in the vagaries of human behaviour, Jameson wondered whether the infamous cult of 'Momism' hadn't originated with the Irish as much as with the Jews.

He spoke to the two vergers on duty at the main door, and to the officer of St Vincent de Paul who manned a special collection plate. Lastly, Jameson went to two men who had been in the body of the church for the last hour.

'Everything all right?'

'Harry has checked all the side altars and I went through the confessionals an hour ago,' the F.B.I. agent answered. 'There's nothing been left anywhere and nobody hiding. Are you satisfied, Monsignor?'

'Sure. You won't find any bombs in the pulpit!' He made a joke of it, but neither man smiled. He thought, irritably, that they were unnecessarily wooden and grim, like characters out of a bad gangster movie.

'Harry and I will stay till around the six o'clock Mass in the morning. Then two more of us will take over before the main group arrives for the High Mass.'

'In my opinion,' the Monsignor said, 'this is a whole lot of nonsense. Nobody's going to do anything inside St Pat's. I don't know why your people don't leave us alone and concentrate on the procession.'

174

'Because none of the priority targets will be walking in it,' the man called Harry answered him. 'Nobody in public office dares to walk the streets any more. You ought to understand why. The last time I was on duty here was the Requiem for Bobbie Kennedy.'

Jameson walked back down the long nave; he was tired out, but still had to deliver the speech to the Cardinal.

Martino Regazzi was in his study reading a paperback detective novel. The first time his secretary found him doing this he kept trying to read the title of the book upside down. Regazzi turned it right way up and remarked that it wasn't as good a murder story as the previous one. It was his only relaxation; that night his nerves were tense and his brain refused to quiet. His whole system raced at full throttle; nothing but an hour of the leisurely mystery story with its classic formula and list of suspects would slow him down enough to get a little sleep.

He put the book away when Jameson knocked and came in. He may not have noticed the older man's weary expression, the forehead creased with the niggling ache behind the frontal bone, but the secretary forgot himself enough to say abruptly:

'Eminence, if you don't get to bed tonight, you won't make any speech tomorrow. I've a good mind to take it away again and not give it to you till the morning!'

'Don't fuss, Patrick,' the Cardinal said. 'I'm in the middle of a really good murder story. Look—*The Mystery of the Boston Bean*—I'll lend it to you tomorrow.'

'I can't read those things,' Jameson said. He laid the typed sheets on the Cardinal's desk. 'I can't read detective stories or holy books. So there's not much I can read these days but the newspapers. It's all finished; I made three copies.'

'Good.' Regazzi began reading the first page. He would have gone on through the whole speech if Jameson hadn't cleared his throat.

'Did you see the N.B.C. programme tonight—the Sons of St Patrick?' Regazzi asked suddenly.

'No,' Jameson said. 'I was working—was it good?'

'No,' the Cardinal answered. 'It was a lot of green soap. All the big politicians, the millionaires, the old racketeers. And the Church was represented by at least four Bishops and two Cardinals. If that's all St Patrick can claim, God

175

help him! Somebody discovered John Jackson had an Irish great-grandmother. So we had a snap profile of him too. Very clever propaganda. Like coming here tomorrow. Do you know, Patrick,' the black eyes blazed with the rage of his Sicilian ancestors, 'do you know if it hadn't been such an opportunity to attack him personally, I wouldn't have allowed him in my church?'

'He thinks he'll get votes,' the secretary said. 'Much good it'll do him with the coloured Catholics. They know where he stands.'

'After tomorrow,' the Cardinal said, 'please God they'll know where the Church stands too. Right up there with them. You went round the cathedral—everything quiet?'

'Just as always. Except for the cops and the plain clothes. They've been poking round, looking for bogies.' Nothing had altered Jameson's irritation at government precautions in the cathedral. The facts of political murder so recently in memory meant nothing to him. It was nonsense to suggest it could happen in his church. Regazzi knew his attitude. He appreciated Federal and City Hall anxiety as Jameson refused to do, but he despised precautions. Death came when it was time, and nothing could refuse it entry. This attitude, with its Sicilian fatalism, made him a very difficult man to protect.

'The only murder that'll be done is when you start preaching, Eminence,' Jameson said. 'I just hope the Holy See doesn't pull down the roof on you.' He sighed; he had his generation's doubts about the liberal attitudes of the Church's centre of government in Rome. 'They're all for the diplomatic touch; nobody's going to like the way you throw your punches.'

'That's where I think you're wrong,' Regazzi said. 'I believe the Holy Father will be delighted. One of those copies you made is going direct to him with a letter from me, explaining my motives.'

'But you'll have delivered it all before he gets that,' the Secretary pointed out. Regazzi's thin face relaxed for a second in a very narrow smile.

'Exactly,' he said. 'This isn't just internal politics, this is a universal principle, applying to every human being made in his Creator's image. There are no inferior races, only ignorant, prejudiced individuals who are so busy looking

176

at themselves they can't see God's imprint on their brothers. One day, Patrick, there'll be a black man on my throne on the high altar, just as there's been a Catholic in the White House. Evil doesn't triumph, because the soul of the people is good. With God's help, John Jackson will crawl out of our cathedral tomorrow on his hands and knees.'

'You'll be accused of losing him the Presidency,' Jameson said.

'That's my intention.' Regazzi glanced down at the speech and quickly wrote something in the margin. 'Thank you, Patrick, I'd forgotten to make that point emphatic enough.'

'Shall I go to bed, then? Will you want me again, Eminence?'

'No, no, there's no more to be done. Tomorrow will be a long day for us all. Good night, and God bless you.'

And you too, the Monsignor said to himself, as he walked slowly away from the Cardinal's apartments to his bedroom. Men have been lynched for what you're going to say tomorrow. It was not a happy thought on which to fall asleep.

Keller left his room at eight-thirty on Monday morning. He carried the money re-wrapped in a parcel under his arm; it was just a neat brown paper package, no bigger than a large box of stationery. He was freshly shaved, and he wore the dark suit in which he had travelled to America. He looked clean and unobtrusive, a foreigner who only lacked his tourist's camera to be perfectly in character. The money had presented him with a problem. He couldn't be sure of coming back to the room. If he left anything there, the room would be searched by the super, who must have a duplicate key. Yet his instructions made it clear that nobody would be admitted to the cathedral carrying anything which hadn't been vetted first. It was a cold morning; he shivered, turning up his coat collar, wishing the overcoat he had bought at Elizabeth's insistence was thicker and warmer. He felt the cold acutely; he stuffed his hands in his pockets to keep the fingers supple. The cotton gloves were no protection.

He had given himself the maximum time, allowing for getting lost and the delays for which an inexperienced traveller in this confusing city was unprepared and unequipped. He had memorised the subway route. By nine-fifteen he was in a self-service cafeteria just down the block from the cathedral. He was hungry, but his stomach closed against the ham and eggs. He felt as if the sight of another ophthalmic egg on its bed of sweet pink American ham would make him heave over the table. He drank the coffee, which was weak by his standards, and ate a doughy roll. There were doors marked 'Toilet' at one end of the long sandwich-and-hot-drinks counter. The waitress clearing away dirty cups pointed out one as the men's room. It was a curious expression; he had never heard it before. He hid his parcel of money behind the cistern. For a couple of hours at most, it was a reasonable place to hide something. He came out and went back to finish his coffee. He could have left the money behind; he could have dropped it in a trash can on his way over. But he would see them damned first. Money was part of the bargain they had already broken. This part of it, at least, Keller meant them to keep. He had been paid to kill a man, and he was going to do just that. Professionals have their pride; the mercenary soldier fights as hard for his employers as the patriot, or he soon loses his commission. The killer takes his fee, and kills as he has undertaken. Even the scum have their code. But it's unwise to trust them if you break it. They can turn very nasty. Keller had bought a paper. There was a large picture of John Jackson on the front page; it was a cheap tabloid, screaming sensationalism from every column. He didn't bother to read it; most of the items meant nothing to him. He studied the picture of Jackson instead. It all made very good sense; he had been thinking it out carefully, keeping his emotions over Souha in the background, trying to assure himself that what he was going to do would really damage the plan inherent in the death of the Cardinal. There was a photograph of him, too, smaller than the Presidential Candidate's—even the cheap journal described him as a champion of the poor and a fighter for the rights of coloured people. When Elizabeth told Keller he was working for the communists, she used the word in a sense that meant nothing to him. It was just another description for the other kind of professionals; the politicians, the princes of graft and grab. All Keller knew of communism was what he had seen at Dien Bien Phu, and he was not impressed. The small fry did the fighting and stopped the bullets; the cry of universal brotherhood seemed a particularly empty slogan when it was accompanied by a bayonet thrust in someone else's gut. Communists were like the rest: purveyors of the familiar opium by which the poor and down-trodden were kept drugged into quiescence. The good things of the earth would soon be theirs, provided they didn't try to anticipate by taking them on their own initiative. Keller hated all organisations; he believed they only worked to the benefit of those at the top. The communists talked about representing the people, but that hadn't stopped them sending in the tanks just like the rest to keep the people in their place. Keller had no more feeling towards communism than any other ideology, civil or religious. He mistrusted them all. If they were genuine in their beliefs, a man like Cardinal Regazzi should have qualified for honorary membership. But they were going to kill him, because he belonged to the opposite side. They wanted a racialist President in America, with the bloodshed, and misery of a civil war as useful adjuncts in their political strategy. So much for their bloody crusade, he thought bitterly. A million lives wouldn't mean any more to them than the life of one Arab girl, throttled to death on their instructions. For that one murder, the man King and all he represented in the world were going to have their global plan frustrated by someone as expendable and insignificant as Souha Mamoulian and all her kind. The displaced person of the twentieth century; the human ammunition, the breathing targets, for ever falling casualty in a game of war they didn't ask to play.

John Jackson would never be President of America and there would be no civil war, no dreadful upsurge from within to open the way for them. Because their hired assassin was going to kill him to prevent it. He buttoned his coat against the March wind in the street outside and began to walk towards the twin grey towers of the cathedral. At ten o'clock the body of the church was filling up with people; there was a subdued sound inside composed of many different noises; the movement of people taking their places; whispering, coughing, and through it all a subdued but beautiful anthem played softly on the magnificent organ high above the entrance. Keller knew every foot of the way he had to take. He had spent an hour there two days before,

179

pretending to visit the side altars, getting every detail fixed in his memory. He walked through the enormous doorway, flanked by the massive bronze doors, elaborately ornamented with Christ and his Apostles above, three figures of saints associated with New York on each of them. Two men stopped him. 'What's in your coat, mister?' Keller didn't argue; he handed it over to them. People passed him, staring, their heads turned. He wasn't the only one. A man carrying a brief-case had also been stopped and asked to open it. He was arguing angrily. Keller gave his coat to the security man, and raised his arms while a second ran over him with expert touch to see if he were carrying a weapon.

'Sorry to trouble you,' they said when he was passed clean. 'Regulations are tough these days.'

'That's all right,' he said. He walked through and turned left up the aisle. He went up the short flight of steps leading to the back of the tall mahogany screen which closed out most of the high altar except its elaborately carved canopy arch. The special confessional was tucked into a corner, wedged into the wall, with one of the huge four-columned pillars as part of its construction. A number of people were in the area; Keller picked out three men who were certainly not worshippers moving watchfully up and down. He saw one of the vergers pause and speak to one of them. In that instant they were occupied; he looked from right to left, and behind him. For that brief moment no one was walking near or glancing towards the confessional. Keller had rehearsed it all so often in his mind that he acted inhumanly fast. He ducked inside the green curtains of the confessional, reaching towards the wall; his fingers found something long and loose; he slipped one arm through it and stepped clear. In full view of anyone coming up the steps towards him, he adjusted the verger's robe and walked to the altar of St Rose of Lima. His heart was beating at a slightly faster rate than normal, but he tested himself deliberately. He went to the candlestand, blazing with votive lights, and adjusted one or two which were dripping wax on to the floor. People went past him, paused to kneel a foot or so away and pray, and accepted him as one of the cathedral staff. He began to walk back towards the confessional again. It was one thing to grab an overall left hanging for him to find; it was not quite the same to get

180

that kneeler rail lifted and extract the gun. Now his heart rate was increasing; he hid his hands inside the robe and eased on his cotton gloves. There was another confessional box on the way; it too had the same curtains, looped to one side. He went up to it and swept them back, peering inside the narrow place where the penitent could kneel. He felt the kneeling rail and the top. It was all in one piece; nothing moved. The other must have been specially altered; probably weeks before. He walked up the steps again and turned behind the altar; the huge carved screens shut out the glittering lights which were being lit round the sanctuary; the passageway was not very wide and in places very shadowy. He knew exactly where the two doors were. The nearest to the confessional was the one through which the Cardinal and his procession of priests and acolytes would enter for the High Mass. Just beyond it was the exit leading to 51st Street, with the man on the outside who would be his final hazard as he got away. He went past both doorways and saw what he expected; four men were posted round the first exit, and one was on duty by the second. The man who had briefed Keller had told him not to worry about the man on duty by the door *inside* the church. He glanced up at him, and saw the security man watching him with unusual concentration. This must be their man; the one who had the opportunity to hide the robe and the gun; the one who would let him rush through after the killing. Keller didn't hold his look. He remembered exactly what Elizabeth had said: 'Immediately you've killed Jackson you'll be killed yourself to stop you being arrested.' Immediately. Immediately after. That would be their security man's opportunity to close the bargain. When Keller tried to get out through that door he would be shot dead. King's executioner would be a national hero for killing the Cardinal's assassin. And there would be no chance of that assassin getting caught and giving any clue away. He didn't raise his eyes or look at the man again. Keller turned back and went up to the confessional. He didn't try to slip inside the curtains. He swept them right back and then moved in, pretending to look at something. There was an electronic headset for use by the deaf, hanging close to the small meshed opening which concealed the priest during the confession. He lifted the edge of the kneeling rail, and a part of the top came up like the lid of a box. He plunged his hand inside the narrow space which had been hollowed out of the wood. The gun was lying in it; it was in his coat pocket under the robe before he withdrew his head from the darkness.

'Everything okay?' One of the men on duty by the Cardinal's entry door had come up behind him.

'Yes,' Keller said quickly. 'I just wanted to be sure.'

'You can't be too particular,' the man said. 'With that bastard attending here today, anything could happen. Keep your eye on anyone coloured in your section; they're the ones to watch.'

'I will do that,' Keller said. He nodded to the man—F.B.I., Police Department, or whatever he was. He kept his right hand in his pocket, holding the pistol. He checked his watch; it was ten-twenty-five. The main doors were closed now; the organ music had increased in volume, the whole body of the cathedral was full of people, their faces turning towards a small procession which was coming down the nave. These were the important, the privileged, coming to take their reserved places. Keller didn't recognise anyone from his position at the top of the steps leading down to the aisle; certainly Jackson was not among the group of a dozen men and women who were filing into the first three rows on either side of the nave. He hadn't come. At the last minute he had been warned off. There had been one attempt to murder him already. Keller knew about that from the TV news programme the night before. Maybe he had just lost his nerve.

But then he saw the other group, approaching from the opposite side of the cathedral, and the hand in his right pocket grew tense as he recognised the thin face, the white hair brushed up, the glint of the steel-rimmed spectacles on the snubby nose. John Jackson had come in with his party through a side entrance. It was an obvious precaution against a hostile demonstration from the crowds gathered round the cathedral entrance. Keller stood close against the huge supporting pillar with its Gothic saint suspended in perpetual levitation above the ground; round the corner, protected by that pillar, he had seen the splendid throne where Regazzi would sit during the Mass. He could see Jackson bowing to some of the people round him; a smile looked uncomfortable on the fanatical mouth. He had a nervous mannerism, more noticeable in the flesh than it had been on the screen, of sucking in his lower lip.

Keller judged the distance to be not more than fifteen feet, with an awkward angle for taking aim. The view was good but the angle was a disadvantage. It needed time to point the weapon and take a correct aim which would make sure the bullet penetrated the front cranial bone and through into the brain.

There was a tremendous chord from the organ; it filled the vast roof with a triumphant peal of music; at the same moment the congregation stood up. The noise was like a roll of distant thunder. Keller turned. Behind him, away down the side passage, the door to the rectory had opened. As the Cardinal's procession entered the cathedral, the choir began the opening anthem of the High Mass.

'What's the time?' King had asked them the same question three times in what he supposed must be the last hour. He got the same reply. 'Time you gave us a straight answer, Mr King.'

They were very polite, very correct. There were three of them, which was the routine number for an interrogation at this stage. Two to ask the questions and one to take it down on a transcriber. They were middle-aged men; the principal questioner looked like a college professor; he was quiet-spoken, his hair greying and cut to a liberal length. He had taken off his jacket, but that was the only cessation so far to the session which had been going on all through the night without a pause. There had been no brutality; King was too experienced to expect this at such an early stage. But he had been afraid all the same when they made the descent in the lift and began the walk down the bare cor-ridors lit with fluorescent ceiling lights.

It had begun politely, impersonally, as if he weren't im-portant and it would soon be over. He had answered their questions with his cover story, and after nine hours he hadn't changed a single detail. He was sick with tired-ness; his head ached with the effort to concentr and there was no aggression being generated against h eded at this

This would have helped; this was what h ind off want-stage to give his energy a shot and keep but it was very ing to lie down. He had been given a ch

183

uncomfortable. His buttocks ached in sympathy with his head and his legs were stiff with cramp. He had been given coffee, which at first he had refused. The chief interrogator had been mildly contemptuous. 'It's not drugged, Mr King,' he said. 'We don't use those methods over here.' He had drunk from King's cup to prove it. In the end King needed the coffee, and drank as much as he was offered. He wasn't really afraid, because he was a brave man, and this was a contingency he had prepared himself to meet for many years. But still he was more shaken than he should have been. The end had been so close, the contingency itself had receded further and further into the improbable until he hadn't really thought of it ever happening; and still it had. With an hour to spare, he had been arrested, and he still didn't know how they had found him out. They hadn't mentioned Beirut or Huntley Cameron; the whole line of attack against him had been directed to making him break down and admit that he was not Eddi King. While this was the worst development for him personally, because it supposed a vital leak in his security cover, it left his final blow against them time to be delivered. They hadn't discovered anything about the assassination which was going to take place that morning. It must be the morning; as his watch had been removed he couldn't tell what time it was in the underground room, and that was why he interrupted to keep asking.

'You're very interested in the time, Mr King.' The second interrogator took it up to give the senior man a rest. 'But time doesn't matter here. You can be here for days if you go on being obstructive. Weeks. You won't like that chair after a while; we don't have any beds.'

'I want to see my lawyer,' King repeated. He said it because an innocent man would do so, but without any hope of convincing them. They knew enough about him to go on and on until he broke. He wouldn't be beaten up or doped. He would just be kept awake until his mind collapsed to hallucination and his body could hardly function except to restore a minimal balance and then woken up to start again. He wasn't expected to stand out indefinitely; in his case he need only resist until he was sure that Regazzi had been murdered and the political conspiracy directed at putting John Jackson into the White House was properly advanced.

Then he could admit just enough about himself to get him out of the interrogation centre. He was allowed to implicate a few minor agents, who were expendable, and couldn't provide any information if they were picked up. He could stand his trial for being what he was: a Soviet agent running an Intelligence network under cover of a magazine. He would get twenty, thirty years, and before long the negotiations to release him on the usual exchange basis would begin. The K.G.B. never deserted their big operators. All the top agents were assured that they wouldn't be left in capitalist prisons to finish their sentences, and by means of blackmail, kidnap and exchange of agents the K.G.B. had kept their promise. But if his part in the Regazzi assassination became known, then not only would his plan misfire completely, because any hint of a foreign conspiracy would distract public attention from the carefully laid frame against Huntley and the Democratic Party, but it would invoke the death sentence against King. And nobody had been able to rescue the Rosenbergs.

'When did you take over Eddi King's identity? 1945—that's when he died in the death camp. We know this, Mr King; we know all about how the deal was set up for you.'

'There was no deal,' King said, as he had been saying all through the night. 'My name is Edward Richard King, I was born in Minnesota, I live in New York and I don't know what the hell you're talking about. I spent three years interned in a concentration camp and then I lived in France till I came home in '54. I've told you this over and over, and that's all I have to say till I see my lawyer.'

The two interrogators said something he couldn't hear. He leaned his head on his hand and shut his eyes for a moment, taking advantage of the pause. Elizabeth Cameron. That was the greatest single mistake of his career; leaving her alive that night at Freemont, waiting until the morning and then killing Huntley's strumpet in error. His people had to get her, or the truth about the assassination could still come out, now that he was caught, and she could connect him with it. She could prove that Regazzi had never been the target, that Huntley himself had been duped and double-crossed. His hand was damp with sweat against his forehead. To be caught was bad enough, but to fail in this, the most important mission of his life; this would forfeit him the protection of his own people. He would be abandoned as a punishment and an example. They must get to her. They would get to her. He had telephoned the best man, the expert who was in charge of the Regazzi operation. He had a long record of successes; he had been recruited by King's people during his army service; he had worked for them as well as for the millionaire crime syndicate in New York. King looked up; the three Americans were watching him. 'I want to have a pee,' he said.

There was a little lavatory leading off the room; he was followed there and allowed to relieve himself, with the door kept open. What was the time? He felt like turning round and yelling at them, demanding to know. It was a human right, the right to know what hour of the day it was. King checked himself angrily. This was just the first sign of nervous strain and physical exhaustion. He had a long way to go before he could afford the luxury of breaking down. And then he noticed three other men had come into the room. The transcriber yawned and stretched, giving his place to one of the new men; the others conferred again, and the man standing behind him said, 'Come on, that's enough. Button yourself and sit down.'

It was a new team taking over. That meant the first shift was being relieved. If they worked in ten-hour shifts that meant he had been there through the night and it was well into Monday morning. He pulled himself together. Hold on for a while longer. Give the man in the Cathedral time to do his job and get killed afterwards; give the organisation's man a chance to reach Elizabeth Cameron. Then he could begin to crack for them, just a little; just enough to take the pressure off himself and keep them occupied. He walked back to his chair, wincing as he sat down again, and looked at the new set of faces.

'Now, gentlemen,' he said, 'maybe *you'll* allow me to call my lawyer?'

Peter Mathews hadn't slept during the night. He stayed in the cramped little driving seat of the observation car, taking Benzedrine tablets and smoking. She hadn't left her apartment; people had come into the building, including several men who might have been her contact, but it was Leary's guess they'd try to leave together. He had given up trying to better Leary's guesses and he stayed where he was supposed to stay, waiting. He put in two calls during the night, reporting himself and asking about King. No progress, was the answer. He hadn't expected any that soon. Leary knew the type: only a fool underestimated the courage and endurance of a first-grade Soviet agent. Personally Mathews thought they were too soft; the method took too long. A man of strong nerves and sound physique could take up to a fortnight without breaking down. Tired, angry with himself and strung up from the stimulant to keep him awake, Mathews wished they'd give up Mr King to him and, with a couple of guys to help, they'd have the answers by the end of the day. By eight o'clock it was light and the city was alive again after the weekend. The noise volume was increasing and the street where he was parked was running with streams of traffic. A traffic cop, cold and truculent at that unpleasant hour on a March morning, stalked towards him.

'Move it! Don't ya know this is a no-parkin' area?' Mathews showed him a card. He didn't say anything, he just held it in his cupped hand and brought it up under the policeman's line of sight.

'Sorry, sir.' He moved away from the window; he called the F.B.I. a dirty name and added the Irish and St Patrick's Day to the Bureau. It was hell on wheels for the police; the traffic got snarled up, the goddamned parade screwed up the whole of 43rd, 44th, 45th, 46th, and Fifth Avenue itself right up 86th Street from Central Park to Third Avenue. He got mad every time someone took him for a Mick because he was a cop, and he spent every March 17th passing out tickets like confetti just to show his feeling to the whole damned circus show. Peter Mathews put the card back in his pocket. He wished he'd brought a Thermos of hot coffee; he dared not leave his post even for a moment now in case Elizabeth came out.

He decided to move the car in and park in the 'Residents Only' space outside the apartment block entrance. He could give the porter a five-buck note to square it with him. They knew each other well, and Mathews had kept on good terms with him. He eased out of the traffic, and disregarding a furious chorus of hooting and swearing from the stream of cars he intersected, he turned across and

187

swung inside the U-shaped enclave. He cut in immediately in front of a TV service van; he took the only available space, put on the brake and switched off the engine. The van had no place to park. It stopped behind him, half blocking the driveway. Mathews expected trouble from the driver. He watched in his mirror and saw him get out. He was young, dark, stockily built, wearing white overalls with the name of the TV repair service printed on the back in red letters. But he passed Mathews without saying anything. He walked up the three broad steps under the yellow and black awning above the entrance with the apartment block number printed on it, swinging a canvas bag in his left hand. Mathews went on watching him, just exercising his eyes without any thought attached, still a little surprised that the van driver should have let him in like that and hog the only place. There wasn't much road courtesy between drivers in New York when conditions were easy. Most repair men would have offered to poke his nose through his face for slicing them out of a spot like that.

Perhaps it was the Benzedrine; perhaps it was that million to one instinct which distinguished Peter Mathews from the other eager young men who worked for Leary. He himself wasn't sure what set the alarm bell going in his mind. Most repair men would have raised hell. Why hadn't this one? Why was he different—Mathews was out of the car in the same second, racing up the steps, pushing through the plate-glass doors. There was no one in the lobby but the porter; a glance towards the elevator showed the red light popping on the indicator as it went up.

Mathews didn't waste time. It wasn't just an instinct now. It was a certainty. There was something wrong with the man in the overalls.

'Where'd that repair man go?' He swung on the porter.

'Miss Cameron's apartment. He said she'd sent out a call her TV wasn't working. He said they got a lot of calls today from people wanting to see the parade . . .'

This was the cover, of course. Mathews was at the second elevator, pulling the door open. A pair of overalls and a van. That was how the man she was protecting could get in and they could leave in minutes of each other without anyone suspecting. And that was why he hadn't complained when Mathews took his space. He didn't dare attract attention

188

to himself. And so it was the effort to blend which had made him stand out, the attempt to hide which made him more conspicuous than the row he would have raised outside. The elevator was shooting up. Peter Mathews had his gun out, and the catch off as it came to rest on the twelfth floor.

Elizabeth was in the drawing room when the doorbell rang. She had woken at dawn, alerted to the slightest sound, her nerves quivering with fear. She had gone to the kitchen and made coffee, trying to calm herself. The front door was bolted; nobody could possibly climb up the sheer face of the building. She had nothing to fear, and only a few more hours to wait before she left for the airport.

She was dressed and ready to leave when the bell rang; it would take an hour and a half at least to reach Kennedy that morning. Her packed suitcase stood near the door; there was a letter in her handbag which had been written in the long night hours. It was addressed to Francis Leary; it would be posted just before she and Keller caught the plane. When the bell rang she froze stiff with fear.

It rang again quickly, and this time there was rapping on the outside. Keller. It might be Keller who had changed the plan and come to her direct. The latch was down and the chain was in place. No one could get in unless she opened it from the inside. She came across the floor.

'Who is it?'

On the other side of the door the man who had given Keller his instructions took a step back; he had his Schmeiser automatic weapon out of the canvas bag, and he got ready to fire it through the door. He wanted to make sure the woman was behind it in the line of fire. One burst would go through the wood like a hot knife through butter. At that range she would be almost cut in half.

'Miss Cameron? Is that you?'

Elizabeth answered at the same moment that Mathews, coming behind from the second elevator, shot the man in the overalls through the back of the head. The short-barrelled weapon clattered out of his hands, and he doubled up, falling from the knees.

There was a small dark hole in the base of his skull, and a lot of blood. Mathews stood over him; he dragged the Schmeiser out from under him and put it on 'safe'. Very neat and professional; with that kind of gun you could kill as effectively through a locked door as if it were a paper hoop.

'Elizabeth? Open up, it's Peter. Come on, open up and take a look at what you've been protecting!' He heard a cry, and then a frantic fumbling with the latch and the rattle of the flimsy little chain. The door opened and she stood there, staring from him to the dead man curled up in a foetal position on the ground. Mathews held out the Schmeiser. 'Your boy friend was just about to let this off at you,' he said. 'Nice choosing, Liz. What happened, lovers' quarrel?'

She looked up at him slowly. 'I've never seen this man before,' she said. 'Oh God, for a moment I thought it was . . .' Then she put her hand to her mouth and stopped. 'Oh God,' she repeated. 'When I heard that shot and your voice, I thought . . .'

'You thought I'd killed your friend, didn't you?' Mathews stepped over the dead man. He gave Elizabeth a hard, angry push. 'Get back inside while I pull him in. You and I are going to have a talk.'

'Don't,' Elizabeth begged, 'please, don't bring him in here—oh, there's blood everywhere.' She began to cry, shivering hysterically, her face turned away. Mathews dragged the body out of the passage and through into the kitchen.

'You can get the carpet cleaned,' he said. 'I've just saved your life. Stop making that bloody noise; if you play with these kind of people you get this kind of mess.'

He went into the kitchen, leaving the door open so he could watch her, and quickly searched the dead man's pockets. He carried nothing which identified him; his pockets were empty except for ten dollars in notes, a comb, a half-finished packet of Luckys and a cheap lighter. Elizabeth was huddled in a chair, shivering. Mathews had saved her life by seconds. What a fool to have thought twelve floors above ground and a locked door could have protected her against Eddi King.

'Here.' Mathews had come back, and she thanked God he had shut the door into the kitchen. 'Cigarette.'

'Thanks, Pete.'

He had thought of finding a drink to steady her and then changed his mind. Let her shake it out; it would be easier

190

to break her down. Looking down at her he thought for a moment how unreal it was, how unbelievable that he and she could ever have found themselves in such a situation. Conspiracy and espionage and violent death. He still couldn't believe the girl sitting in front of him had any connection with it at all. He had to remind himself that he had found a hired killer outside her door a few minutes before. That was how truly involved she was in his uneasy world.

'Now,' he said. 'I want the truth. That wasn't the guy you brought back from Beirut—who was he? Why was he going to kill you?'

'Eddi King must have sent him,' she said. She felt numb and desolate with horror; even so the full significance hadn't sunk in, it was still cushioned by shock. 'King was staying at Freemont this weekend. I found out what he and my uncle were planning and he wanted to shut me up. He murdered Huntley's girl friend Dallas Jay, thinking it was me. Huntley called last night to warn me. I wouldn't listen; I thought I'd be safe here.' She closed her eyes for a moment: Mathews thought her colour was so bad he might have to produce a drink to keep her conscious.

'Where's the other one,' Mathews said, 'the one you're going to meet?' He jerked his head towards the suitcase still standing on its side near the front door. 'You can't stall any longer, Liz. You've got to tell me.'

Elizabeth turned her wrist and looked at her watch; it was a pretty Cartier model in white gold, with a tiny face. She could hardly see the hands through tears. It was almost ten o'clock.

'I love him, Peter. I'm not giving him up to you. He's done nothing wrong.' If she delayed long enough, he would get to Kennedy. He'd wait for her, but when she didn't come, he'd catch his plane and get away.

'What was the plan you discovered at Freemont?'

'They were going to have Jackson assassinated, my uncle and Eddi King.'

'And you brought in the killer,' Mathews said. He looked down at her and shook his head. 'We knew you came back with someone; we've known for some days. He was with you the first time I called you up here, wasn't he?'

'Yes,' Elizabeth said. 'He was. He'd nowhere to go and I let him stay here. I didn't know what he was supposed to do; you won't believe this but he didn't either. Not till yesterday. I saw him, Pete. I persuaded him to double-cross them; that girl in Beirut who was strangled—she was his girl. He was fond of her. They were paying him a lot of money; I offered him more, but he wouldn't take it.' She raised her head and looked at him; she had no defiance left, only a desperate plea for his belief. 'He's not what you think, Pete. He wouldn't take money from me. He promised we'd meet today and leave the country. There won't be any killing now. You've no reason to want him.'

Mathews didn't try to bully her. He had noticed that glance down at her watch and he had guessed immediately that she was holding out with a deadline in mind. She wouldn't tell him anything until the man was clear. The place they were going to meet was most probably Kennedy Airport. She hoped to go on talking until he had got there and was on his plane. He lit a cigarette. 'Jackson,' he said. 'So that was it. That figures, I suppose. I can't say I'd lose any sleep about him.' He relaxed, deliberately unbending his body from its taut, hostile pose above her. He produced his usual grin and to her surprise he came close and put a hand on her shoulder.

'You look rough,' he said. 'I'm going to get you a drink.'

'I don't want anything,' Elizabeth said. She turned away suddenly and began to cry. 'Thank God you came,' she sobbed. 'One more minute and I'd have been shot dead.'

'A burst from that little toy would've carved you up like a side of beef. Drink this down, and you'll feel better.' She did as he told her. It was a relief to have him take command, to lean on him, even for a few moments. It was exactly what Mathews wanted her to feel; he bent down and put his arm round her. 'Look,' he said gently. 'Look, Liz, I don't want to be a bastard. I have to do my job, you know that. You've just seen the kind of people Leary's up against. We had to get Eddi King, and, honey, I've got news for you. We got him. He was arrested last night.'

'You've got him? You're sure?'

'He's being questioned now,' Mathews said. He was very close to the soft mouth, and the scent was in her hair. That son of a bitch must have made hay with her, shut up alone in the apartment for two weeks. He must have really enjoyed himself, getting her so hooked on it that she would go away with him, knowing he was no different to the killer lying behind the kitchen door. Maybe killers were good at making love, maybe the two skills had something in common. Maybe women just found the extra thrill in going to bed with them.

'You really love this guy, don't you?' Mathews said. He could see her watch too. It was ten-twenty; time was passing.

'Yes,' she whispered. 'I love him, Pete, And he loves me.' A wild hope brought her round to him, almost in his arms.

'You wouldn't let me go to him? Oh, Pete, I beg of you, let me go to him!' He didn't answer immediately; he pretended to think about it.

'I don't think I can, Liz. My orders are to bring him in for questioning.'

'But you don't need to do that—I've told you everything, look, I wrote a letter to Mr Leary, explaining everything. You don't need Bruno. He doesn't know as much as I've already told you! Oh, please, if you've any feelings, Peter, if you've ever cared about anyone—let me leave here, and don't follow me!'

He went on holding her; he patted her shoulder once or twice and let her beg and plead, giving a little more and a little more. When he got up she thought she had won him over.

'I was always soft on you,' Mathews said. 'Maybe I was scared to marry you, Liz, but there must be something left. I've never cared a damn for anyone, except you. Okay. If he means this much to you, he must be worth something. I'm going now. I'll take the letter to Leary, and fix the police about our friend through there. You take your bag and just slip through the door. Don't let me see you do it.'

She came up to him and threw her arms round his neck. She kissed him on the lips and left the taste of her tears for the other man in his mouth.

'Thank you, Peter.'

He went into the kitchen and slammed the door. The tradesmen's entrance at the back was bolted top and bottom. He opened it and ran out into the corridor. Both elevators were still at the floor; he was inside the nearest with the gates closed when he heard Elizabeth's front door slam. He reached the lobby a minute ahead of her; the porter was not in sight. He was trying to move the TV repair van from its position in the driveway, watched by an angry tenant whose car could not get through. Mathews was in his own car and on his way out before Elizabeth had come down to the lobby.

CHAPTER SEVEN

The Cardinal was smaller than Keller had expected; on the TV screen and in newspaper photographs he had appeared a tall man. He had passed within a few feet of him and he looked slight and borne down by the weight of his scarlet robes and long train. The face was much more alive, thinner, with a sallow Southern skin and bright black eyes that seemed to burn like coals. It was the face of an aesthete, of the gaunt, medieval martyrs engulfed by pagan fires. Keller didn't even notice anyone else; the single small figure in blazing scarlet reduced his attendant priests, even the child acolytes in their white linens and dark cassocks, to a dim mediocrity. The procession pace was slow and dignified; a tall gold cross was carried in front of the Cardinal. It swayed and glimmered in the lights above his head. Keller had stepped back into the shadow, as close to the wall as possible. This was the moment when he had a perfect target; the skull-cap in bright scarlet bobbed ahead of him like a little ball on the tree in the Lebanese orchard. He could have killed the Cardinal with a single shot. He began to walk with the rear of the procession; he found himself level with the three priests in their gorgeous white and gold vestments who were to celebrate the Mass. They went down the short flight of steps leading to the main body of the church; the Cardinal had already turned left to the high altar to take his place on the throne. The priests followed slowly, keeping time to the stately organ music. Keller went down the steps after them and slipped among the crowd standing in the side pews. Behind him, the detective Smith, who waited by that door to 50th Street, fingered his gun and raised himself on the balls of his feet to get a look at what was happening below. The timing was wrong. The shot should have been fired before the Cardinal descended the steps. It should have been over by now. He couldn't see the

194

assassin; one moment he had been in position, waiting by the wall, shielded from the lights, the next he had gone and the procession was dispersing at the high altar. The magnificent choral *Kyrie Eleison* was just beginning; the two thousand people in the congregation were on their knees. The Cardinal was now out of range of anything but a direct shot from in front of the altar. The man looked round him quickly. Something had gone wrong; the killer had balked at the last minute. He began to walk away from his post, down towards the steps and the nave. 'Hey!' He turned, finding one of the C.I.A. men right beside him. 'You're not to leave that exit . . .'

'Okay,' he glared back at him. 'Okay, I just wanted to have a look . . .' He didn't try to move away again. He had been with the Police Department for fifteen years, and he had never made it beyond the detective grade. He was forty-three, greedy, sour and disillusioned. For the last four years he had been taking bribes. His fee for planting the gun and the verger's robe in the confessional was a mere thousand dollars. He had been promised ten thousand for shooting Regazzi's assassin before he could get through the exit door into the street. He had put the gun in its place as soon as he came on duty that morning at eight. Someone else must have cut the ledge and made the hiding place some time back; probably when the confessional was discontinued. Whoever was behind this business, they worked like real professionals. Shooting a man down didn't worry him; he had killed at least eighteen people in his career, including a woman who had happened to get in the way during a hold-up. He regarded his opportunities to assert himself as one of the few compensations in a lousy, badly paid job. If he regretted anything about himself it was the length of time it took him to get bent, and make some money out of the badge. The thought of the kind of money the professional ghoul must have been paid for putting a hole in Martino Regazzi made him so sick he would enjoy blasting him, just for that. But if he had ratted on the killing and didn't try to run through that door, he wouldn't get the chance. He wouldn't get his ten thousand. He retreated right back into the doorway, and slipped his gun out of his pocket. The safety catch was 'off'; the hot sweat in his palm had made the stock greasy. He wiped it with a handkerchief, swearing in furious panic. Ten thousand. For Chrissake, why hadn't the bastard fired—why had he let the chance go by—knocking him off on the way back would be much more dangerous; it meant firing at him face on. The detective could have cried with frustration.

In the body of the cathedral, Keller was watching the Mass. He had no time for memories; there was so little behind him that was worth remembering and so it was much easier to forget. It was the smell of the incense that brought back the chapel in his orphanage so vividly. It used to make him sick every time there was a High Mass. It didn't go well with an empty stomach; he could remember the feeling of light-headedness and the slow heaving inside him. The chapel had always been cold; the floors were stone and the nuns didn't indulge themselves with cushions to kneel on. He knew the words of the *Kyrie* by heart; he knew everything the choir sang in response to the priest's intonement on the altar, amplified throughout the huge building by microphones. Christ have mercy. Christ have mercy. Lord have mercy. *Gloria in excelsis Deo.* People round him were singing. The men who had hired him didn't believe in God. He had that much in common with them. Souha had believed; the only time she had ever questioned his word was in her childish attempt to defend the name of Allah when he dismissed her Muslim precepts as a myth. She had believed in her God; so had the nuns who looked after him and all the other rejects in the orphanage. So did the priests in the scarlet robes. It wasn't a comparison prompted by sentiment. It was a fact, like hunger and poverty and vengeance and wanting one woman more than anything else he could imagine. He had never quarrelled with facts. The congregation was standing for the Gospel. One of the officiating priests came down from the altar and read it out through a microphone. Keller didn't listen. He had moved near the steps again, taking a position by the pillar with the statue of the saint suspended; its stone feet were right above his head. This gave him John Jackson at a range of about ten yards. He was in the front row, with two large men on either side of him with florid, barbered faces and a look of prominence in the way they held themselves and the cut of their dark suits.

One wore some green stuff in his lapel, like cress. Jack-

196

son's spectacles glittered in the lights, hiding his eyes like shields. Then the whole mass of people made thunder again as they sat down, and from his throne near the high altar the Cardinal began to speak.

Mathews phoned through to Leary's office. What he had discovered was so important that he dropped the cover. He was told that Leary was engaged on another line; Mathews insisted. He knew his chief. He was still so sore-headed that he didn't want to talk to him direct. It was one of the signs of being in disfavour. 'I've got to talk to him,' Mathews said. 'Tell him I've broken it.' There was a long wait; he passed a second set of traffic lights, keeping a close tail on Elizabeth's taxi. It wasn't difficult; the traffic was like treacle. He couldn't have got separated if he'd wanted to do so.

'Leary here!' The voice sounded rough and irritable; Mathews guessed he hadn't been to bed.

'It's Mathews, sir. I've got a report to make; I can't come in. I'm following my client. How's King coming along?'

'He isn't,' Leary said. 'But it's early yet; he seems pretty confident. But I'll crack him. I'm taking the next session myself. Report in and make it brief. I'm busy.'

He was still bitter towards Mathews. Everyone was permitted one mistake before he tossed them out, but he hadn't forgiven him for it. Nor would he, till Mathews did something outstanding to make up for it.

'Huntley and King were planning to knock off J.J. That's what this was set up for. The guy was brought in exactly as we thought. But he won't be operating. She's on her way to meet him now. I only got to her in time; there was a contractor with a Schmeiser outside her front door. She said King must have sent him; she also said he murdered Huntley's piece of tail, Dallas Jay, thinking it was her. He knew she'd found out everything and he wanted her mouth shut. She gave me a letter for you; I promised to let her meet the lover boy and look the other way.'

'You've done a good job, Pete.' The use of his Christian name was Leary's way of saying he was back in favour. He sounded different now; intimate, friendly. 'A damned good job. Now I've really got something to use on Mr King. And don't lose her, whatever you do. I want that guy and I want

197

her. I want to bring them face to face with this bastard here, right at the end.'

John Jackson. Leary put the phone back and poured himself the dregs of the coffee. He had drunk so much during the hours while he awaited his team's report on Eddi King that he was too jacked up to feel tired. That was who the target was. Personally, he thought it was a good selection. But it was curious to find Huntley Cameron planning the death of a man who was dedicated to the principles of white supremacy and right-wing reaction. A more obvious victim for King, the communist, to choose. But politics were like marriage; he had thought of the saying himself and he often used it. They brought some ill-assorted partners into the same bed. He heaved himself out of his chair and stretched. There wasn't any point in waiting; now it was his turn to take Eddi King on. He was really looking forward to it.

In the slow line of cars creeping along Park Avenue, Peter Mathews stopped in yet another jam and lit a cigarette. Women were such fools; a little flattery, the suggestion that they were still important to you, and vanity could persuade them to any improbability. Like the chance of his keeping his word and letting Elizabeth and the killer get away. But it would be interesting to see him. To see what it was that Elizabeth had found in this one man which was so different. It must be sex, Mathews decided. With a capital 'S'. Sex on such a scale that the well-bred, self-contained girl he had known and never succeeded in arousing properly had lost all sense of proportion or even of personal safety. She talked about love; the memory made him a little uncomfortable; it was so obviously what she thought she meant when she begged him to let her go. To let them both go. He loves me. That was what she had said, and she believed it. Mathews wondered what would have convinced her that the word was not in such a man's vocabulary. Maybe the sight of someone lying in their own blood after he had gunned them down. He picked up speed, keeping the cab in full view. She had lost one of Leary's best men when she was being followed for exactly the same purpose. She was not going to slip away from Peter Mathews.

In the cab Elizabeth looked at her watch again, and called

198

through to the driver, 'Can't we find a different way out—
I'm going to miss my plane?'

'You won't be the only one, lady,' the driver answered,
glancing at her in his driving mirror. She looked agitated,
almost dishevelled. He wasn't interested in her one way or
another. Passengers were another species to him, slightly
less than human. 'There's no quicker way out today. You
forgotten it's St Patrick's?'

'No.' Elizabeth sank back against the seat. 'No, I couldn't
forget that.'

Perhaps Keller was as delayed as she was. He had promised to leave the hotel early and get to the airport by
eleven. How long would he wait for her—an hour, two
hours—outside the East Airlines' office, that was their arrangement? He wouldn't go without her. He would surely
believe that she was on her way to join him, that something
she couldn't control had kept her late. She lit a cigarette, and
shivered. If Mathews hadn't come she would have been
lying in front of her own splintered door, as dead as the
Arab girl who had been strangled. They had arrested Eddi
King. The man sent to kill her had been killed himself. She
paused a moment to give her Uncle Huntley his due for
being right. She hadn't been safe in the apartment, but she
was safe now. Now there was no danger to her, only to
Keller. Mathews had given them a chance; she cried suddenly, almost hysterical in her gratitude to him. But unless
she and Keller left America that morning Leary would have
them found and brought in. He wouldn't be moved by anything but his professional duty. They came out of F.D.R.
Drive through to the Triborough Bridge and she relaxed,
seeing the clearway ahead of them. Kennedy Airport lay
about eight miles ahead of them. She tried the driver again.
'Please,' she said, 'please hurry as fast as you can. I'll give
you double fare.'

'Okay,' he said. 'But I ain't got wings, remember.'

He put his foot down and the cab began to travel at its
maximum speed.

Martino Regazzi stood on the top of the crimson carpeted
step, framed against the magnificently carved canopy of the
throne. He held the speech in his left hand. He didn't read

199

from it; he spoke direct into the microphone facing the congregation·

'My dear children in Christ,' he said gently. 'Today is not just the feast of a great saint in the Church's calendar. It's a special day for America and Americans because St Patrick came to our shores as surely as to the shores of Ireland, brought here in the hearts of an immigrant people, driven by want and injustice from the place of their origins, seeking,' his arms opened for emphasis, 'seeking the chance of a good life. Seeking freedom, and opportunity. Dignity, liberty of conscience. To the Irish, to my people the Italians, to men and women all over the world, America has been the Gentiles' promised land, a country unsullied by old tyrannies, bright with a new Christian spirit of universal brotherhood.'

He paused for a moment; there was not a sound in the body of the cathedral. Not even a cough, or a movement. The Cardinal had caught them as a great actor does his audience. 'A century ago, my dear children, the leaking ships of profiteers brought Christ's poor to our country, with nothing but hope to sustain them, and faith to give them strength. Faith that for their children life would be full and good in God's sight. They brought us much of what we have today; some would say all. Their culture, their talents, their individuality, their music, their saints. St Patrick, St Stanislaus, St Anthony—we honour them and know them. They are part of us, part of America. That is surely the genius of our nation! To unite through love and Christian fellowship, instead of conquest!' Again he paused. In the choir stalls, a few feet away, Monsignor Jameson couldn't take his eyes from the Cardinal. The theatrical diction used to irritate him. Now he appreciated the performance for what it was, a beautifully honed and polished weapon designed to transfix the enemies of God. His own parents had travelled to America exactly as Regazzi had described. Even though Jameson knew the speech by heart, the way the Cardinal said it made him hot behind the eyes.

'But long before the immigrant ships from Europe—a whole hundred years before their coming—other ships dropped anchor here.' The Cardinal pointed, almost accusingly, at the field of faces below him, upturned, listening. 'Ships bearing our black brothers in Christ into bondage, not liberty! In the living death of slavery instead of the life of the Spirit—which is Man's right to dignity and freedom. And that right has been denied these same people ever since.' He took a step forward, both hands outstretched towards them now, pleading, not denouncing, the passion of a passionate race in every movement, every tone of his voice.

' "Give me your tired, your poor, your huddled masses yearning to be free." That is the message of our country, carved on the Statue of Liberty. America! The Motherland. But not to one race, one colour, one creed, but to all! America, her arms outstretched to all in need of shelter, owes to these, the first of her suffering children, that liberality she gives so generously to the rest of us. And no man,' the burning eyes turned downwards, the gesturing hand dropped until it seemed to point directly to the place where Jackson sat, 'no man, proclaiming himself a Christian and an American, can deny to his fellow Americans, his fellow Christians, the fruits of our great liberal tradition. To do so is to damn our society and defile our nation. Any man who preaches the continuance of hate, social injustice, and repression must at all costs be returned by the people of America to the obscurity—the darkness—from which he came!'

Above the Cardinal the TV camera concealed in the passageway over the high altar zoomed in close to John Jackson. He showed no reaction; throughout the whole speech so far he hadn't moved or made a comment; several people sitting near were looking uncomfortable; two of his supporters were whispering. His wife, a large dark woman heavily swathed in a fur coat, was as still and impassive as her husband. There was such a silence, such a shocked expectance, that when someone sneezed it was like a gunshot.

Up by the 50th Street exit door, Smith the detective listened to the words coming over the amplifiers, and felt his temper bubbling. He lost it over insignificant things; a trifling mistake in the office brought it seething over into yelling and swearing. All that sentimental hogwash about the Irish and the immigrants. What about Tammany Hall, what about the Mafia—culture and music and saints? He answered the lilting voice over the loudspeaker with obscenities of his own. And the poor. All the yapping about them. The hell with the poor; they made trouble, and Smith hated them for it. He hated most people, but the Negroes occupied a special place. When the Cardinal talked about the Negroes and slavery, Smith's nervous system jumped, as if he'd been given an electric shock. Black shit, that's what they were. The right place for them was where shit ought to be—in the gutter, off the sidewalk. He loved arresting them; he loved the way their eyes rolled up when they were hit. A numbness came over him; it was like a fog, closing him in with his hate and the raging, erupting fury in his mind. The Commie Cardinal. By Christ, a nigger-loving Red—he should have a hole in his head bigger than his big mouth—where was that dirty fink who'd lost his nerve—he'd lost Smith ten thousand bucks by losing his nerve—where was he? He'd fix him, the fink. He'd find him and fix him—he'd knock the Bejesus out of him.

Martino Regazzi let the silence hang for a moment. He waited, as the two thousand people in the church were waiting, for history to be made. For the Catholic Cardinal to throw his challenge down in the arena of a Presidential election. He was about to do it, and it must be done with due solemnity. He spoke at last; evenly, quietly, in contrast to the ringing oratory of a moment earlier. He spoke as one man to another, and he looked down at John Jackson as he did so.

'In my church today, before the Altar, in the very presence of Almighty God, there sits a man who publicly proclaims himself the enemy of Christian love. To this man, before you all—I say this. Renounce the doctrine of hate and ignorance. If you believe in our great country, if you are fit to offer yourself for leadership—tear prejudice and repression from your heart! For if you cannot represent *all* the people of America you're not fitted to represent any of them.'

There was a massive gasp, a sudden involuntary movement among the congregation. The Cardinal raised his right hand.

'In the name of the Father, the Son, and the Holy Ghost. Amen.' He turned and took his seat on the Episcopal throne.

That was when Mrs Jackson rose from her seat; at a nod from her husband she picked up her handbag, and looking straight ahead began to move out of the pew. There was a rustle and a murmur; it started in the Jackson vicinity and quickly spread. People here and there in the side aisles stood up to see what was happening. Keller saw the woman get up; she was nearing the end of the pew, easing past the embarrassed public worshippers from City Hall, and then John Jackson moved to follow her. Everyone in the cathedral who was in sight of the altar and the front pews was watching Jackson. Nobody saw Keller bring the gun out of his pocket. He took careful aim at the head, its white toque of hair shining under the lights. When the muzzle was in exactly the right place, allowing for trajectory and recoil to put the bullet into the left temple, Keller pulled the trigger. No silencer had been fitted because it made the weapon more conspicuous and difficult to hide; the original plan for Regazzi's assassination counted upon the organ anthem muffling the sound of one shot. There was no music at the moment Keller fired. There was a single sharp crack and then a loud scream. Jackson fell sideways against the back of the pew; his spectacles slipped off, hanging for a second grotesquely caught on one ear. His body slid and slumped, unable to collapse out of view because of the narrowness of space, caught up on both sides by people grabbing at him, shouting in horror. The single scream had become pandemonium. The aisles were filling with people, the security men were punching and fighting their way through; still the screaming continued as the hysteria spread, as the shriek went up. 'He's dead. He's been shot!' At that moment the victim's identity wasn't clear. But the fact of assassination was enough. Keller stood with the crowds rushing past him, holding himself against the pillar for support to avoid being dragged into the mob. Police and plainclothes men were in the middle of the group in the pew; the people were being pushed back. Somebody shouted at him. 'For Christ's sake get them back; put up the ropes!' Keller didn't understand what they meant. He stayed where he was, the pistol hidden under the skirts of the verger's robe. He had got Jackson right in the left temple; he had seen the little hole appear as if a fly had settled on him, just before he fell. He was dead. As dead as Souha; as dead as Mr King's plans. He had killed a lot of men in battle whose names he would never know. He felt nothing about killing the man Souha's murderers wanted in power. The time had came to get to that exit door. King's man would be on duty there, and he would need his gun again.

When the shot was fired, Smith was on his way down the passageway at the side of the altar. The massive mahogany screens concealed what was happening. All he could hear was the hysteria and the shouting; he saw men from his own department, and from the F.B.I., run past him, weapons in their hands, and he began to run with them. He didn't even see Keller in the mob. 'What's happened?' he kept on shouting it as he struggled to get through. 'Jackson,' somebody yelled back at him. 'He's been shot.' He had his gun out, and he was using it like a club, swearing and foaming with aggression. He didn't know it but he was screaming at the top of his voice. 'Where's that bastard—where's that fucking bastard . . .' He didn't even know who he meant.

When the shot was fired the Cardinal leapt to his feet as Jackson began to fall, pushing aside the priests who ran to crowd round him, acting as a living shield against a second bullet. He came down the steps with his scarlet robes flying out behind him, forcing his way through to where the stricken man was lying, propped up on the pew. Blood seeped steadily from the hole in the side of his head.

'Get back from here,' a detective turned on the Cardinal and bellowed at him. 'You want them to get you too!' Regazzi didn't seem to hear; he was beside Jackson, bending over him; the spectacles splintered under his feet. He was praying, holding the slack hand between his own. He didn't hear the angry warning, but close behind him, shaking with horror, Patrick Jameson did hear it and turned round. Smith reached the perimeter of the crowd surrounding the front pew. The noise was a crescendo, broken by high-pitched sobbing, and the repeated shouting for a doctor. The emotion hit Smith like a sea wave; it hurled against him, battering him with the hysteria all round him, tearing his emotions up by the roots. He wasn't a Jackson supporter; he had never bothered about politics or taken the trouble to vote since the war. But if there was nothing he loved, his life was full of hates, of unsettled scores, of faces he had wanted to beat in, bodies he had wanted to pump full of bullets, institutions he had resented and wanted to tear down. He saw the scarlet robes of the Cardinal, washing over the body of Jackson; he saw him bending close over the lolling white head, and suddenly something broke loose in his mind. It was like the fraying of a rope so tautly held that as it breaks it cuts down everything in its way until it falls, spent and useless, to the ground. He pointed his gun and screamed. 'You bastard, you nigger-lovin' bastard ...' That was when Jameson turned round. He didn't think; he leapt with the wild agility of an old man finding his last reserves of strength. The bullet meant for Martino Regazzi hit him in the chest.

The exit door to 50th Street was unguarded. Keller had almost reached it when two men on duty by the rectory door ran up to him.

'Where you think you're going?'

'A doctor,' Keller said. 'He's still alive. I must get through here. The other doors are blocked.' He bluffed for his life. 'It's like a mad-house down there.'

'I'll go,' one of the men said. 'You stay on duty by this door.' He opened the exit door and Keller caught a glimpse of a second man outside. He waited for little more than a minute. Then he slipped the gun out of his pocket again and gripped it by the barrel. As he opened the door, the man on duty turned round.

'Nobody's allowed to leave, bud,' he said. Keller didn't move, and the man did what he hoped. He came closer to him. He wasn't expecting an attack.

'Is that a doctor coming?'

He turned round to look as Keller asked him; the butt of the little gun cracked down on his head. The verger's robe dropped in a heap. Keller walked away and turned left towards Madison Avenue. It was eleven-twenty, the sun was shining, but the cold was intensified by an unpleasant wind which patrolled the wide street in long gusts, driving the crowds before it. The café where he had hidden the money was only a few minutes' walk away on Madison itself. But at the end of the street he saw the crowds, gathered in density, with the red flashing lights of ambulances and police cars winking above them. The sirens wailed, the fluctuating note growing louder as he came closer to them. Twenty-five thousand dollars were hidden behind a lavatory cistern. They were also protected by half the police force in the city. He felt little sense of disappointment; his mind was insulated against emotion. He didn't even care about

205

the money. He felt a fierce, sick longing to be with Elizabeth. Further than that he was unable to think or to feel. He walked part of the way back and then out down the block till he came to Madison Avenue. After waiting for a long time—he didn't know how long—on the sidewalk, Keller picked up a cab.

'The airport,' he said.

'Which airport?' the driver asked him. 'What the hell's goin' on back there? They got enough sirens for the San Francisco fire . . .'

'The Kennedy Airport,' Keller said. He saw his own face in the driver's mirror. It was grey and expressionless. 'There's been some kind of accident. Hurry, will you, I have to catch a plane.'

He would be late. He was already late. Perhaps she had tired of waiting for him and gone away. Perhaps she had changed her mind and not come at all. He leaned back and closed his eyes. He felt very tired; it was his only nervous reaction now that the worst danger had passed. His chances were very high now. He had got out of the cathedral. That was the miracle he needed in order to escape. By the Eastern office; that's where Elizabeth would be waiting for him. He didn't care about not being able to get the money. He had never cared, not since she told him what had happened to Souha, not since he had decided to strike a blow on his own account, to pull the trigger for himself. The money didn't matter. Nothing mattered but to find Elizabeth and get away.

They had carried Patrick Jameson behind the marble altar rail and laid him on the ground. There were several doctors in the congregation of distinguished Irishmen; two had examined John Jackson and declared him dead. The assassin was in the vestry behind the High Altar yelling and fighting with the police who had managed to handcuff him; his crazy shouting could be heard from a distance, and it went on until a senior detective from his own precinct smashed a fist into his mouth and shut him up. A third doctor was with Jameson. He was unconscious; he knew nothing after the split-second pain in his chest. Martino Regazzi was on his knees beside him, and his scarlet robe was stained with the old priest's blood.

'He's dying, Eminence,' the doctor said. He had examined

the bullet wound and its position was mortal; the man's fluttering pulse and feeble respiration would soon stop. It was extraordinary that his heart could go on beating even for those few minutes.

'He should have the Sacraments; there's not much time.' The Cardinal didn't answer him. He didn't pray for his secretary as he had done for Jackson, whom he had hated. He stayed on his knees and watched his life seeping away, and before them all he bowed his head and wept. In the limbo before death Patrick Jameson, the son of a labourer from County Kerry, received the last rites of the Church he loved from the Cardinal he had also loved, albeit without understanding very much about him. He never regained consciousness, but during the anointing he smiled. The smile remained on his lips at the moment he died.

The chief of the New York Police Department gave orders to clear the cathedral and draw the crowds outside away from the exit leading to the rectory. He had worked it out that Smith could be hustled through into the rectory and from there taken away to the police station.

When the body of the cathedral was clear he saw Smith borne out of the door towards the rectory surrounded by police. He was still struggling and yelling. Crazy like a dog. Thank God for that, the chief said privately to himself. Thank God he hadn't been bribed, and gone political. Any department could have an officer who suddenly went berserk. When a junior detective came up to him he brushed the man off angrily. He was trying to complain about being knocked out by someone in the crowd. The chief didn't listen. Neither had his captain, or anyone else but a harassed C.I.A. man who had told him to report it. Nobody listened or cared about the verger who clubbed him and disappeared after the two shootings. It wasn't until well into the afternoon that he got himself a hearing, and the authorities realised that there had been more than one killer in the cathedral.

'Tell me, Mr King, how long have you known Huntley Cameron?'

This was a new man; the teams had been changed over in so short a time that Eddi King was worried. The lightly built man sitting behind the table, a percolator full of fresh coffee set in front of him, had a hard, triumphant look on his face. But that too was an old trick; pretending to know everything, playing the cream-fed cat to the victim's cornered mouse. King looked surprised. 'For a number of years. We're close friends. He won't be pleased to hear about this.'

'I don't suppose he will,' Leary said. 'I guess he'll wonder how long you'll be able to hold out. If you're obstinate, of course, he'll probably get out of the country. A man with his money can usually find some place to hide in. So you'll just have to carry the can for both of you.'

'I don't know what you're talking about,' King said. 'You're not making sense.'

'Then let's try something else, shall we? When were you planning to have Jackson killed?'

King had been well trained; his self-discipline didn't desert him. He didn't change colour or show any sign of the terrific shock he had been given. Elizabeth Cameron had got her information through. He hoped she was dead, because at least she couldn't be a witness. But she had given the whole plot away; that was why he'd been arrested. He hoped the man he'd sent to kill her had shot her in a way to make her suffer. He hoped she had lain alone for a long time, in agony, before she died. He just hoped the girl hadn't been taken in for her own safety. That brought a few drops of chilly sweat out on his face, above the line of his hair. He turned his eyes on Leary; they were stony with his determination not to give way. He still didn't know what time it was.

'I want to see my lawyer. I want my constitutional rights. You can't keep me here, throwing these crazy accusations at me!'

'I don't intend to,' Leary said. 'I know you're not Edward King from Minnesota; you don't have any constitutional rights, because you're not an American. You're a Russian agent. I know that. You know I know it.'

The door opened; all of them turned round, including King. A woman came into the room; she didn't look near him. She went straight to Leary and said something. He sprang up, his face grey-white. He turned on King like a snake.

'You did it, you son of a bitch! You sat here stalling, and you brought it off!' They were all looking at King now. He glanced from face to face, ending with the man who a moment ago had been taunting him in his confidence. Now it was his turn to show that elusive glint of triumph which could never be pinned down in words.

'What's the matter,' he said. 'Bad news?'

Leary was shaking. The caffeine was playing a devil's toccata on his nerves. He looked into the good-looking face of the man in front of him, a little beard showing through the smooth skin, the light eyes watching him beneath that vaguely Slavic forehead, and he felt sick with himself. He'd been too late, too slow. Not seeing the date screaming at him from the calendar. If he'd clamped down on King as soon as he was arrested the murder in St Patrick's might have been prevented. He hated the enemy in front of him at that moment with an intensity enough to kill him, but he hated himself more.

'You got him,' he said slowly. 'Right in the middle of the Mass. You bastard.' He stepped forward and suddenly hit King. For a lightly built man he struck hard. King's head jerked back and his lip split. He brought out a handkerchief and wiped his mouth.

'If you're going to do this I'd better make a statement,' he said.

It was over for him now. He couldn't hope to hold out against them; he had done what he had been ordered to do. He mightn't see that Moscow flat and write a letter at his expensive French *bureau plat* for a few years, but he could wait. His own people woud get him out. All he had to do was admit to running an espionage ring under the cover of his magazine, and deny that he had done more than listen to Huntley Cameron's assassination plot. Elizabeth Cameron was the key; Huntley could only implicate him at the cost of his own safety. Only Elizabeth could bear personal witness against them both. And the word had gone out for her. If she hadn't been reached already, she'd never live to testify in court against him.

'I'm ready to make a statement,' he repeated. There was blood on his handkerchief. Leary watched him; he was rubbing his fist.

'Okay,' he said. 'Okay. We'll take it down.'

No questions were asked of King; Leary wouldn't allow him to be interrupted. He talked for some time, admitting

209

espionage, admitting his identity as a Soviet agent. He even gave his real name, Alexander Turin, major in the Soviet Army. He implicated three minor agents, two in West Germany and one in France. Beyond that, he had nothing more to confess. He expected them to have his statement typed and brought back for him to sign. But nothing happened. Leary stayed where he was, drinking coffee, tapping a pencil against the table surface until it began to get on King's nerves.

'I've told you everything,' he said. 'I'll sign my statement.'

Leary's tired eyes considered him with dislike. 'I'm not charging you on that,' he said. 'I don't give a damn whether you're a K.G.B. man or Eddi King from Minnesota. You're not going to get rapped for spying, Mr King. As far as your function as an agent is concerned, we don't give a damn. I'm passing you on to the police. For the murder of a woman called Dallas Jay.' He got up and walked towards the door. Before he went through it he turned round. 'You'll get a life sentence,' he said.

Two men came towards King; he stood up without them having to touch him. He swallowed with some difficulty; the room seemed very much smaller and darker than when he had come into it. 'I had nothing to do with it,' he said. 'I didn't kill anyone. I didn't kill the Cardinal either. He can't do this to me.'

'Nobody killed the *Cardinal*,' a man's voice said, quite close beside him. 'You got it wrong, Mr King. It was John Jackson who was shot dead today.'

It was five minutes to noon when Elizabeth walked through into the Eastern Airlines building at Kennedy. The doors were operated electrically; they swung open to let her through and silently closed behind her. She had always found the innovation eerie. Less than a month ago she had stood waiting in the Arrivals Building surrounded by much the same human maelstrom which flowed perpetually through all airports, waiting for someone to take charge of Keller. Nobody had come, and they had left the building together, his hand on her arm to prevent the escape she was contemplating. It was less than four weeks, but it seemed as if her whole life had been lived out within that period.

210

They had come together like characters in a Greek play, with the same inexorable Fate directing them. Elizabeth had never believed in a predestined future; she wasn't sure what she believed about the purpose of human life. It was a common escapism for the uncommitted to protest they were too busy living to wonder about life itself. Before she had met Keller she might have said this. But not now; not as she pushed her way through the crowds, looking for the place they had arranged to meet, the place where their tickets would be waiting.

She was so late; she felt a return of the impulse to break down and cry which had come on her during the taxi ride out. If he had given up and gone away. If he had just taken another plane, thinking she had changed her mind. If, by the malignancy that dogged the Greeks, to whom she had likened herself and him, they were to come this far, defeating all the obstacles gathered against them, and then miss each other. People turned to look at her as she brushed past them. She had always caused attention because of her elegance and her beauty; she appeared the glossy American socialite with the extra burnish associated with successful models. Now the Yves St Laurent suit, and the black mink coat falling off her shoulders, only emphasised the desperate look, the frantic struggling to get somewhere ahead of time. She came round a big bookstall, crammed with magazines; there were crowds round it, she didn't notice the fact that they weren't buying anything. They were listening to a transistor, giving a newsflash. Elizabeth didn't hear it; she was way past, running towards the ticket desk. She would have picked him out of any crowd. He wasn't there. She stopped for a moment, fighting back the tears of disappointment. She mustn't be a fool, imagining the worst immediately. There might be a message for her. It was difficult to gain attention. There were half a dozen people lined up for their tickets; she joined the queue and waited, watching from all directions in case he came. 'Two tickets to Mexico City booked in the name of Miss Elizabeth Cameron,' she said. She was trembling so visibly she had to hold on to the counter. The clock directly in front of her said noon. An hour; an hour late. He must have come and gone away again. Unless he was delayed by traffic. And of course he would be; he would have started so much later, not realising what the St Patrick's Day procession did to the transport system. She was so relieved, again she could have cried; her only reaction to anything, she thought hysterically, was tears. Of course he was late. They would miss the flight, but it didn't matter. They could take another plane to Mexico City. Where was he—Oh God, where was he?

'Here are the tickets, the noon flight passengers were boarded twenty minutes ago. I'm afraid you'll have to take our next available, which doesn't leave till five this afternoon.'

'We must get there sooner than that,' Elizabeth said. 'We'll take the next plane to Mexico City, whatever the line.'

How long could she wait without losing hope? An hour, two hours. She still had the address of his rooming house in her handbag; she could try to telephone. She opened the bag to make sure it was still there; she looked at it and put it away. Then she did what every woman does when she's waiting for a man. She remembered to look at her face. It was pale, and her mouth needed lipstick. In the circle of mirror, set in its tooled Van Cleef vanity case, she saw the figure of Peter Mathews standing on the perimeter of the crowd round the bookstall.

She painted her lips, and pressed them together to set the colour; she powdered her face with the little flat puff, and went through every natural motion. He stayed reflected in the glass until she closed it. When she turned a little he had disappeared.

'There's a Braniff flight to Mexico City leaving in an hour. I can fix that for you . . . Is anything the matter, madam, aren't you feeling well?' The clerk was a pretty Mexican girl, with satiny skin and black grape eyes. She thought the American was going to pass out. 'Would you like to sit down?'

'No,' Elizabeth said. 'No thank you. I'm quite all right.'

'It leaves in an hour. The BN703, there are two first-class seats available.'

'I'm sorry—I've changed my mind,' she said. It was Mathews; there wasn't any doubt. He had stayed in her mirror, watching her for as long as she was using it. He had never meant to let her go. He had lied, determined to get her to lead him to Keller. He had put his arms round her

212

and lied, pretending to be sympathetic. She didn't feel angry; everything had reversed like a spinning wheel.

Before, she had searched every distant group of people advancing towards her in the hope of seeing Keller among them. Now, ice cold with fear, she swung round to make sure he wasn't walking into the trap Mathews had set for them both. She opened her bag again and screwed the paper giving his address into a tiny ball. She dropped it in the wastepaper bin. The moment of sick panic had passed. She was thinking with the fierce clarity of someone protecting the person they loved, and the power of that love gave her confidence. What happened to her didn't matter. Nothing mattered but Keller's safety. 'I'm cancelling my ticket; I won't be travelling today,' she said to the clerk. 'My friend will take the Mexico flight. His name is Teller.' She remembered the false name on his passport. 'Could you give him a message please?' She dared not write; Mathews could be watching from any vantage point hidden from her. He mustn't see her leave any note.

'I'm sorry—we're not supposed to take messages.'

'Oh please,' Elizabeth said. 'Please—it's so important. Just tell him to go ahead. Tell him I'll join him in Cuernavaca as soon as I can. And give him my love.' The girl shrugged and then she smiled. 'Okay. I'll tell him.'

Where she went Mathews would follow. As she turned to the left, to the back of the bookstall, she saw Keller come into view framed in a group of people with children and overnight bags. For a moment she faltered; she fought off the impulse to bring disaster upon them by forgetting about Mathews and rushing to him.

'Give him my love,' he would hear that from the girl behind the airlines desk when he came to collect his ticket. And he would take the other flight to Mexico. He would be safe in Cuernavaca in her mother's house.

Peter Mathews slipped back into the crowd around the bookstall. He could see Elizabeth at the office, leaning across the counter. She was picking up the tickets; all he had to do now was find out which flight she was on and call through to have Leary order a search of the plane before take-off. He didn't even have to arrest the man when they made their rendezvous. He didn't have to do it, but he was going to; he was going to come up behind them both and

213

take the bastard in himself. And while he was waiting, pretending to look at the magazines while he watched Elizabeth, he heard the newsflash of Jackson's assassination. He didn't lose his head. Danger had never panicked Mathews; he reacted with the stillness and caution of an alerted animal. He didn't disclose himself, or try to push deeper into the crowd to hear more. He stayed where he was, keeping watch upon the girl. He put his hand in his pocket and slipped the safety catch off his gun. Jackson had been killed, and it was confirmed that a member of Cardinal Regazzi's staff had also been murdered.

A woman standing near began to cry; she wailed into a handkerchief, and immediately others joined her. Someone was swearing, using the same obscenity over and over again.

King had succeeded in spite of everything. He had brought his killer and let him loose. If Elizabeth Cameron hadn't lied to protect him, it could never have happened. But she had lied; she had loved the man enough to cheat and beg on his behalf, deluding herself that he was harmless, that everything was absolved by what she chose to describe as love. Mathews saw her making up her face, and a sick rage gushed up in him like bile; he could taste his anger, he could feel it, making him cold with sweat. Only a woman would have done it. Only a woman would have put her heart where her conscience was, and given it a fancy name. Elizabeth had not only helped kill two men, but she had also ruined Mathews' career. He had never realised it before, but his hatred of her at that moment reflected his basic dislike of the whole sex. Elizabeth had turned away from the desk; Mathews stepped back into the crowd, completely hidden from her. She was obviously worried; her face was drawn and anxious. He could see by the way she moved she was hurrying away from the ticket office as quickly as she had tried to get there. He went round the back of the bookstand. She had a wide area to cross to any exits, and a longer way to go towards the bars and restaurant at the other end. He would have time to get to the ticket desk and make sure where she was booked. Then he could catch up with her.

A queue was forming at the desk; several family groups with children were making a noise and there was a lot of excited talk in Spanish. Mathews pushed right to the head

214

of them, his official card in his hand. He showed it to the pretty dark-eyed girl. She was dealing with a group of two adults, one baby and four children. 'The woman you were just talking to—Miss Elizabeth Cameron—what flight is she booked on?'

The girl hesitated; the identity card was thrust at her.

'One moment please.' She had forgotten the blonde woman; there were six seats in tourist and a baby cot to sort out, and the queue had grown up like a patch of mushrooms. 'What name was it?'

'Cameron.' Mathews could have taken her by the front of her well-filled blouse and shaken her silly. 'Elizabeth Cameron. You were talking to her just a minute ago.'

'Oh, that's right. But she's not booked on any flight, sir. She had a booking to Mexico, but she missed the flight and she cancelled.' Mathews swung round—Elizabeth was some distance off, walking fast towards the restaurant, or one of the bars. A minute more and he might lose sight of her. He didn't risk it. She had cancelled her ticket; that lead was blocked now. He didn't wait to hear anything else, and the clerk had just started to mention the other ticket, booked in a different name, when she found he had gone.

Keller walked towards the counter; he moved slowly, looking round him. Twice he bumped into people going the other way. He couldn't see Elizabeth anywhere.

He was late. Too late, perhaps. Perhaps she had given up and gone back home. Perhaps she had heard the news, which was coming through a transistor on the news stand, and walked out on him. He stood in the middle of the crowds, looking round him, left and right and back again to the airline office which was their rendezvous. He had promised her not to do anything; he had promised to come to the airport and begin their life together clean of murder. He had broken that promise. For the larger issue he had sacrificed her happiness and his own; he knew this, but he also knew that he couldn't have done anything different.

He went towards the ticket counter, caught up in a crowd of other passengers, shuffling forward with them, part of an anonymous queue.

There was a long hold-up, while a passenger argued over seat allocations; the noise peculiar to airports hummed all round Keller, who heard nothing, not even the angry whine

215

of the inevitable spoilt child just ahead of him, whose mother refused to let go of his hand. He was watching for Elizabeth; once while he waited he saw a blonde head, bright as a sunflower, among a group of business men, but he turned away, seeing a different face coming towards him. He annoyed the people immediately behind him by turning round, searching for her from every angle. When he reached the desk he hadn't made up his mind what to do. He had only joined the queue of people to see if there was any message for him.

He faced the same girl as Elizabeth had done. He hesitated, not knowing how to ask.

'Can I help you, sir?'

'My name is Teller, is there anything for me?'

She looked down at a list, and then back at him. 'There's a ticket for you, sir, on Braniff flight BN703 to Mexico City. There were two tickets for our flight booked in the name of Cameron, but you missed it, and the lady re-booked for you. She cancelled her own ticket.'

'Where?' Keller said. 'When did this happen?'

'Oh, only about fifteen minutes or so—you must have just missed each other. She asked me to give you a message.'

So she had heard about Jackson and decided not to go with him. He looked down at the ticket lying in front of him on the counter.

'She said to tell you she'd follow as soon as she could, but you were to go ahead and wait. She asked me to give you her love.' The girl was smiling at him; he had looked really sick when he heard about the one ticket. A lot of people went to Mexico on honeymoon or to get married. 'Here's your ticket,' she said. 'And you'll have to hurry over to the Braniff lounge. Check your luggage over there, sir.'

Keller took the ticket from her. 'Thank you,' he said. 'I have no luggage.' He had missed Elizabeth by minutes. He hesitated for a moment, wondering whether even now he might find her, and to hell with the plane to Mexico. Her mother's house at Cuernavaca. He remembered what she had said to him in the room after they had made love: 'We'll be safe there. It's tucked away below the gardens. She loved it so and she left it to me. We'll be happy there . . .'

She had left him the ticket and the message; she had sent her love. He wasn't just running from something; for the first time in his life he had a place to go, and this was his only chance to get there. Any moment all planes might be grounded, every airport in the States closed to prevent Jackson's killer escaping abroad. If he took that flight to Mexico he would be ahead of the United States police, and the sinister contacts of Mr King's organisation would have lost track of him. If he didn't take that plane he couldn't go back to look for Elizabeth; he'd be found by one or other of the forces looking for him if he stayed in New York. He passed the baggage counter and went through into the departure lounge. The flight was being called again, for the last time.

Elizabeth heard the announcement as she reached the bar at the other end of the building. She had almost run, knowing that Mathews must be following her; leading him as far away from Keller as she could. She went up to the bar, and looked at her watch. In a few minutes they would be going out to board. The flight left at one o'clock. It was twelve-forty exactly. She leaned against the counter, her sleeve in a circle of damp Scotch; a man on her right was looking at her, but the barman chose not to notice while he checked something at the till. He was feeling bad-tempered; he had little sympathy for the scared travellers, drugging their jumpy nerves before take-off. He thought the woman in the fur coat looked a bad risk to sit next to on any flight. It was the man on Elizabeth's right who spoke first.

'Hear about the shooting?' he said.

'No.' She turned towards him, suddenly finding movement difficult. She could feel herself beginning to shake. 'What shooting?'

'Jackson,' the man told her. He took a swallow of his beer, and offered her a cigarette. 'He got shot dead in the cathedral this morning.'

The barman had come over at last. 'Yeah?' he said in Elizabeth's direction. 'Whaddya want?'

'I guess the lady needs a brandy. Make it a double.'

Peter Mathews gave the order from behind. He spoke to the man on her right. 'I'd like you to identify yourself. Here's my authority.'

Elizabeth hadn't spoken; she watched Mathews blocking off the man's route to the door. She even saw his left hand in his pocket and guessed that he had a gun in it. The man

217

was flustered, staring at Mathews, slowly recovering himself and beginning to show truculence.

'My name is Harry Wienerstein, and I live in Hampton, New Jersey. What the hell's this about? Here's my driving licence, and my plane ticket to San Antonio.'

'Brandy, one double; a dollar fifty.'

Elizabeth picked up the glass; Mathews hadn't even looked at her until then.

'What the hell's all this about?' The man was getting louder, more self-confident.

Elizabeth slowly shook her head. 'He's not the one, Peter. You're just making a fool of yourself.'

As he looked at her, Mathews knew it was true. He examined the driving licence, and the details on the ticket. He could have taken the drink out of her hand and thrown it in her face.

'You want to check on me, call my office,' the man called Wienerstein said. 'So what the hell are you guys bothering ordinary citizens for—why don't you pay more attention to the criminals, eh?'

'Shut your mouth,' Peter Mathews said. He caught Elizabeth's arm. 'Leary wants to see you.'

She walked with him, watched by the customers; even the sullen barman looked shaken out of his determined apathy.

'He cheated on you after all,' Mathews said. 'He wasn't going to do it, was he? He'd promised you.'

'Like you did,' Elizabeth said. 'Just like you, promising to let us go.' They were at the exit door. She stopped for a moment, pulling back from him. On the far runway a giant jet engine began to whine and scream before take-off.

'You're going to tell us where he's hiding,' Mathews said. 'You never were going to meet him, were you—that was just a blind! But we'll find him, I promise you that.'

High above, the massive aircraft rose into the sky, its engines thrusting in a shattering roar of power, pulling the nose higher and higher in an almost vertical climb, Elizabeth glanced down at her watch. It was one o'clock, plus two minutes. Then she looked up at Mathews. 'I don't care what he's done,' she said. 'You'll never find him. That's all I'll ever tell you, Peter. Now I'll go and see Leary.'

A week later John Jackson was buried in his home state; his

obituaries were mixed. The reactionaries mourned, the Left rejoiced, the coloured people said nothing, because they saw Jackson as a symptom of a disease which nobody had cured with that bullet through the brain. Detective Richard Case Smith was committed to the state criminal asylum, being found unfit to plead to the murder of the Presidential Candidate and of Monsignor Patrick Jameson of St Patrick's Cathedral.

Rumours that the bullet which killed Jackson was a different calibre from the one fired at the priest were ruthlessly suppressed. The State Department had sent word. There was not to be a political scandal; relations with the Soviet Union were entering a crucial phase with the President about to make a prestige visit to Moscow. Smith was a paranoid schizophrenic who had committed both murders. There was a greater sensation over the trial and conviction of Edward King, publisher, socialite and millionaire, for the killing of Huntley Cameron's mistress. One of the maids at Freemont testified to seeing Dallas go into his room in the early hours. The fear of being blackmailed provided him with the motive; instructions from his own people and ruthless pressure by Leary prevailed on King to plead guilty and accept a life sentence. Not long after his trial a cleaner found twenty-five thousand dollars in notes in a bag, hidden in a men's lavatory in a cafeteria off Madison Avenue. It was claimed. By the end of May, Leary stamped and closed the file on Eddi King. He called Elizabeth Cameron personally and told her she was free to travel anywhere she pleased. She wouldn't be seeing him or Peter Mathews again.

219

The Tamarind Seed

EVELYN ANTHONY

'Even better than Mary Stewart, I commend this book
without reserve'
Anthony Hern, Evening Standard

Judith worked for the United Nations Secretariat, handling
classified information. She never suspected that the
attractive stranger she met on holiday in Barbados might
be connected with Russian espionage. Until the secret
police intervened in their love affair to suggest that Judith
might help them obtain the secrets she dealt with at the
UN – or see her lover die.

'A most enjoyable mixture of espionage, diplomacy and
romance'
Daily Telegraph

30p

A Selection of Historical Fiction from Sphere

A Selection of Popular Fiction from Sphere